Four
Winds

Four Winds

River of Time: California

LISA T. BERGREN

FOUR WINDS

Published by Bergren Creative Group, Inc.
Colorado Springs, CO, USA

Cover design: Bergren Creative Group, Inc.
Cover images: Jennifer Ilene Photography

Printed in the United States of America

Dedicated to Ashley, who was so captivated by the original series,
that she read it forty-two times (and then "lost count after that"),
and is now a medieval and Renaissance major in college.
It's readers like you that convinced me
to keep writing time-slip romances—even in other eras.
Thank you for your passion!

CHAPTER 1

ZARA

Javier laughed and shook his head as we reached the top of the sand dune, Centinela loping in a wide circle around us. "I do not know if I can court a girl from the future *and* have a pet wolf," he said in Spanish. "That is a lot to ask of one man."

I gave him a half-smile, not yet ready to admit it—that I might be his girlfriend, that I might be here to stay—still trying to accept that it seemed I didn't really have another option. I was relieved and yet still pulled by my own time, all at once.

He reached for the reins of his hobbled mare and peered toward the setting sun, barely visible behind a dark, gray cloud bank. "We best hasten to the harbor. It looks like that storm might be upon us soon."

I studied it and lifted my cheek to the breeze, closed my eyes and took stock of the moisture in the air. The cloud bank appeared to be building in intensity, not moving. I had a thing for weather; in my own time I had wanted to study meteorology in college. "I'd wager it's all for show; the real storm is behind it. This one will not even make landfall."

Javier put his hands on my waist and gave me a sly look. *"¿Deseas apostar sobre el clima, chica? Con el Don de la Ventura?" You wish to gamble on the weather, girl? With the Don de la Ventura?* "I fear no *don*," I replied saucily, lifting my chin, sliding my arms around his neck and smiling as his warm hands pressed me closer to him. "What shall the stakes be?"

He bent down to hover his lips near mine. "A kiss," he whispered huskily, his breath practically a kiss of its own. "If I win, I get to kiss you. If you win, you get to kiss me."

I giggled and lifted my chin, inviting him with my eyes. "Shall we not kiss now and make certain that's a wise wager?"

"Clearly you have much to learn if you are ever to be a true gambler," he said, leaning away from me and pretending to scoff at my suggestion. "Does one pay his opponent before the cards are played?"

I grinned and pulled him closer again. "No, but does not one put the potential winnings on the table so it's clear what the stakes are?"

"But it is, my darling girl," he whispered. He lifted an index finger to stroke his bottom lip slowly as he studied mine. "Here are our lips, between us, simply waiting for the prize to be claimed when the hand is *played*." He gestured back to the storm, still brewing, making the sea beneath it a charcoal gray.

I hit his arm and grinned, half delighted by his teasing, half completely frustrated. I'd make him *beg* for a kiss when I won. He'd see it wasn't wise to mess with this particular señorita!

Still laughing under his breath, he tucked my bundle of things in the saddlebag. Then he lifted me to the back of his mare and mounted in front of me. Gleeful, I wrapped my arms around him, inhaling his scent of leather and oranges and salty, clean sweat as we set off.

"How come you have never named your horse, Javier?" I asked.

He shrugged a little. "When I was a boy, my father bought me a beautiful filly. Her name was Valentina, and she was very dear to me. She was not as big as this one," he said, leaning forward to pat his mount's neck with affection, "but she was sturdy and fast. We grew up together, in a way," he said, sounding a little shy over this admission. "But then my father's heart failed him, and the same day we buried him, Valentina came down with the colic. She died three days later. Ever since, I've never named my horses. But you may name yours, Zara. Given that you've named your wolf-dog, it seems appropriate to name your gelding."

I thought about that. When I was given the horse to ride, I'd been thinking of it as a temporary thing. Now, the idea of staying here long enough to name him struck me, like it was foundational somehow. Something that would ground me here…in a good way. We climbed the hills that surrounded Tainter Cove and reached the road, moving north to join Javier's family on the *Heron*, where we were to have dinner with a visiting sea captain, Alistair Craig.

I remembered the odd exchange between Craig and Javier the night before—the veiled meanings, the subtle warnings. Javier seemed both drawn to the man and agitated by him.

"What is it about Captain Craig, Javier?" I asked. "What must I know about the man?"

He glanced over his shoulder at me, then back to the

setting sun—now illuminating the bottom edges of the clouds in a brilliant, brief rim of orange—but he remained silent.

"If I am to remain here," I urged, "to be a part of life at Rancho Ventura, doesn't it make sense for me to understand what concerns you and your mother about him? What your secret is?"

"He is a nationalist," Javier said at last, as we reached the far end of the cove. "A lobbyist, bent on making Alta California the newest of the United States. And he does not fear a potential war with Mexico in order to accomplish what he wishes."

"I gathered that much from your mother's clear distaste."

"Refusing to receive him…" Javier spoke over his shoulder, as I shifted my arms around his waist. His big, broad hand covered my own, and he seemed to forget what he was about to say as he peeked again at me. "Zara, the feel of your arms around me…" He swallowed hard. "Coming here this day, I feared I'd never experience that again."

I gave him a gentle smile and leaned my cheek against the center of his back. "But God had other plans."

"And I will forever praise Him for that."

I grinned and gave him a squeeze. "You were saying… Refusing to receive him…."

"Honestly? You wish to keep talking when you are holding me so close?"

I giggled. "We have ridden this closely before."

He shook his head, and even with just a glimpse of his profile, I could see the wonder and joy in his expression. "But now…with the thought of you with me forever…" He said no more.

A shiver ran down my back as I thought of the hope and promise in his tone, and then I blinked, forcing myself to concentrate. I felt a sense of urgency, a deep need to know. What was it? "All right. No more hugs to distract you," I said, easing slightly away. "Tell me of the captain."

Javier sighed. "The issue is this: Craig's hinted that if I refuse to support his cause, he will convince other Americans to stop trading with us. Upset all we have built. As a ranchero, I must keep good relations on both sides of this political wall, regardless of what my mother wants. You've seen that the soldiers of the presidio do little to intervene, other than collect what they deem to be their due. And yet I trade with Spanish and Mexican ships too. So if they learned that I'd turned traitor—regardless of the disarray of our mother country in the hands of General Santa Anna—we would be swiftly cut off by both sides. Therefore I continue to gamble, playing my cards on both tables."

"But what do *you* want, Javier? For Alta California to remain a territory of Mexico or for it to become the newest state in the Union?"

He thought on that a moment, and absently stroked my hand with his free one as he looked along the beach and then to the hills. "I think it is only a matter of time before the United States turns her eyes upon this beautiful land. Our trade in tallow and hides has already caught her interest. And Mexico has all but abandoned us, seemingly lost in her constant uprisings and poorly managed wars. Her treasury is empty, so they gladly take our taxes, but do they send patrols to help keep cattle rustlers in check? Do they sail our coast, keeping alert to those—like Captain Craig—who might block our trade, holding us captive? No," he said bitterly. "They think they can occupy this territory, but at no cost. They do not realize that the power is slipping from their grasp."

He pulled up on the reins suddenly and glanced over his shoulder at me again, eyes alight. "But you...you know what transpires here. You know!" he cried, his face splitting into a beatific grin, his dark brows arcing in wonder. He squeezed my arm. "Tell me, Zara. In your time, is it Mexican or American rule? Or perhaps Russian? They have some holdings in the north, but seem mostly interested in pelts."

I stared at him. Was I supposed to tell him such things? Would it interrupt the space-time continuum or something? Might I...change the future? And yet my heart wanted to help him, to protect him and his family.

"I...I need to think about that, Javier. Maybe I shouldn't tell you what happens. Maybe what is meant to happen will unfold because you make the decisions you're supposed to make, without my interference."

His brow furrowed. "But you will tell me, if I choose wrongly?" he asked. "Can you not do that?"

I studied his handsome, earnest face, regretting that I couldn't immediately say yes. "I don't know, Javier. Let me think about it, all right? I need to decide what's wise."

Centinela whined then, her ears pricking forward as she trotted beside us. I thought her sound spooked Javier's mount, making the mare shy and whinny.

Javier yanked the horse's reins back and stroked her neck. "Whoa, *whoa*."

But a second later, we heard what had upset both animals. A low boom reached our ears, and then another, identical to the first.

"What is *that*?" I asked.

Javier was already gathering the reins tighter in his fist. "Cannon fire," he said grimly. "And from the sound of it, coming from Bonita Harbor. Hold on."

I clung to Javier all the way to the harbor, about a mile and a half distant from Tainter Cove. By the time we reached it, my arms and legs were trembling from the effort to hold on, even with Javier's firm grip on my hands in a knot at his sternum. I'd forced him to pause so that I could switch to riding astride, at least—not caring how it might chafe or how it might look, only wishing not to get bounced right off the horse's rump.

We reached the harbor and saw a newly arrived three-masted ship, right beside Captain Craig's damaged, listing *Heron*. The *Heron*'s deck was crowded with men, all in hand-to-hand combat with their attackers. We could see smoke rising from a fire belowdecks through two massive holes in her side, visible even from the beach.

"Who…what…?" I stammered.

"Pirates," Javier ground out. He was off the horse before we'd completely reached a stop and thrust the reins into my hands. But my eyes were on the new ship, flying a black Jolly Roger flag. *Crescent Moon* was painted on her back end. "Move forward to the saddle, Zara!" Javier demanded. "Now!"

I did what he asked without thinking. I tried to shove my boots in the stirrups, but they were too long for me.

"Go now, Zara!" he said, running his fingers over the grip of his pistol and reaching to pull his sword free. "Ride to the villa! You will be safest there!"

"But Javier, I—"

With a quick touch behind her withers, Javier turned the mare in the direction of the villa and then slapped her hard on the rump, sending her skittering ahead. Obviously surprised by his rash action, she surged from a canter into a mad gallop. I rode up and over several hills before I felt I had control again, and cresting the last rise, I pulled up on the reins in horror.

Because there I found Mateo's mare and two villa guards lying on the ground, all of them deadly still. Mateo—Javier's younger brother—was not with them. I leaped from my mount and quickly felt for a pulse at each of the men's necks, but they were clearly gone. And his horse—unlike Javier, Mateo had doted on his pretty Palamino, named Justina. If she was gone…I swallowed hard and looked back to Craig's burning ship again, only her topmast and the *Crescent Moon*'s visible above the dunes and hills between us.

"No, no, *no*…." Mateo had surely been taken captive. I glanced toward the rancho, thinking that the men there must have heard the cannon fire, as we had. How long until reinforcements arrived?

Too long?

I circled around, and then again, slowly beginning to understand what I must do.

If Javier de la Ventura was wading into that fight, a fight that might save his brother's life, I was determined to be by his side.

CHAPTER 2

I left Javier's mare on the landward side of the dunes, hobbling her just out of sight from the shore. I grabbed the long, curved knife he'd left in the saddlebag. Then I crouched over and scurried to the edge to peer down at the storehouse. There were no guards in sight, no sounds of bullets fired or men fighting. I could hear only the crash of waves, swollen by the approaching storm.

Along the shore, pirates were launching one rowboat after another, loaded with crates and barrels and bundles, systematically removing the rancho's treasured exports that had been stored here. Stacks and stacks of hides—which I'd learned the sailors called "California dollars"—two freshly butchered sides of beef, coils of tanned leather and rope, barrels full of tallow, giant spools of wool, and crates of oranges. In addition, I glimpsed bolts of cotton fabric in several patterns, casks of wine, an elegant mahogany rocking chair, rounds of cheese, and other barrels labeled SUGAR and SALT, all of these presumably just obtained in trade from Captain Craig.

So they were not only pillaging the *Heron*; they were also raiding our stores.

Fury washed through me. I thought of how hard the people of the rancho worked for all of those products…how they depended on the rest arriving on a timely basis to supply the villa and feed the rancho's hundred or more people. And these pirates had killed some of the kind guards who had protected Mateo—*please, God, let their lives have at least protected Mateo*—and perhaps others.

I gathered up my skirts and hurried over the dune and to the sidewall of the storehouse. I was standing with my back against it, holding Javier's dagger, when I saw Mateo lifted from one of the first boats to reach the pirate ship. He struggled against his bonds as he was picked up and bodily hauled aboard like nothing more than a wriggling sack of grain. "Oh no," I whispered. *This can't be happening.*

Did Javier know they had his brother? Was he already finding his way out there? Where *was* he?

I peeked around the corner and saw four men struggling to lift a massive, heavy safe, one of the last things in the storehouse—something that I dimly remembered Javier's dear friend, Rafael Vasquez, asked him to obtain. But my mind was trying to cope with the idea that two more dead guards were on the ground, with blood pooling around them. *Four men… dead! Dead, dead, dead….*

I whipped my head back, swallowing the bile that rose in my throat, and took several breaths, fighting my tunneling vision. There were still at least two other Ventura guards that lived. I'd seen them sitting, bound and gagged, backs against a pillar. If I could free them, could we, together, overtake the four remaining pirates and use that last boat to come to Mateo's aid—and Javier's?

The men counted together and then heaved the crate

upward. With grunts and straining sounds, they began to move together, out from under the rooftop and down through the soft sands to the last rowboat. When they were twenty paces away, fully focused on their task and gaining momentum, I eased around the corner and went to the two young Indian guards, where I used my knife to cut away their bonds.

The first staggered to his feet and reached for me, looking anxiously about. "You must be away from here, Señorita!" he whispered frantically. The other rose more slowly, and I saw that he had blood trickling down the other side of his head.

"No," I whispered back. "They have Mateo! We must go after them!"

The first guard reached for the nearest dead man, rolled him over, and grabbed the sword from his still-clenched hand. "We will go. You go to the villa!"

"I can help," I insisted, frowning in frustration as they both just stood there, staring at me with wide eyes. Too late, I realized they weren't looking at me, but rather past me—

"Oh, that you can, Señorita," said a low voice behind me, in tandem with the cocking of a pistol. I felt the smooth, round circle of the gun at the base of my skull. "You will most certainly be a *great* deal of help in future negotiations with Don Javier, if you are who I think you are. Now drop that dagger," he demanded gruffly.

I looked down the beach and wanted to cry. The four men had set down their heavy load and were returning to us, all drawing weapons. I dropped my knife.

"You should have stayed where we had left you," said one of the pirates to the Ventura guard. And then he drew his sword, whirled, and practically cut the man's head from his body.

I gasped as blood sprayed across my face and chest, nauseatingly warm at first, then quickly chilled by the breeze. I turned and vomited, and as I did so, I heard them murder the second Ventura guard. I threw up again, not daring to look.

My stomach empty, I rose and looked at my captor for the first time—and by the way the other men gave him sway, I assumed he was the captain. He had long, straight black hair and creamy skin the color of *café con leche*, not as dark as the rest of his crew. Pointing the gun at my chest, he lackadaisically looked me over from head to toe and back again, a slow smile lifting the corners of his mouth—as if he'd just captured a rival's trophy. I supposed he was handsome, in a way, nearly as big as Javier and with sculpted cheeks, a long, straight nose, and full lips. There was a dimple in the cleft of his chin. But in that moment, I thought I'd never seen anyone uglier in my life.

"You...*murderer*," I seethed, hands clenched. I was aware of the others, moving in on me from all sides, just waiting for their boss's order to grab me.

"Me han llamado peor," he continued in perfect Spanish. *They've called me worse.* "And I tried to leave two alive, to demonstrate that I am not a complete villain. Did you not—?"

I used his momentary distraction to shove upward, grabbing hold of the gun with one hand and ramming my fist into his throat with the other, hard enough to make him let go. The gun went off, and the other men hesitated, as if stunned that a girl could do such a thing. As the captain staggered backward, clutching his throat and gasping for breath, I swung

my body, lifted my skirts and roundhouse-kicked the nearest
man, my boot connecting with his jaw and sending him reeling.
I cocked the heavy gun again—one bullet left—and fired at the
man barreling toward me.

I turned my head before I saw the bullet's results, confident
that it had to be a crippling blow, if not lethal. Another man
grabbed me from behind, pinning my arms against my chest
as he pulled me toward him. I managed to wriggle my left arm
free, reached behind me, and grabbed his nose, tearing away
the soft flesh at his nostrils. He screamed and flung me away.

But the next man tackled me, driving the breath from my
lungs. I was just thinking about a move in which I might be
able to get my leg up and in front of his neck—if it weren't for
my cursed skirts—when he lifted a fist and belted me across
the cheek.

I felt the blow as if I were outside my body. I recognized
the pain, but it was distant. And my last thought as I lost
consciousness was this: *I'm sorry, Javier. Mateo. So, so sorry.*

I felt the rise and fall of waves before my other senses finally
helped me figure out where I might be. Slowly I lifted my head.
It was throbbing so hard, I could barely open my eyes.

I was at sea. As in, *on-board-a-ship* at sea.

"Ahh, there you are, my dear. At last," said the captain,
stroking my cheek, making me wince from the pain there, even
though his touch was light.

I forced my eyes open. Or one eye, actually. The other

refused to open—because it was swollen shut? I struggled to remember what had happened. But as I blinked, I saw that I faced an enraged, red-faced, and gagged Javier, bound in a chair across the table from me. And to my side was Mateo, similarly bound but unconscious.

Slowly, I took stock of my situation. I was in a chair, bound heavily around the chest, wrists, waist, and feet. Totally immobile. My head began to throb at twice its previous beat.

I struggled against the scratchy ropes for a sec, which seemed to amuse the captain. Then I tried to yell at him and realized I was gagged, a filthy rag held in my mouth by a band around my head.

Recognizing the disgusting, salty taste of someone's sweat, I began to choke. The captain watched me a moment, waited until Javier began to rock his chair in agitation and fury, until he casually reached forward and untied my gag. I spit out the wad in my mouth, retching for a moment, dizzy. I gasped, regained my composure, and sat up straight, closing my eyes and forcing myself to breathe slowly. *Get a grip, Zara. Think. Think!*

I felt his finger along my jaw line. "She is lovely, is she not, Don Javier? Pity my man had to punch her to bring her down. She is rather…feisty." He began to circle us, arms folded. "It shall be something of a challenge to keep her from further harm unless she chooses to be more docile. How much is she worth to you, Don Javier, if I return her to you unharmed?"

I blinked and stared up and over at him as he moved to Mateo, trying to pull four images into one. "Or how much is your little brother's life worth?" he asked, waving to Mateo's inert form. He was still unconscious, his head lolling down against his chest. "It must eat at you, thoughts of your elder brother, dead and gone, and now this one, so near to his own death…"

"What did you do to Mateo?" I spat out, my voice raspy and dry, wanting nothing more than to end his taunting of Javier.

The pirate captain glanced back at me before studying Mateo again, as if appraising artwork in a museum. A curiosity. "The boy thought he might be a hero," he said, glancing back at me over his shoulder as he continued to pace in a circle around us. "Let's just say he's young yet."

My eyes met Javier's.

I'm sorry. So sorry, I said to him silently. If I had done what he'd asked—gone home, rather than stay and try to fight—well, he and Mateo might have still been captured, but I would likely not have been a part of the stakes.

He frowned, but his whole expression was protective rage. Love. Worry.

Which *encompassed* me, warmed me, in a way.

"And you—Señorita Zara Ruiz, I take it? You, my dear, have *cost* me. Two men dead. Injuries to two others." He refused to admit that I'd hurt him, too, but I saw him lift a hand to his collar and pull the starched edge away from a purpling bruise.

I wanted to laugh.

"Who are you?" I said, my voice still raspy.

"I am Captain Santiago Mendoza," he said, waving a small circle in the air as he gave me a courtly bow. "I'd kiss your hand," he added, rising, a wry look in his dark eyes, "but well, you recognize my difficulty in that."

My skin crawled as he slowly perused me again, one inch at a time. I knew it was a scare tactic. Menacing, a threat somehow, to Javier, more than me. When his eyes returned to mine, I was staring straight at Javier. *It will be okay. Somehow, some way, it will be okay,* I willed him to know.

Because something in me, in spite of these crazy odds, told me it was so.

Had God brought me back a couple of centuries to fall in love with a man and his family, only to die at the hands of a pirate?

N*o way*.

The knowledge of it sent a surge of adrenaline through me and I lifted my chin.

But Javier stared back at me with nothing but fear and righteous, impotent rage.

Which made me feel the same, of course.

"What is it that you want, Captain Mendoza?" I rasped out.

Wordlessly, he poured a cup of wine and brought it to me, obviously recognizing that my throat was killing me.

I accepted a sip, desperate to ease the pain in my throat, but I soon felt the tart wine fill my mouth to the full and slop out the corners of my mouth and down my cheeks, chin, and neck. He laughed. I gulped, trying to stay ahead of the flow, feeling the wine continuing to flow down my neck and drench the bodice of my gown.

Captain Mendoza pulled the empty cup away at last as I panted for breath and glared up at him. His expression of delight didn't change in the face of my anger.

Javier was rocking again, infuriated, wrenching at his bonds.

Captain Mendoza looked…thoughtful. As if he were testing me, trying to figure me out.

I swallowed hard and wished I could get free and teach him what came of such disrespect. I hated him with an intensity that made me tremble. How could someone be so horrible?

Then he turned his thoughtful gaze upon Javier and resumed his circuit around the three of us, hands clasped behind his back. "You asked what I want, Señorita," he said, as if still trying to figure out his demands, when it was more than clear that he'd long since determined them. "As near as I can fathom it, the vast reach of Rancho de la Ventura is at my fingertips," he said, pausing to lift my chin and look over at Javier for a long moment. Then he moved on to Mateo, grabbed hold of his dark curls, and roughly raised his head.

Mateo stirred, squinted, and squirmed, starting to rise to consciousness.

"Free Javier's gag," I said to the captain. "This is *his* deal to make, not mine."

Mendoza considered me. Behind him, I saw the swing of the light on a chain, moving in an arc with the waves. All at once, I became aware of the creak of the timbers all around us, the thrum and energy of sails unfurled. The washing sound of water moving past, surging with each wave, deep enough to make us all lean one way and then the other.

We weren't simply at sea; we were on the move. Away from Rancho Ventura. Farther with each wave.

How long had we been at sea? How far were we from home?

Home, I acknowledged internally. *Rancho de la Ventura.*

The captain moved to free Javier's gag, and he spit out the rag from his mouth.

He turned away when Mendoza offered him a cup of wine, sneering in his direction. "When I am free—"

"When you are free," the captain easily interjected, resuming his pacing around us, "you and I shall sup on occasion as good friends. Perhaps even accept a friendly wager? I hear of your fondness for a hand of cards. But for now, *Don* Javier, you are *not* free, and these are the terms of my demands…"

We waited, the three of us—the gradually rousing Mateo, Javier, and me. Surrounded by four burly, armed guards in the shadows—my brain finally took them in—beyond the pacing captain.

"I am going to set you free, in a rowboat, to make your way to shore and back to the rancho to collect the same sum you handed to the presidio scum. That is my price for your precious little brother," he said, miming an arc across Mateo's throat with Javier's own dagger. "And as for *this* sweet, intriguing creature…" He lifted my chin with the cool flat of the blade.

I stared only at Javier.

"I take it she has stolen your heart? This girl, whom no one knows?"

"Verda deramente," Javier whispered, staring back at me, pledging his love with those two words in a way that I didn't think any other might ever match. *Indeed.*

He hadn't had to say it, admit it. But he had.

"Be wary of women without roots," Mendoza said with a humorless laugh. "There is a reason that our mothers wanted to know those who might lure our hearts—and their kin."

"I know all that I need to know," Javier said softly, still looking only at me. As if…as if he might never get the chance to say it again. My heart lurched.

"Well then," Mendoza said wryly, "her freedom shall cost you another chest of gold."

Javier's eyes moved to Mendoza, deadly still a moment. "I shall not give you two chests of gold for these two, Mendoza. I shall give you four."

"Javier!" I gasped.

"Four," he repeated. "But you shall deliver them to me in Monterey. Unharmed. *Unmolested,*" he emphasized, looking to Mendoza with a deadly intensity that sent a shiver down my back. "And I shall never see you or your crew again. Ever. We shall *not* sup together or play cards. The next time I see you shall be the last time."

The captain cast him a wry grin, brows lifting. "Four chests of gold when I asked for but two? Clearly, you are not the gambler that others said you were," he scoffed.

"You, Captain," Javier said, staring at him with a sneer, "have no idea *who* I am and *what* threat I might be. Harm either of these two, and I shall *hunt* you down. *Destroy* you. No, *kill* you…in a slow, *exacting* measure," he growled.

"Such grand talk!" Captain Mendoza scoffed. "May I remind you that it is I who hold your loved ones' lives in the balance? To say nothing of what might transpire for your widowed mother, sisters, and brother, far behind us? Ahh, yes, Señor Ventura, I am well aware of *all* who hold your heart. We dropped anchor and took much of what you had. What would keep us from taking the rest?"

I closed my eyes again, unable to combat the fear of what I might have brought down on those I loved, by not doing what Javier had asked me to do. But only part of that thought turned in my head and heart.

Those I loved.

I *loved* them.

Not just Javier. But Estie. Francesca. Jacinto. Mateo. Doña Elena.

I loved them as my own.

My own *family*.

And Javier?

As I stared at him, I couldn't imagine him gone. Away from me. It baffled me that I had ever been ready to leave him for my own time. *What had I been thinking?*

It came to mind, then, my third wish. *Adventure.*

My blood was pulsing at a faster rate than I could ever remember. *Okay, God, maybe this is a bit too much adventure.*

Somehow we had to get out of this. Some way.

Because this love that I felt for Javier, for his family, couldn't end here or now.

And I didn't want to leave his side. Not ever again.

"Bring them," the captain grunted to his men over his shoulder with a casual wave of his hand. "Bring all of them to the deck."

CHAPTER 3

Two men, about my height but twice as wide and strong, untied me and hauled me out of the captain's quarters and onto the deck. Two others brought Mateo. I squinted, trying to see the shoreline as night closed in. They were shoving Javier toward the rail and then worked on his bindings.

"What? You can't send him to shore now!" I said, trying to wrench away from the iron grip of my captors. "Not at this hour! Not on these seas!"

The captain glanced back at me. "If we wait until morn, your man will have even farther to walk once he reaches shore," he grunted, and waved at his men to continue their task of untying Javier.

"But he might not make it to shore!" Mateo cried. "Do you not wish for him to get to the rancho and obtain our ransom?"

The captain shrugged. "It would be nice, but I'll find other means to make our kidnapping profitable, if Don Ventura fails us. We secured a fine sum from the Ventura storehouse in the harbor." He moved over to Mateo. "You, my boy, might have the makings of a sailor in you." He eyed me, arms folded. "And you, my dear..." A wicked grin split his face.

Mateo, enraged by his disrespect, tore free of the sailors'

hold on him and barreled into the captain. The captain almost lost his footing but then succeeded in turning to the side and sending Mateo sprawling across a heap of rope. The boy fell headlong and then rolled off to the side. The crew erupted in laughter. Mateo gathered himself, as if to spring at the captain again, but two sailors took a firmer grip on both of his arms.

"You'll receive ten lashes for that attempt," the captain growled. "I shall suffer no disrespect upon my own ship." He gestured to the crew with his chin. "Tie him up."

It was Javier's turn to try and charge him, but he only succeeded in getting one arm free of his captors, and two burly men stood between him and the captain, arms folded. "You promised that you would not harm my brother and Zara," he grit out, straining toward Mendoza, the veins in his neck bulging.

The captain let out a scoffing laugh. "You promised me two *additional* chests of gold if I didn't. I made no promises of my own. And these two will get no better treatment than anyone else on my ship. If they fail to obey me—or dare to try and attack me again—they will get exactly what my men would get. Punishment. Now, off with you, Don Ventura. Before you are hopelessly lost at sea."

Javier was pushed to the rail again. "Do me the decency of allowing me to say farewell."

The captain scoffed. "Nonsense. On with it. A lack of farewell shall make your reunion all the sweeter, no?" He lifted his chin to his men. "Now get him down to that rowboat. If he resists any further, toss him overboard."

"Captain Mendoza!" Javier shouted.

But the captain ignored him, turned, and strode to me. He took hold of my arm and wrenched me along, away from Javier. I looked back, desperate to catch one last glimpse of him, but Javier was alternately fighting the men and trying to keep his hold on the rail as he climbed over. I thought about using my self-defense moves—it would be easy enough to escape the captain's grip—but then what? We were a good mile offshore, and I was in long skirts. Even if I helped Javier and Mateo get free and made it to the edge, I couldn't swim that far, especially in a dress. And there was no guarantee we could secure a rowboat.

Mateo was shouting, struggling, but the men were doing as the captain had said—lashing him to the mast. I heard them tear his shirt away, taunting him, as the captain opened his cabin door and thrust me inside. "Stay here, my dear. I shall return to you shortly."

Then he slammed the door in my face. I could hear his muffled orders, setting guards outside. I began to pace the small cabin, trying to think, trying to figure out what Mateo and I would do without Javier. *Without Javier.*

I scurried to the tiny window, the ancient glass too mottled to see more than odd forms beyond it. *Javier.* He was going. He might already be gone. *Gone.* The thought of it made my heart ache. My breath came out in panicked gasps.

I leaned my forehead against the glass and closed my eyes. What was happening? What on earth had I gotten myself into? This was way over my head. Way beyond anything I'd ever even thought I might have to deal with.

Gangs on the street at home? *Check.*

Boys thinking they were all that and making a play for me? *Check.*

Life on my own as an eighteen-year-old? *Check.*

But this? Watching my new love get tossed off a ship as night closed in? My friend tied to a mast to be whipped? Getting locked into a pirate captain's cabin?

The bile rose in my throat.

Oh, God, I prayed, the rest of my plea wordless. He knew. Somehow, he knew the answer even when I didn't have all the words to ask for what I needed.

At least I hoped he did.

Oh, God, oh, God, oh, God...help us.

CHAPTER 4

JAVIER

"Don't fret over your pretty pony," a sailor said to me as he kicked my rowboat away from the ship, bequeathing me a gap-toothed grin. "Cap'n said we could each take a turn with her if she doesn't take to her bridle. By the time you get to Monterey, I'd wager she'll be as tame as a brood mare." He stroked the scraggly beard about his chin, as if appreciating the thought of it.

I gritted my teeth and ignored him. Captain Mendoza, despite his bravado, would want those extra chests of gold. Tying Mateo up, dragging Zara into his cabin, had all been saber rattling. Had it not? I could bear to think of it in no other way than that. Grabbing hold of the oars, I took stock of the wind, the sea, and what I could see of the coast in the distance. As much as everything in me wished to return to my brother and Zara, to fight to the death in order to free them, I knew it was futile. The best thing I could do for them was to return home and find my way to Monterey…the fastest way possible.

As I settled into the backbreaking work of rowing across deep waves—half the time leaving nothing but air for one of my oars as I crested and descended—I let out guttural cries of rage. Again and again, I raged at the storm, my circumstances, even God on high. How could this have happened? There hadn't been pirates along Alta California's shores since the year that men pillaged the missions for altar treasures. Most found it more profitable to import and export than to bother with such treachery. Why now? And what had happened to Captain Craig, his crew, and the *Heron*? Were all lost?

Worst of all was thinking of facing Mama, and telling her that Mateo had been taken. *I must get him back. I must.* She'd lost Papa, Dante…and Adalia and little Alvaro had just left us. I could not fathom telling her that Mateo was lost to her too. No matter how angry I'd been with her, no matter how she'd failed Zara and me in not telling us the truth about her own mysterious travels through time…she was still my mother. And I owed her a great deal.

I cursed the waves as they fought me and the night grew darker still. I thought of Zara—my beautiful Zara—her skirts drenched by the sea, torn between staying with me and returning to her own time. I complained to God for giving her to me the first time, not answering her call to return, then allowing her to be taken away. I grumbled at Zara for not obeying me and returning to the rancho as I'd asked…for becoming a prisoner right along with my brother. And then I laughed through my tears, forced to admit my admiration for the girl-woman. So strong. So willing to wade straight into a fight to try and aid us.

I loved her. God help me, I loved her with an intensity that threatened to drown me. Never had a woman captivated me so. I didn't want it…hadn't wanted marriage. It chafed, this idea that my mother had cornered me this way, tying me back to my home with the aid of but a wisp of a woman from another time. And yet Zara had awakened me to all I had here, now. The importance of family. The steadying influence of a woman's love. The idea that this was but one chapter in my own book of life.

And I would do anything—absolutely anything—to get her back.

I dug into the water all the harder, my fury at the thought of Captain Mendoza's hand on her slender arm making me seethe. Manhandling my intended! When she and Mateo were safe, I would take great pleasure in exacting my revenge. I'd make the man wish he'd never weighed anchor in my harbor.

Again, I wondered how he seemed to know so much of me and mine. As if some spy had told him the best ways to cripple me. It was one thing to see the entirety of my stores in the pirate ship's hold; it was another to see my brother and my beloved at his mercy. Had it been purely poor luck that both ended up in his hands? Or had he set out to kidnap someone that he could hold for ransom, in addition to what he could steal?

I paused and searched for the shoreline. Getting closer. The tide was with me, thank God. I'd only need walk a few hours to make it back to the rancho. Mama would be beside herself; at least in my return, she'd find some relief. And there was the matter of Captain Craig and his men. Had he survived? Were all murdered or maimed in the attack?

I dug my oars into the water as a wave rolled past. Stars were beginning to peek out above me, and grimly, I admitted that Zara had won our wager. I laughed, mirthlessly, thinking she'd want to collect on that wager, and yet now, we were hopelessly far apart. The storm had drifted south of us, but I could feel the edge of another on the wind. I shook my head slowly, mulling it over again. Pirates, in these waters? Or had someone engaged Mendoza to deliberately cripple Craig and me, under the guise of "pirate"? Craig was a Unionist, determined to win me over for the American cause. Mendoza spoke with a fine Castilian accent—belying his Mexican or Spanish roots. Perhaps the captain from the Mexican garrison, Lieutenant de la Cruz, had paid him with my own gold to come after me? To remind me that I was in need of protection? Or had it been one of our rancho's neighbors, figuring that if I was weakened, they could take advantage of my distraction? Perhaps the Vargas family, who had stolen our cattle at every turn and then claimed innocence?

It mattered not. In time, I would discern what nefarious things were unfolding about us. What mattered now was getting the gold I needed and getting to Monterey before Captain Mendoza considered other options with his prisoners.

CHAPTER 5

ZARA

To my surprise, the captain did not return to his cabin that night. I spent a miserable, restless night inside, either pacing or dozing at the foot of the bed—because hello, who wanted to get under those disgusting covers?—all the while half-awake, waiting for his return. I didn't like the idea of him coming in and finding me totally out and vulnerable, so I resisted the I'm-gonna-die-if-I-don't-sleep urge.

But by the time I heard the low-timbred clang of four bells—andthe sky showed no hint of morning—I knew I was in serious trouble. My eyes burned, and my body ached. I was chilled, and despite my reservations, I finally pulled the top cover across me, bundled up the bottom corner of blanket as a makeshift pillow, and was out in seconds.

I woke some hours later to the sound of water filling a basin. I blinked, squinted, and then hurriedly sat up. My heart pounded in my chest when I saw what had made the sound. Captain Mendoza was stripped to the waist and faced away from me. His back was broad and strong, but a slight thickening around the waist told me he was well into his thirties.

Scars here and there marred his olive skin. He dipped his hands into the water and splashed his face several times, then wiped it with a cloth. He then dipped the cloth in, wrung it out, and wiped his chest and armpits. Without looking back at me, he said, "Why did you sleep across the foot of the bed, Señorita?"

"I didn't dare to truly sleep," I returned.

"Why ever not?" He pulled on a clean shirt and turned toward me. I could see the purpled bruise left on his neck from my blow on the beach, but he ignored my drifting eyes as he tucked the shirt into his breeches and reached for his coat.

"There is no need to feign ignorance, Captain," I said, not dropping my gaze. "I am on my captor's ship. My beloved has been cast off in the middle of the night, and my friend lashed to the mast. None of that makes for a good night's sleep, does it?"

"Pshaw," the captain scoffed, flicking out his hand. "Ventura likely made shoreline before midnight. And the boy was lashed to the mast, yes, but I wager you never heard the crack of a whip or cat-o'-nine, did you?"

It was true. I hadn't. But I thought it might have been too difficult to hear over the creak of the ship's timbers, the rush of waves and wind.

Captain Mendoza gave me a small smile. "The boy spent a miserable night outside, and he is likely quite stiff with cold, but his skin has not suffered the cut of a whip."

"So it was all for show, your threats?"

He squinted, and his lips thinned. "For show? No, my dear. I prefer to think of it as *encouragement* for your dear Javier. I don't wish for him to tarry. He must hasten to Monterey, if he intends to collect you and Mateo before I discover other ways in which I could capitalize on your unique…virtues."

He moved over to a chest in the corner, flipped open the creaky lid, rustled through it a moment, and then tossed a blue gown onto the bed. He dumped the basin of water into the chamber pot, refilled it with the pitcher, and set out a fresh cloth beside it. "Now clean yourself up and change out of that gown. We shall break bread together after I fetch Ventura the Younger from his post."

He winked and then exited the cabin, leaving me feeling a bit bewildered. Half the time I read subtle threat from him; the other half I believed he simply enjoyed toying with me. I again wondered how I was supposed to cope with this. It was one thing to take on a jerk in my own time; it was another to deal with a freaking pirate. And this guy was nothing like Johnny Depp.

I blinked, my eyes feeling dry and weary. I had to get a grip if I was going to be able to figure my way out. For my sake, but also for Mateo's. He was just a fifteen-year-old kid— he'd need me. I lifted the clean, blue gown—similar to my green, but with white lace instead of black—and glanced down at my wine-soaked bodice. It would feel good to get out of the dress and into something new, as well as take a quick basin bath. My skin was itchy with saltwater spray and sweat and wine.

I went to the cabin door, barred it, and then hurriedly stripped off my gown. I washed as fast as I could, pulled on the blue dress—which was cut a little lower in the bodice— and then dipped the cloth again to continue my bath. Spotting a comb that appeared carved from bone, I let down the remainder of my hair, carefully setting the pins to one side, and combed it out. Sand tumbled to the table and floor, reminding me of my last hours with Javier, and then at the harbor storehouse. It was all such a nightmare. I longed to escape it.

My hand, holding the comb, slowly lowered as I stared at the warbled glass window, thinking about being back in my apartment I'd shared with my abuela.

What if I'd dodged all this? Been able to travel through time again?

Gazing into Javier's loving eyes yesterday morning, I was certain I'd been saved from a very bad decision—that I was meant to be right here, in this time, in his arms.

But now? Take him out of the equation and I wondered just what kind of mad drug I'd swallowed. Yes, I loved him. Yes, I loved his family. But was it worth my life?

I set my hands on either side of the basin and looked down at the water as if it might give me an answer. The captain's last words echoed in my mind. *Before I consider other ways I could capitalize on your unique…virtues.*

I'd seen enough documentaries on the sex trade in my own time to know what he might be hinting at. And yet it seemed to me that it was all part of some game for him, and he was using that threat to try and keep me in line. I was reasonably confident I could fight him off, if worse came to worst. But I could not fight off his whole crew. Even my Krav Maga instructor would have told me there's a logical time to fight, as well as a logical time to flee. But where was I supposed to run when I was trapped on a ship sailing five miles from land?

In all the pirate movies I'd seen, there was an air of play. But here? Now? This was nothing but a deadly game, and I didn't feel I knew even half the rules.

CHAPTER 6

JAVIER

It was dawn by the time I reached shore. By the time I'd run the twelve miles south, it was noon. Sweat dripped down my face and chest, drenching my shirt. But finally, finally, I'd reached Bonita Harbor.

I stood there panting on the northern crest, surveying what remained. Happily, Captain Craig's *Heron* no longer listed, her hull apparently patched and pumped dry. Crews were already working on taking down her damaged mainmast, and I could see mules hauling a straight new one onto the beach. We always kept a supply of ten or more, curing along the edges of the mountain forests high above; yet we only sold one or two a year. My brother's thinking had been that in wartime, there might be a bigger need, and bigger needs equaled greater profits. To date, no wars had impacted Alta California's shores or ships. We did, however, have occasional need like this…but usually the damage was wrought by storm, not attack.

For the thousandth time, I considered what it would feel like to wrap my hands around Captain Mendoza's neck. To squeeze it until he gasped and silently begged me for release. He deserved to suffer. After all he'd done, after all he'd killed, stolen?

I would take him his gold. Get Mateo and Zara back.

And then hunt him down again to deliver his own share of misery and grief.

I was almost to the storehouse, and none of the men had yet caught sight of me, so intent were they upon their work. The empty storehouse again made my pulse quicken with rage, but I knew we could send a man to Santa Barbara to obtain what we needed until I could trade with the next supply ship that came through.

Concentrate, Zara, I told myself. I needed a ship to get me to Monterey with the chests of gold, or horses, if no ships were fit to sail. I needed additional gold, which would have to be borrowed from Rafael. I needed men to accompany me, and weapons. And yet some of my best men had been killed in the attack, their weapons taken from their dead bodies.

I edged around the storehouse and saw two villa guards—Hector and Rodrigo. Their eyes lit up and mouths dropped open. Hector recovered himself first. "Don Javier! *Estas aqui! Estas a salvo!" You are here! You are safe!*

Word spread quickly, and in seconds I was surrounded by perhaps twenty men, all clapping me on the back and asking me questions in a rush. But it was Captain Craig, just arriving on shore via rowboat, that I turned toward first. I patted men on the shoulders and face and back as I passed them, thanking God that not more of my friends had perished in the attack.

Captain Craig rushed forward and embraced me, then held me away from him at arm's length, as if trying to ascertain if I was but a mirage in the desert. "My friend, my friend.

Where have you been?"

"Taken by the pirates, along with Señorita Zara and Mateo."

He nodded and dropped his hands, face grim, then looked over my shoulder, as if hoping to spot them on the bluff behind me.

I shook my head and rubbed my aching neck. "The pirate set me to rowing late last night, and I made shore twelve miles north. I ran from there. But he kept Zara and Mateo."

"He is intent upon a ransom, then?" Craig said, taking my elbow and urging me away from the crowd so that we could speak frankly.

"Indeed," I said. "He demanded double what I paid the Mexican garrison in taxes during the rodeo."

Craig's hazel eyes widened in surprise and then narrowed in consternation. "How would he have known what was paid to Mexico if Cruz himself didn't tell him?"

I shook my head and let out a deep breath. I wasn't yet ready to believe that Cruz could betray me in that way. As much as I despised him, he was still my fellow countryman.

"There were likely many who witnessed those greedy bottom-feeders pilfering your hard-earned gold, who could've informed the pirate," Craig allowed, pinching his chin and staring out to sea, thinking. "But I'll tell you this: we haven't seen a blackcoat yet on the rancho, even though we sent a rider to town last night to inform the authorities of the attack."

I frowned and clenched my fists. This was but one more reason for my blood to boil. Captain de la Cruz or Lieutenant Gutierrez had not bothered to come and take a report, check on my mother, my sisters? When an attack had been made upon Mexican land, her people killed, her property stolen, and others kidnapped?

Craig lifted one eyebrow and his hands, leaning forward from the hip. I was grateful he said nothing more, though he clearly wanted to. It was like salt on a fresh wound, this latest injury from my own homeland and its representatives.

"There hasn't been a pirate attack here in years," I said, pacing away, running my hand through my sweat-soaked hair. "Not since those men attacked the missions back in '18, pillaging them for altar valuables."

Craig nodded in agreement, arms now folded, watching me. "I know."

"And yet this, *this*," I said, waving back across my beach, still blood-soaked where my men had died, "was not enough for them to ride out and observe for themselves? When Mexican citizens perished?"

Craig kicked at the sand with his boot. "To those of the presidio, your men were but Indians. *Servants*. Perhaps they do not consider them Mexican citizens?"

I frowned. "They were *employed* by a Mexican citizen," I ground out, bringing my fist to my chest. "A citizen who recently paid more than his fair share of taxes."

Craig crossed his arms, bit his lips, and ducked his head, as if reluctant to report what he had to say next. "Your messenger. He said the garrison door was open, and the men were…*incapacitated.*"

I froze and then shook my head in disgust, moving to stand beside him, looking out to sea, thinking, thinking. The men were drunk. Likely, they'd done what I most feared and merely distributed my gold among themselves, to spend on wine and women. I ran a hand through my hair again. Why? Why did I remain loyal to the mother country when her representatives were so despicable?

I took another long, deep breath and let it out slowly. It mattered not. Clearly I could not depend on the soldiers to help me restore order. It would have to be up to us. As it had always been, no matter how much I hoped it would someday be different.

I turned back to Craig. "How soon until the *Heron* is seaworthy?"

The captain glanced out toward his ship. "Three days. Maybe four. But no later." He shrugged and looked uncharacteristically weak. "And yet the pirates stole every crate and barrel from my hold. I have no idea how I shall pay my crew, let alone obtain any further cargo."

"I shall take care of that," I said, setting a hand on his shoulder. "Get your ship seaworthy and ready to sail for Monterey, my friend, and I shall fill your hold with all the cargo you can manage from Rancho de la Ventura."

CHAPTER 7

ZARA

Captain Mendoza brought Mateo in. The boy was groggy, squinting in the relative dark of the cabin after the bright sun on deck. I winced as I saw his swollen eye and bruising cheek, even as he frowned at me. "Zara?" he said, dumbfounded. "What have they done to you?"

He turned furiously toward the captain, but the much larger man just forced him into a chair. "Settle down, boy. You're my captive, as is Señorita Zara, and there is no fight here that you can win." One of his men shut the door behind him, but one stayed inside, folding his work-hardened arms and keeping an eye on Mateo and me in case we thought about trying some crazy escape plan.

"I'm all right, Mateo," I said, reaching out to touch his arm. "Despite what it looks like." I knew from my limited vision that my left eye was really puffy. My cheek ached, where the man had punched me and knocked me out on the beach. "We're on our way to Monterey."

"As I've heard," Mateo said, glaring at the captain as he sat down across the table from him and casually sipped from a mug. "Where this thief intends to rob my brother."

"Thief?" the captain repeated drily. "I prefer to think of it as seeing through an agreement between two gentlemen."

"You, Captain, are a pirate. You are not a gentleman."

"And you are an insolent boy," he sneered, rising to come after him.

Mateo bravely stared at Captain Mendoza with nothing but belligerence as the pirate took hold of his tattered shirt at the neck. I definitely could see he was Javier's brother. The resemblance, along with his defiance, strengthened me too.

Mendoza tightened his grip on the shirt, making it look like he was choking him. "Javier offered to pay you double what you asked for our return," I said hurriedly, "if you did not harm us."

The captain slowly dropped Mateo's shirt and then turned to approach me, leaning close to speak in my right ear, and then my left. "Make no mistake, my dear. I have already won in this deal, regardless of what gold I fetch from Don de la Ventura in the end. Your fate, and the whelp's, is entirely in my hands."

I frowned. The cargo was undoubtedly worth a great deal, but so much that he could turn down four chests full of gold? I tried to swallow, but my mouth was suddenly dry. Was it a game? An idle threat to keep things interesting for him? Or was that a note of truth behind his words? I shifted in my seat but then abruptly stilled as his eyes lazily moved from Mateo back to me.

He rose and walked around the table, reaching out to place his finger beneath my chin, gently forcing me to look him in the eye. "You shall answer a few questions for me, Zara, if you do not want us to lash young Mateo to the mast again and fulfill our threat of last night."

I pulled my chin away, not agreeing to anything.

He sighed heavily. "Let us begin with Javier de la Ventura. I wish to know where his loyalties lie."

"I don't understand," I said, shaking my head.

"Does he remain loyal to Mexico, or does he side with the Americans? More and more of them sail these waters. Did the good Captain Craig fill his mind with the Unionist claptrap?"

I frowned. "I...I don't know."

"I believe you do," he said, pinching my chin and forcing me to meet his gaze.

"She will tell you nothing," Mateo spat out. "You wish to know something about my brother? Ask him yourself when you see him in Monterey."

One look at Mateo and I knew what Captain Mendoza would discern—the boy would not be forthcoming, and he didn't want me to be, either. But at what cost? Clearly, this man wanted what he wanted and wouldn't hesitate to use either of us against the other. As mature as Mateo was, maybe he hadn't lived long enough to know people like I did. How wonderful... and horrible they could be.

"Oh, I believe she will," the captain said, continuing to round the table. He pulled a long knife from his belt and put it under the boy's chin as he looked over at me. Mateo's eyes widened as he leaned back, and the captain pressed the blade into his neck.

"He will not kill me," Mateo said bravely. "If he does,

he receives no ransom."

"Ahh, true," the captain said. He took hold of the boy's ear and moved the knife to it. "But a simple maiming would still get me half of your brother's gold."

Mateo swallowed hard.

"Captain—" I began.

"Does Don Javier de la Ventura remain a loyal son to Mexico?" the captain asked, ominously caressing Mateo's earlobe. He focused his steely gaze on me. "Or does he fancy the Americans' advance into this territory? He does a fair trade, after all, with Americans like Captain Craig." He spit out the captain's name as if it tasted rank.

"He…he is loyal to Mexico," I said, deciding on Javier's own last, known public proclamation. "Did he not just pay his taxes?"

"Reluctantly, it was said," the captain said. He moved behind Mateo, grabbed his forehead and pulled it back. His dagger hovered near Mateo's open eye, the tip terribly close. He stared down at the boy even as he continued speaking to me. "Was he reluctant because he listens too often to the rhetoric of those such as Captain Craig, with their idle notions of the Union expanding?"

"I-I have no idea."

His dagger got even closer to Mateo's eye. I could see beads of sweat forming on the boy's lip.

"Think, Zara," the captain said. "You must tell me something. I know you know something that would be of interest."

I wondered why he cared. Why it mattered. Was he not a pirate? Did pirates around here have an alliance with Mexico or something?

He edged the knife closer, and Mateo sucked in his breath.

"He has wondered!" I blurted. "Considered what would be wise!"

"Wise?" the captain asked, pulling away the knife a tiny bit. "In what way?"

"Whether it would be best to remain true to Mexico or consider the Unionists' cause."

Mateo's eyes widened again, but this time he looked at me. He frowned. "Zara! That is not true!"

He was like his mother, Doña Elena. He wanted to believe that Javier would never betray the mother country. And yet if the mother country did nothing for them but bleed them of necessary resources without giving anything in return…

"Why do you care?" I asked the captain. "What business is it of yours? You'll take your gold and run, will you not?"

He shrugged and sheathed his dagger, bringing me some measure of relief. The tension in Mateo's shoulders eased a little, but his face was still white. "That remains to be seen," Mendoza said. "And in my line of work, knowledge is power. Now"—he paused to lift his hands, once again assuming the role of cordial host—"do either of you play chess? I have hungered for a good game for some time and have already beaten every man aboard ship."

"Sail ho!" came a shout, distant, as if from the crow's nest. "Sail ho!"

The captain's smile vanished, and he strode toward the door. The guard posted there opened it for him and both exited, leaving Mateo and me alone for a sec. Outside, we heard the captain shout, "Hoist the red and green!"

A flag, I assumed. Mexican?

"Do you think it's Javier?" I asked Mateo. "Someone in pursuit?"

He shook his head, his face rueful. "There's not been enough time. Most likely just another merchant ship en route north to Monterey or south to San Diego. But whoever it is, Mendoza won't want them to know what he's done or the cargo he carries."

"What if we went out on the deck?" I asked him in a whisper. "Signaled them for help?"

"To what end?" he returned. "Even if they could somehow discern that we were in need of aid, if they attacked the ship, we would as likely be hurt in the skirmish as rescued." He winced. "Do you think you might be able to get my bindings loose? My shoulders ache terribly."

I hurriedly rose and went around to him, chagrined that I hadn't thought of it myself. As I worked on the knot, I asked, "Did they hurt you, out on deck last night?"

He shook his head. "They ripped my shirt, as you can see, and bound me to the mast, as if they had every intention of flogging me. But then the captain simply waved the rest off and left me to stand there through the night."

I frowned, trying to figure that out. Why go through the motions but then not follow through? The knot came loose at last, and Mateo slowly rolled one shoulder and then the other, touching each one in turn. He turned partway in his chair and took my hand. "And you, Zara?" he asked, gazing at me intently. "Did the captain do you any harm?"

"No," I said, feeling my face warm at what he obviously

feared. His eyes were so much like Javier's, chocolate-brown and laced with thick lashes. "In fact, he didn't return to the cabin last night after he'd escorted me here. Not until this morning."

It was Mateo's turn to frown as he rose and paced to the porthole to look out, obviously thinking as he rubbed his raw wrists. "So he suggests he might do us harm, but then doesn't."

"Because he wants the extra gold that Javier promised?"

"Perhaps. I think it's as he said; his mind is not yet settled." He turned to me, and I realized that he was just taller than I was. Had he always been so, or had he grown in the last weeks I'd been here? Or was it that I was simply looking to him as more of an equal rather than as Javier's little brother? "I think we'd best do all we can not to taunt him, Zara. If these men were willing to murder our own and kidnap us, then they may well follow through on their threats."

I nodded, and he placed a gentle hand on my shoulder, quietly encouraging me. "If we can get to Monterey," he whispered, "there might be a chance for us to escape the ship, and save the rancho the cost of freeing us."

"Do you know the city?"

He squinted. "Have you not been there?"

I shook my head, electing to say nothing more. Mateo did not yet know what Javier and Doña Elena did—that I hadn't seen much of Alta California...at least, in 1840. What I'd seen in my own time was much, much different. "Tell me of it."

"There will be a great number of ships," he said, pacing back and forth. "We may be able to swim to the nearest and enlist their aid," he added in an undertone. "Or if we can get to town, there are as many saloons as ships. Surely we could find aid in one of those."

"I can't imagine that we'll be left unguarded," I said.

"No. But if we behave as docile prisoners, resigned to our fate and merely waiting for the exchange between the captain and Javier, they may very well relax and not be as vigilant."

I nodded and paced a bit myself. "We can hope," I said. "How soon until we reach Monterey?"

"Depending on the weather, another day, maybe two. There's another storm on the wind, and rounding Point Ruina is always a risky pass."

"And how long until Javier reaches us?

"He'll get there in time, Zara. Trust me. Even if he has to come overland, my brother will come for us in time."

CHAPTER 8

ZARA

It was a good plan. But that night, we dined at the captain's table along with the first mate, the second, and the steward. The brush with the other ship had seemed to cool the captain's attitude toward us; perhaps he now was just eager to get us off his ship and into Javier's hands, before he was caught with a hold full of Rancho Ventura's inventory and two kidnapped victims. But the second mate, Gonzalo, leered at me so much that I had a hard time eating. Not to mention the fact that just watching the short, wide man shovel food into his mouth was disgusting in its own right. He chewed with his mouth open, ignoring the bits of food that got caught in his beard and mustache. And when he found the bits, he plucked them out and popped them in his mouth, half-grinning at me all the while.

The first mate, Emilio, was a more educated man who seemed to disdain Gonzalo but refrained from chastising him with words, even though his eyes did a fair job of it. He asked a couple questions of Mateo, which were grudgingly answered, and then turned his sharp-eyed gaze on me. "And you, Señorita Ruiz? How did you manage to capture the heart of one of Alta

California's most eligible bachelors?"

"Do you not have two eyes to see, man?" slurred the second mate. His eyes slid down to my cleavage and back again for the hundredth time that night. The captain merely sat back in his chair, lifted his glass in silent toast to me, and sipped.

"It must be more than mere beauty to draw a man like Javier de la Ventura," said the first mate, his eyes still on mine. "We've waited a long time to find a way to corner the man's attention. What a joy to finally hear of you," he said, lifting his own glass in silent toast to me.

I puzzled over his words. They'd had their eyes set on Javier for a long time? Didn't pirates just swoop in on the next conquest and swoop back out?

Emilio took a sip and considered me further. "So tell us, Señorita. From where did you come? Some fine family in Mexico? Or are the rumors true that you washed up on shore with no recollection of whence you came at all?"

"She's a siren," slurred the second mate. "Stole the man's heart and then traded her tail for legs!" He glanced under the table as if he wanted to make sure they remained legs, which made the captain laugh.

But the first mate's light brown eyes remained on mine.

"It is true," I said, setting down my fork. "I have no recollection of where I came from, only that it wasn't too far from Rancho de la Ventura."

"Such a mystery," the captain said. "Not far, and yet no one knows you or your family. Judging by your grace and countenance, you are no orphan. And yet your Spanish is…far from genteel. You have no family in search of you?"

"I don't know," I said.

"She suffered a terrible head injury," Mateo said. "My mother and brother believe it caused her to lose her memory."

"Convenient, that," said the captain. "There are parts of my own past that I'd rather forget."

"Perhaps she was a whore in Mexico City," said the second mate.

Clearly horrified by such an accusation, Mateo shoved back his chair and rose. "You dare to say such a thing to my brother's intended?"

"Sit down, boy," the captain said coldly. Slowly, jaw and fists clenched, Mateo did as he was told.

The second mate raised his hands as if sorry, but his expression was anything but apologetic. The corners of his mouth still quirked upward.

The first mate leaned back in his own chair, wiping his mouth on a napkin. "It is not such a preposterous notion," he said. "We meet prostitutes in every port, with dreams in their heads of a new start in Alta California. A rich ranchero would only sweeten the pot. Perhaps you were a stowaway and the captain found you, knocked you over the head, and tossed you overboard."

"I was not a prostitute," I said flatly.

"Oh?" said the captain, leaning forward. "So you remember that much. Curious."

"Give me a chance with her this eve, and I'll give you a full report, Captain," said Gonzalo. "I'll tell you if she's untried or well versed in the ways of men."

I shifted in my seat.

"I think not," said the captain drily.

"Zara is an accomplished cook," Mateo said, obviously trying to steer the conversation back to safer territory.

"Truly?" the captain said.

"Truly," I returned.

"So the girl draws Ventura's appetite in more ways than one," said Emilio, pouring himself a second glass of wine for himself and then topping off mine, though I had barely touched it.

"But his mother is not one who is rumored to fancy a common cook as the future bride of Don Javier," Gonzalo said.

Mateo and I shared a glance. Obviously, these men had been gathering information about Javier and his family for some time—beyond the taxes, beyond the likely stores in Bonita Harbor...

"Look at her," the captain said, gesturing toward me with his goblet. "There is nothing common about her. It is almost as if she is from another country. Her Spanish is not like others' in this region. And yet neither is it like any I've heard in Mexico."

I pretended to toss him a conspiratorial grin and raised my own goblet. *"Algo misterioso acerca de una mujer es siempre buena cosa para un hombre, ¿no es así?" Some mystery in a woman is always a good thing for a man, is it not?*

The captain grinned and lifted his goblet higher, then took a swig while I ventured a tiny sip. I wanted them to think I was relaxing, maybe even partly enjoying their company. But there was no way I could allow myself to get tipsy. That would be stupid.

"Perhaps she's a witch and has entranced Don Ventura," the second mate said, squinting at me as if he could see an aura about me.

The candelabrum at the center of the table slid a little as a big wave washed past us. The first mate reached out and caught it, then looked to the captain. *"Las olas están creciendo más pesado."* *The seas are growing heavier.*

"Indeed," Mendoza said, turning to the second mate. "Go to the deck and report back."

"Aye," Gonzalo said, lumbering to his feet. He held on to the table a moment, as if gaining his balance, then set off, opening and closing the door loudly.

The captain was just asking Mateo about the year's citrus crop when the second mate knocked and ducked his head back in. "Best you come straight away, Capitán. A storm is soon upon us."

The captain swore under his breath, tossed back the last of his wine, and rose. I was surprised he could stand at all, but then maybe he routinely drank a lot. The candelabrum was again sliding. The silent steward rose and blew out the five candles, then strapped it on a shelf in the corner of the room, where it could safely be stashed in any seas.

Emilio gestured to the guard by the door. "Take the boy belowdecks and leave him in one of the storerooms. He can do his best to sleep through the storm." He turned to me and pointed. "Stay here in this cabin, and only here, Señorita. *¿Comprende?* The deck is no place for a woman in stormy seas. To come out would likely give you as much chance at a watery grave as an escape."

There was a measure of compassion in his steady gaze, a sincere warning.

I nodded. "I understand." Already the waves were bigger, making me lean more distinctly against them in one direction and then the other to keep my footing.

He and the guard exited the cabin, Mateo firmly in hand, and I glimpsed rain beginning to spatter the deck. It was very dark outside, the sky roiling with ashen clouds, even though we had a good two hours of daylight left. The cook came in through the open door and followed my glance backward, even as the guard moved to close it. "We have just begun to round Point Ruina," he said, moving to help the steward gather the remaining dishes. "Famed for her four winds."

"Four winds?" I said, automatically stepping toward the table to help before realizing that a lady and a guest in this time wouldn't do such a thing.

"Sailors carefully choose their timing rounding the point, for just as soon as a ship sets her sails for one wind, it switches. If the crew is not quick enough, sails set for one wind will allow a shifting wind to send us keel-to-sky. The storms are fierce here, and many have gone down on the rocks of her shores. It is only because we hasten to Monterey that the captain chooses to push through the storm." He shook his head and muttered to the steward, "He tempts the fates by daring the four winds to take us down."

"Best we get there, collect our payment, and move on, or there will be greater forces than *wind* that threaten to take us down," the cook grumbled back, glancing my way.

Javier, he meant. And his friends. Or the Mexican troops?

Perhaps they would aid Javier, now that pirates had dared to attack one of their own.

"The winds can be a boon to sailors," the cook went on, gathering the last plate, "or our doom. One must always pay attention to them."

The guard led the way to the door and let the cook out first, leaving one hand free to close the door behind him. "Best you remain seated, Señorita," he told me, looking out upon the deck and then back to me. "It's bound to get much worse before the night is over. You will be safe in here."

But as he shut the door, I couldn't help but think over his words. I settled into a rocking chair and shifted it, trying to move with the waves rather than fight them. This was more than the four winds—this was the storm behind the one we'd seen last night.

You owe me a kiss, Javier de la Ventura, I thought wistfully. *I won our wager.* And in that moment, he felt farther from me than ever.

Hour upon hour later, dark was fully upon us and I was panting, trying to keep from throwing up every bite I'd taken at dinner. I rocked to the end of my chair legs with each wave— so far that after a while, I feared falling over—and then so far forward I had to stabilize the chair with my legs and use my arms to keep my seat. I finally lay down on the floor, feeling the waves wash beneath us like giant whales, pushing us over neck, hump, and tail.

Somewhere in the middle of that terrible night, I heard a high-pitched, faint shout over the howling wind, then two, just before something crashed into the side of the ship.

I rolled in a backward somersault, feet over head, and then again, hitting the far wall.

The last candle on a side table sputtered out, drowning in its own wax, leaving just one tiny flame somehow flickering in the corner, an urn beneath glass that swung on a chain, back and forth like a hypnotist's enchantment. Water seeped under the door and ran toward me. I scrambled up, trying to avoid it, but then another wave hit us. The ship leaned so far over that I slid across the wood floor, crashing against the table and then tumbling over it. I could hear a scream outside above the wind—a horrific, fading scream, as if a man fell from the rigging—and more shouts.

Still another wave hit us, and we leaned even farther over. My eyes widened in terror. Were we going to capsize? We were practically on our side!

The cook's mention of *keel-to-sky* echoed in my head.

But then the boat rocked back, and I tumbled in the other direction, so wrapped up in my stupid skirts that I could do little but roll. I hit the chest, and it was then that I realized that all the main furniture had been anchored to the floor. Even the three chests that contained the captain's clothing—and apparently a spare gown—were set between brackets screwed to the floor so they could be moved but would not slide.

The wind sounded like a living thing now, a haunting, terrifying screech of coming death. I could hear the roaring shouts of both the captain and the first mate, echoing him, but wondered how the sailors could hear them if they were farther away than I was from them. Another wave rammed us, and again I slid across the floor, yelping in terror. Again, we hovered almost sideways. I prayed that another wave wouldn't send us over, that God would send another of his four winds.

But he apparently didn't hear me. Because at that moment, another wave struck the lower, exposed side of the ship, and with a creak and groan, we began a sickening roll.

CHAPTER 9

JAVIER

Having heard the news in town, my friend, Rafael Vasquez, arrived late that afternoon, with twelve fresh horses in tow, as well as a dozen of his own men. "In case you elect to go overland," he said in his elegant, offhand way. That was part of what I so appreciated in Rafael; he seemed ever-ready to be my aid, my guide, my help. A brother in every way.

We gripped arms as he dismounted, and he gave me a hard look with his dark blue eyes. "We shall get them back, Javier." He set his jaw and said again, "We shall get them back."

I knew he was thinking of his own sister as he considered the prospect of my losing Mateo as well as Zara, and my hand tightened above his elbow. "Yes. We *shall*," I pledged.

We were just heading inside the villa when a guard shouted, "Riders, Don Javier! From the harbor!"

I turned and watched as Juan Diego, one of the new guards just assigned to the harbor storehouse, tore down the lane. Behind him, massive, dark thunderclouds rolled toward us. There was an eerie green light beneath the coal-gray… an odd distorting of the setting sun? Or something worse?

The guard pulled up at last, his horse panting and prancing. I grabbed the mare's bridle and looked up. "What is it? A ship?"

"A ship, yes," he said.

"Will she agree to take us north?"

A shadow crossed his face. "The captain refuses. He says that storm was building around Point Ruina, and his cargo demands he hasten south, as soon as it passes. He has taken shelter in our harbor only because he fears he cannot make Santa Barbara before it is upon us."

"Did he see the pirate ship?"

"Sí, Don Ventura. They saw her this morning. But she was flying the Mexican flag."

"They did not hail her?"

"No," he said with a shake of his head. "As I said, the captain is in a hurry to sail south, and the storm was chasing them. They took note of the ship, though, because it did not appear as if the captain intended to weigh anchor, closer to shore, and wait out the storm. The *Crescent Moon* was heading directly toward it, as if they intended to round Point Ruina tonight."

"The *fools*," I muttered, turning to Rafael and shaking my open palms. "Why would he take such a risk? Mendoza gets nothing if—" I couldn't bear to finish the thought aloud. *If they all go down.* I swallowed hard. *Zara! Mateo!*

"He likely wants to gain some distance from Rancho Ventura and any support you might rally," Rafael said. "As well as sell your cargo long before you arrive."

"Or get to Monterey and plan his escape, once your gold is in his hands," Mama said. Behind her, my sisters, Estrella and Francesca, interlocked hands with my youngest brother, Jacinto. All stared at me with wide, round, brown eyes, and I felt their collective trust as a weight, even as I felt Mateo's and Zara's from afar.

I turned away from them, gazing at the fearsome, roiling cloud bank, perhaps thirty miles distant. And yet it was so close, in turn, that I felt like I could feel the rumble of its thunder in my chest, as if I should wince at the cracks of lightning.

"They shall turn back," I said, willing confidence into my voice for my beloved family behind me. "To head into what comes would be to tempt death. And Mendoza wishes to collect my debt when he delivers Mateo and Zara to me."

"Fear of death did not keep them from attacking Rancho de la Ventura," Mama said, holding an embroidered handkerchief to her nose. Estrella wrapped her arm around her waist in comfort and laid her cheek on Mama's shoulder.

"If they are wise and make harbor as you suggest, and this storm persists," Rafael said, "we might have a chance at catching up with them. If we ride *now*."

I eyed him. "Are you prepared for that? You've ridden all day to get here."

"As you saw, we each have a spare horse. Give us all a chance to rest a bit, let the horses take their share of grain and water, and we'll be ready. Together, we can each have an extra horse, allowing us to ride hard." He reached out and grasped my shoulder. "I stopped in Santa Barbara. There were no ships headed north. Craig's *Heron* won't be seaworthy for another few days, from what I hear. We must go overland, even if we don't come across the pirates until we reach Monterey."

"And the soldiers of the garrison?" I asked, not feeling any real hope. But I had to know. "Did you speak to them? See them?"

"I stopped there too," Rafael said grimly.

Doña Elena and Francesca edged closer, Estrella and Jacinto right behind them, hopeful for news of rescue or reinforcements.

But Rafael shook his head, looking abashed. The soldiers of the presidio would not prove to be our deliverance.

I bit back a curse and turned away, hands on hips. It was one thing to suspect, another to know. "What was their rationale?" I asked angrily, tossing a hand in the air. "What will it take for them to move to protect Mexico's own?"

"Lieutenant de la Cruz said it is the risk *you* assume," Rafael reluctantly reported, using a careful, delicate tone, "residing so far from the outpost. There is no way that they can protect anyone 'so distant, and since the danger has moved on,' he sees no reason to make the journey. As he put it, he couldn't 'bring your dead men back to life.'"

His tone turned reluctant, reporting the last of it, but his eyes told me that he shared my loathing of the soldiers. *Despicable, no-account, untrustworthy....*

My mother let out a sound of disgust, and Francesca brought upturned fingers to cover her mouth, tears in her eyes. Despite my anger, I acknowledged that it was good that my mother heard this. She was so loyal to the Mother Country.

And despite her obvious dismay, I saw hope flash across young Francesca's pretty face. I knew Captain Craig had caught her eye; while I did not condone his suit—my sister was a good two or three years away from marriageable age—I knew that if Francesca became more receptive to the Unionist cause, it would still be a challenge to persuade our mother.

But that was a problem for another day.

"So we are on our own," I said to Rafael.

He shrugged. "I brought twelve of my best. Choose twelve of your own, as well as every dagger, sword, and pistol you have, and when we find these pirates, we'll make them wish they died at sea."

"Rafael!" Mama said, aghast, pulling Jacinto slightly away, as if that would keep him from absorbing words already uttered.

But little Jacinto squirmed away from her and squared his small shoulders. "No, Mama. I am with Señor Vasquez. I hope every last one of them suffers. Killing our men! Stealing away with Mateo and our goods. And Zara."

His tone and eyes softened as he glanced at me. For the first time, I could see he was a boy on the brink of manhood, just as my sisters were truly growing into womanhood, capable of marrying and seeing to their own households. I blinked. When had that happened?

While I was dreaming about being anywhere but here, I acknowledged to myself. Perhaps if I'd spent as much time fortifying the harbor, the villa, as I had in dreaming about a return to university, I would have seen my brothers and sisters growing up before my very eyes, and protected everyone I loved from these travesties.

Oh, my dear family. Oh, Zara. I am sorry, so sorry.

I'd failed them all. Would they ever forgive me?

Could I ever forgive myself?

And what had I done, chaining Zara to this place, this time, with my love? If I really loved her, if I were truly willing to let her go—rather than praying with everything in me for her to remain—might she be back in her own time, safe and sound?

The truth of it settled in my chest like a heavy weight, square and sure. She'd been ready to go, not at all certain that this time was to be her own. Yes, she'd confessed that she thought she'd made a mistake, trying to go. But that was *after*, after I made her stay.

As much as she'd begged God for a return, I'd begged him to keep her here.

It was my fault. All of this was my fault.

And now I had to find her…to free her. Forever?

CHAPTER 10

ZARA

The cabin door burst open as we crested such a massive wave of water, that a good ten feet of it must have washed over the deck. As I stood to the side of the door and watched as the room flooded to knee depth, I thought through what I must do to survive. It was almost as if this wasn't happening to me, but rather some other person, so I could calmly figure out that other girl's plan.

But then another massive wave hit us and I was pitched forward, falling facedown in the shallow, cold water. I sat up, sputtering, coughing, and rubbed my head where I'd hit the table leg.

For the moment we were upright but listing heavily. I had to get out of the cabin. To stay inside would mean certain death, and I had to get to Mateo, free him, if there was any way to do so. But how was I supposed to do that in a long dress? It'd be very bad to end up shipwrecked with a bunch of pirates naked, but neither could I swim in a full-length gown. The only light was the periodic flash of lightning out the cabin door. Stepping out of the water and onto a chest, I leaned down, gripped the back of my gown and brought it up between my legs like a diaper. Then I grabbed the two corners and tied it at my waist. I knew the men would gape at me if they caught sight of my legs, bare to the thigh, but for the moment, they had bigger concerns before them, as did I.

Like how to stay alive…

We remained listing to one side, and it made me distinctly uneasy. Because we'd taken on so much water as we rolled? Or because there was damage belowdecks?

Mateo.

I had to get to him. There was no way I could face Javier and tell him Mateo had…. Even the thought of it made a big ball form in the back of my throat and brought to mind the sad day when Javier's sister-in-law, Adalia, holding her little son, Alvaro, left their family. The Venturas couldn't lose another family member. Not after losing their dad and their brother Dante too…. They just couldn't. *Please, Lord. Please, please, please….*

I jumped into the water and made my way to the door, holding desperately to the frame as another wave washed over the deck. What I could see outside—as one bolt of lightning after another flashed—stunned me. Rain fell in sheets, pelting my face with icy bits—*hail?* Sails hung at awkward angles everywhere, making it seem like a ghost ship. The mainmast had cracked nearly in half and leaned ominously with every new gust of wind, threatening to pierce the deck.

There were few men left that I could see. I could make out the wide form of the second mate, Gonzalo, scrambling up the mainmast—dagger between his teeth as if intent on cutting sails loose—but then I lost sight of him among the mass of sails and sheets of rain and intermittent darkness between lightning flashes. A sailor moved past me, helping a friend who was clearly dazed and injured. Another moved in the opposite direction. Emilio, the first mate, appeared, shouting orders—at who?—but I grabbed his arm. "Please!" I cried. "Where did they take my friend? Where is Mateo?"

He frowned and stared at me as if I were a ghost, but he glanced toward a dark doorway to our right before shaking his head. "He's likely long dead, Señorita!" he yelled over the wind. "Leave him and spare yourself!"

He moved to a water barrel, pulled a cork, and it began to drain from the bottom. He took my hand, put the cork in my palm, and then placed my other hand over the handle on top of the barrel as he locked down the lid. "We're going down!" he shouted over the wind. "Once it's drained, cork it, roll it to the edge, and send it overboard. Jump right in with it. Hold on to it. Do not lose it!" he cried. "With luck, it will carry you to shore!"

He disappeared into the dark abyss of the windswept deck, crawling over a fallen mast and piles of sailcloth, obviously intent on helping how he could. My heart pounded as another big wave hit us, and five feet of white water crossed the rail and collided into me. I lost my footing and went under again, all too aware that I hadn't taken a breath. I clung to a pile of thick rope and waited for the water to recede, then once it'd passed, turned onto my back and gasped for air. The ship listed to the other side now. The broken end of the mast looked even worse and teetered directly over me, like the blade of a guillotine threatening to impale the condemned.

A *little help, Lord?* I prayed silently. *Can you send us just three winds instead of four?*

Get out, came the reply to my heart. *Quickly. Away! Away!*

For the first time, I considered my situation as a blessing rather than a curse. There was no one watching me. My captors were dead or distracted. Was this a divine path toward freedom? I glanced back at the water barrel, still draining at the bottom, and considered corking it, rolling it to the side, and doing as Emilio had told me to do—tossing it overboard and praying it would take me to shore. To remain on the ship meant certain death. That much was clear.

Everything in me urged me to leave the ship, as fast as possible.

But then my eyes went back to the doorway as lightning flashed.

Mateo.

I had to try. Had to see if he was still alive.

Biting onto the cork so I wouldn't lose it, I scrambled to my feet and made my way to the hold and braced myself in the doorway, trying to see below. Useless; it was pitch black just a few inches in.

I turned and felt for the steps with my feet. It was steep—more a ladder than stairs. After the next wave passed, I scrambled downward but remained where I was, trying to let my eyes adjust and get some sort of bearings. "Mateo!" I shouted, tucking the cork into the bodice of my dress. "*Mateo!*"

I listened but heard nothing but the whistle of the wind,

the wash of the waves, and the terrible creaking of the ship that sounded horrendously *weak* to me—as if she were slowly cracking apart beneath my feet. The water down below in the hold was up to my knees and rising.

"Mateo!" I cried, working my way down a hall. Behind me was a cavernous area—what I assumed held cargo and rows of hammocks, if the *Pirates of the Caribbean* movies were accurate at all. But they'd talked about putting him in a storeroom. Locking him in. Emilio had mentioned that, right?

Was there more than one hall of storerooms? More than one deck? What if I was in the wrong area of the ship? What if I drowned down here, in the dark?

One step at a time, Grillita, my grandmother's voice said in my head.

I put a hand to my chest. It had been so clear, her voice. And she was right. I had to focus, not give into panic. Panic would be the death of me for sure. *And Mateo.*

I continued to call his name as I worked my way down the narrow hall, all the while trying to keep track of where the ladder to the deck was in case we capsized again and I had to swim for it. "Mateo! *Mateo!*"

I thought I heard something and cocked my head to listen first in one direction, then another. Nothing but storm and sea filled my ears.

"Mateo!" I screamed, my voice higher and more stressed than I'd ever heard it.

For a blessed moment, the wind and thunder seemed to pause. I made out his voice then, even though it was faint. "Here! I'm in here!"

He wasn't far. *Farther along and to the right,* I thought.

I moved forward, and my fingers found the splintered wood of his door first. What had happened to it? I could see nothing. "Mateo?"

"Over…here," he said again.

I didn't like the weak nature of his tone at all.

"Where? *Where?* Are you hurt?" I felt my way through the doorway, trying to make out anything in the inky darkness. "Keep speaking to me, Mateo! I can't see anything!"

"Hurt, yes. But it's…this that holds me." He was short of breath, as if pinned.

I moved, hands sprawled before me in the pitch dark, trying to feel any obstacles in the absence of sight.

When my knuckles brushed the cold hard edge of steel, I knew.

A *safe.* The safe the pirates had stolen from the storehouse and so laboriously carried to the boat. It must've been stored in the room across from Mateo's…and burst through to his, right through the walls or doors.

"When we were hit by that first wave?" I guessed.

"Yes," he wheezed, crying out when the hull shifted, pressing the safe against him.

I winced and moved around the hard edge of iron. "Perhaps I can help you push it away."

"Impossible," he panted. "Too…heavy. Even for the both of us."

I ignored his words and tried anyway. But he was right. The way the ship was listing, it held the safe against him.

"Perhaps if we…rolled…the other way," he tried to joke,

between gasps for breath.

"Shhh," not laughing. "Save your strength. How injured are you?"

"It…isn't good."

"Ribs?" I guessed.

"Yes. Perhaps…more."

I swallowed hard, suddenly thirsty in the midst of all this water. I shoved away my fears over internal injuries and tried to think of a way out. *A lever. We need a lever.* If I could lodge something strong against the wall, perhaps that would help me raise it far enough from Mateo that he could escape. And with the aid of the right wave at the right moment…

I moved around the room, feeling for a strong piece of wood. I tossed aside one option after another, knowing they were too flimsy. But finally my fingers closed around a splintered corner post of a sturdy doorframe, four inches square. My heart surging with hope, I sloshed back to Mateo; the water was as deep as my thighs now. Even if we didn't capsize again, this ship had to be going down. Would the water make it easier or harder to move the safe?

"Okay, I found something I can use as a lever. When the next wave washes past, I'm going to try this. If you are able to wriggle out of there, you'll have to duck this piece of wood. Comprendes?"

"Sí," he panted.

I waited, wishing for a giant wave, just big enough to help me, but not big enough to capsize us. I wasn't sure I could keep my bearings and get Mateo, injured, out to the deck again. Especially if we had to swim.

Please, Lord. Please, please, please....

But there was no perfect wave. I tried on two, three, then four small waves, but I wasn't strong enough. I leaned against the safe, panting, trying to think up another plan.

The fifth wave surprised me, and I acted almost too late. "There!" I cried, lapsing into English in my excitement. "There! Come out, Mateo! Move! Move!" I could hear my bar beginning to crack under the strain, and the wave was moving past. In a second, the safe would be pressing against him again.

He scraped toward me, obeying my tone if not my native language. *He was close, so close.*

"Hurry!" I grunted, beginning to feel the weight of the safe bear against me as we lost our edge of gravity.

He leaned and came under the bar, just as my strength gave out.

The safe slammed against the wall with a thud.

"Mateo?" I panted, half-panicked that he didn't get out in time.

"*Estoy aquí,*" he said. *I'm here.*

I grappled in the dark for his arm. "Oh, thank God! Let's get out of here before this ship takes us down with her."

CHAPTER 44

JAVIER

The storm hit us well after dark. We'd been traveling for hours with urns to light our way, slowing to a walk but feeling pressed to get as far as we could before sleep claimed us.

There was an icy glint to the rain, and Rafael's eyes met mine in the shadows of our lantern. Out on the water, it had undoubtedly been hail. I wondered what had pressed the captain to round the point in such hazardous weather. Why had he not even waited for morn? It made no sense. No one rounded Point Ruina during a storm, and certainly not without the aid of daylight.

Lightning flashed, and from our vantage point high on the hills, we could see the angry seas, roiling, the waves battering the shore as if aiming to expel all their energy. I pulled up with a start, not wanting to lose track of where I'd been looking—out near the point. *Had I seen—? Was it a—?*

Thunder cracked, so close, I felt it in my chest, as if it had rumbled about inside my ribs. Rain pelted my hat and dripped off the rim, but it was the lightning I was waiting for. Just another glimpse. Rafael pulled around and waited in silence beside me. "Did you see something?"

"I thought so," I said, looking out toward the point again.

The other men stopped behind us, asking questions, but I ignored them.

Lightning flashed again, a terrific bolt that zigzagged down to the water and illuminated miles of empty waves racing toward shore. My eyes madly shifted left and right.

But there was no ship.

My heart paused and then pounded. There was no way Mendoza's *Crescent Moon* had been there a moment ago and now was gone.

Unless it had simply slipped past the point?

"Did you see anything?" I asked Rafael.

"No, friend. Come. Even if they ran into trouble, they'd still be miles ahead."

I nodded and followed him, thankful that the men behind us had fallen silent.

It embarrassed me, this desperate need to know what had transpired for Mateo and Zara. It made me feel vulnerable. Weak. Which unsettled me.

Worse was the thought of losing them both forever.

CHAPTER 12

ZARA

I urged Mateo up the ladder-like stairs, fighting against the waves as one after another poured down on us. The cold dumps of water reminded me of dirt dropped onto a coffin by a small bulldozer—intent on covering us forever. Again and again, Mateo fell against me, losing ground every time, until I decided to climb with him, my arms on the rail to either side, bearing his weight against every new wave that came down upon us. He was just too battered, too weak to take this on by himself.

"Leave me, Zara! Save yourself!" he shouted over his shoulder, sounding disgusted and humiliated.

"No! I will not! Go! Hurry!"

He forced himself to take another step, a new handhold, before the next wave hit us. Water was steadily rising beneath too. We were halfway up the ladder and the water was sloshing around my calves.

"Go, Mateo," I urged. "You can do this."

"If anything happens to you—"

"Stop thinking about that. Think only of getting to the top and out of here. Do it for me. For Doña Elena! Your sisters!

Your brothers! Go!"

This seemed to galvanize him. He took two steps and was halfway through the door when the next wave hit.

I almost lost my hold on the rail. I'd been ready to burst through right behind him, not set to withstand another rush of water. I prayed madly as the wave passed me, one arm giving sway to the surge, each ounce of seawater seeming like clawing tendrils, pulling at each of my last five fingers to let go.

But then it was past and Mateo was through, turning, hand to his belly, to watch me come after him. Lightning flashed, and I could see him clearly outlined, bent over, heaving for breath. I couldn't believe it, standing there, on deck at last. We'd made it this far. Could we possibly make it to shore?

I fished in my bodice for the cork I'd stashed there, praying it had remained. It had. Lightning flashed constantly, and I thought I glimpsed land. But it was much, much farther than I'd hoped. I turned away, not wanting Mateo to see my fear as another bolt of lightning came down, so close that I could smell the ozone and feel the soaked hairs at the nape of my neck practically rise. I hurried over to the water barrel, shoved the cork into the drain, then tipped it over and rolled it to the edge.

I grabbed a length of rope that was floating against my legs and tied it around the barrel lid handle. Then I made a loop around Mateo, fastening him to it.

"What? No!" he said, weakly pushing my hands away. "Tie yourself!"

I batted his hands away in irritation and tightened the knot. "I will!" I shouted as thunder cracked. "There's plenty more behind you!"

The rope was long, and I knew it'd be better if I cut it off so it wouldn't get entangled on anything else, but I didn't exactly have the blade I'd need to do so. I was casting about for anything I could use—or something to at least wrap the excess length around—when a hand grabbed my hair and pulled me upright and against a broad chest.

"Where do you think you're going?" shouted a voice in my ear.

The second mate, Gonzalo.

Hot tears came to my eyes—I always cried when I was angry, and it seemed like I'd finally broken through constant shock to pure fury. After all we'd made it through, there was no way—*no way*—that I was going to let this jerk stop us.

I was just about to ram him in the belly with my elbow and then turn and bring his head to my knee, when the ship lurched beneath our feet and we began sliding to the side rail. The man released me with a cry, grasping about to grab hold of anything that would stop his fall. Side by side, we bumped and skittered across the planked floor of the broad deck. I looked behind me in terror, knowing that the ship was going down, stern first. I rammed into the front wall of the captain's cabin, just as Gonzalo did beside me. We stared at each other as lightning flashed constantly.

I'd only had to see *Titanic* once to know what would come next. The ship would go down and pull us with her, creating a suctioning whirlpool that we wouldn't be able to escape before the oxygen in our lungs ran out. We had to be away, as far away as possible, when it happened.

"Mateo!" I screamed as I scrambled to my feet. "Jump! Swim!"

But he and the barrel were already gone, presumably tossed overboard. Only Captain Mendoza, clinging to a side rail with soaked tendrils of black hair coiling across his cheek, glanced back at me before diving off. Two others followed him.

The two-hundred-pound Gonzalo knocked the wind out of me as he literally crawled over me in his crazy desire to be free of the ship. I choked and gasped for breath, holding my belly, watching as the lightning—which was so frenzied and frequent now it was like an odd sort of strobe light—illuminated his progress. He reached the railing and made a flailing jump overboard. I remained where I was, stunned, trying to breathe again and wondered if this was all some terrible dream.

Surely I wasn't the only person left alive on this ship, was I?

I forced myself to move, even before breath returned to my lungs, crawling to the railing. I'd gone swimming almost every night of the summer, back home in my own time, loving the feel of natural space and peace and freedom. Only God, the waves, and me. Time to feel the surge of the tide, the living breath of the sea. I loved it, looked forward to it each night with the same anticipation I might in seeing a dear friend.

But as I teetered on the edge of the rail, praying for breath enough to surface after my dive, I had one thought.

This ocean I've always loved is now determined to kill me.

CHAPTER 13

ZARA

I hit the water hard from about fifteen feet up. It hadn't been my most graceful dive. But as soon as I surfaced, I began swimming, thankful that the corners of my dress seemed to be staying put in their knots at my waist. Perhaps the water had tugged them even tighter. I did my best to do a breaststroke, but the seas were too wild, the water constantly washing over my face. I took a deep breath, went under water and did several strokes, came up for another, and then went down again. I felt I was making more progress this way.

Help me, Lord. Help me get far enough away.

I'd lost track of where the ship was, but from the direction of the waves, I thought I knew where *shore* was. I went with them. Even beneath the water, I could hear it when the ship finally gave up and with a tremendous *crack* and boom, she screeched and gasped, as if fighting the sea and losing with her last gasp. As expected, I felt the pull of water around me, sucking me backward, but I'd managed to get far enough away—or the ship had been full enough with water—that it wasn't as bad as I had feared.

I rose to the surface and waited for one flash of lightning after another to help me see in all directions. I didn't see Mateo, and I fought off the urge to call out to him. While all I'd glimpsed was wreckage from the ship—no people—among the waves about me, if any of the pirates had survived, I didn't want them to know where I was.

I had to get to shore. That's where Mateo would head too, the best he could. I hoped and prayed he'd made it over the rail, still attached to the barrel. That he was alive. *Give him strength, Lord. Give me strength too.*

My fingertips brushed past wood, and I desperately cast about until I found it again. A timber, of good size—nearly as wide around as I was. I wrapped it in my arms, bobbing partially out of the water, feeling a surge of real hope for the first time. I admitted to myself that I'd been worried I wouldn't have the strength to make it to shore. Not on my own, after all I'd endured over the last couple of days.

Silently uttering thanks and praying that the storm would send any great white sharks in another direction, I got my bearings again and began kicking with everything I had in me. I felt buoyant, hopeful, for a good long time, but after some hours, the teeth-chattering chill won out over my energy, and I began to give into despair. I was shivering, sending my teeth rattling, and my throat ached with thirst. My eyes burned so badly from the salt and fatigue that I let them close, resting my cheek against the rough wood of the timber as I feebly continued to kick.

I caught myself dozing off, my grip on the timber beginning to loosen, as the sea beckoned me deeper. Distantly

I considered the relief of it, letting go. Giving up. Stopping this fight that never ended, quitting the hope that this cursed storm would cease or the sun would somehow rise again.

I wondered: if I gave up and let myself sink into the sea, would she spew me back up in my own time? *What good is this, Lord?* I complained. *To come to this time for love, family, adventure, only to die? Did you just want me to recognize that my wishes had been fully granted before you took me home…to you or to my own time?*

But I didn't hear his voice…or my abuela's in answer. Only the constant waves, rising behind me, passing beneath and around me, building again, as if I were nothing but a dull rock they could ignore. Over and over again.

It took me some time to realize that the sound of the waves had changed…that I was hearing them crash on shore.

On shore.

My head popped up, and a pitiful sound left my mouth. I cast the timber away and began swimming in earnest again, a brief surge of energy fueling my path forward. In a minute or two, my toes brushed sand. Sand! In my excitement, the next wave took me by surprise and I came up choking and coughing. But I was close to safety. So close. A minute later, I was chest-deep, then waist-deep, then stumbling on numb, tree-like legs, then crawling, my cold fingers clenching handfuls of sand.

When I was mostly clear of the surf, I collapsed.

And I succumbed to sleep, thinking that the feel of sand on my cheek might be the best sort of pillow I'd ever had.

CHAPTER 14

ZARA

I awoke to the feel of a blade tip at my throat. I blinked, my heart pounding with hope, dreamily remembering the first time I'd met Javier. But it wasn't Javier, of course, I told myself groggily. Javier wouldn't be awakening me with the tip of a sword. He'd be sweeping me into his arms…

"Get up," growled Gonzalo, running his hand over one scruffy cheek.

I groaned and closed my eyes, wishing I could go back to sleep and not wake up to the continuation of my nightmare. Of all the people that had been on that ship, this was the dude I was stuck with? I was tired, so utterly spent.

My thoughts moved to Mateo, but I didn't dare look around for him or call for him. If this guy got him too because I reminded him that I wasn't the only shipwreck survivor who might fetch a ransom, I'd never forgive myself.

"Get up, I said," the second mate repeated gruffly, pressing the blade hard enough that I lifted my chin and eyed him. "We must be on our way. Indians might come to pick through the wreckage."

I forced myself to rise partway, propping myself with one arm. "To where?" I said with a scratchy-throated scoff, glancing south and north. There was nothing but miles of raw, untouched beach as far as I could see.

"We will continue north to Monterey," he said, ignoring my question. He slid the sword aside as I wearily rose and began to work at the damp, sandy knots of my gown. "No need to let down your skirts," he said.

I didn't have to look up to know the jerk was leering at my bare legs, so I continued to work on the knots. If he made a move on me, if there wasn't a sword between us, I'd show him every move my Krav Maga instructor had ever taught me. But first thing was first. "Do you have any water?" I asked, wincing at the effort of even speaking those few words, given my parched, salty throat.

He shook his head. "We might find a stream as we move north. We're just south of the point. I know there's a watering hole on the other side."

That was something, but I didn't know if I could make it an hour, let alone hike for five or six hours, before my thirst would cripple me. I wished I'd spent more time surfing survivalist Internet sites; maybe then I'd know which plant I could dig up for some sort of nourishment and water, or if there was cactus up in the hills above us worth cutting down for the liquid inside…I thought that was a thing. Wasn't it?

Gonzalo was agitated, constantly looking about as we began to walk. Surely it wasn't Mateo that made him so uneasy. "Did others from the ship make it?" I asked. There were several sets of footprints in the sand, and they couldn't all be the second mate's. Maybe one set was Mateo's.

"How comforting that you would think about our welfare," said a voice I knew too well. Captain Mendoza moved out of a cleft in the rocks, lifting his trousers and fastening his belt as if he'd just relieved himself. "Your concern is touching, my dear," he said, waiting for us to reach him. The mate grabbed hold of my arm and pulled me to a stop in front of the captain. Mendoza reached out to pinch a tendril of my salty, stiff hair and looked me over like I was nothing more than a bag of stolen goods, surprisingly returned to him.

I pulled away. "Concern for you?" I scoffed. "I hoped you'd gone down with your ship. Isn't that what the best captains are supposed to do?"

He laughed under his breath, putting his hands on his belt. "I'm certain you did. But here I am! Unfortunately, with the *Crescent Moon* and her cargo lost," he said, bending toward me, "*your* safe delivery is my only way to redeem that loss."

His only way. I blinked. *No. Please, no.* "Mateo?" I asked in a whisper, in spite of myself. But he seemed to know, seemed to be sure that I was the only one....

The captain pursed his lips and tapped them, then looked out to sea. "He apparently did not survive. We traversed the length of the beach, looking for signs of him, but there was nothing."

"What about all the footprints?" I looked from them to the captain's face again.

"Indians, it appears," he said, dismissing the prints. "Probably down here fishing before the storm." It was as if there was not a bit of care in him. No bit of care for a boy's *life.*

I wrenched away from the mate, let out a howl, and crashed into the captain, like a linebacker training for a game. It surprised him, and he went tumbling backward, and I immediately pounced upon his chest, straddling it. I punched him once, twice, before the mate wrapped his burly arms around me and bodily lifted me away by several feet.

Captain Mendoza rose, sputtering curses and wiping his mouth, grimacing when it came away with blood from the corner. "That is the last time you shall ever strike me," he seethed as he strode toward us. He leaned toward me, waggling his finger in warning.

I snapped at it with my teeth, narrowly missing.

He gaped at me, even as he took a step back. "What sort of woman *are* you?" he asked. "By turns you are a lady and— a vixen."

I just glared at him. I hoped he was scared of me. Because the first chance I got, I wanted to take both these men down and see that they had a very hard time rising again.

"You are not at all the sort of woman I'd heard Don de la Ventura would give his heart to," he said, still staring. "You are like a…a *wildling*."

I laughed under my breath. "You have no idea."

"I like her spirit," said Gonzalo, nuzzling his scruffy cheek against my ear. He had my arms pinned against my chest, holding me so tightly that I couldn't head-butt his nose. "Give me a night with her, Capitán. I'll hobble her and break her to the saddle by morn."

The captain clearly didn't miss the surge of fear washing through me. A slow grin eased the grim, tight corners of his mouth. He dared to lean closer again. "So you fear *that*, do you, wildling? Well, be good, or I'll give Gonzalo what he asks… a night with you, alone."

Again, I tried to swallow. Even if I hadn't been deprived of water since yesterday, I knew I would've been scared spitless.

"Am I not your only remaining prize? The only thing that you might trade for a ransom of gold? Remember that you could yet claim *double* my bounty, if you deliver me unharmed." To my own ear, I sounded desperate, and my desperation grated at my heart.

"Ahh, but some pleasures," Gonzalo whispered in my ear, pulling me even tighter against the hard width and breadth of his body, "are worth the cost."

I panted for breath beneath the mate's rocklike grip, staring in grim fear at the captain, waiting for him to come to his senses. Above any base desire, greed *had* to fuel him the most. Wasn't that what led him to attack Bonita Harbor and kidnap us in the first place?

But he made me uneasy, as his eyes shifted to the sea and back to me, as if considering it.

"The gold is a fine treasure," said Gonzalo. "And yet if we made Don de la Ventura hate us even more, would that not build our future treasure?"

I frowned in confusion. *Future treasure?*

"You should have seen her lying there, so sweetly. And those bare legs, Capitán. So beautifully curved, that I—"

"Enough," the captain snapped. I fought the urge to close my eyes in relief. He'd apparently decided, at least for the moment. He reached down in the sand for a span of rope that had washed ashore with all sorts of other wreckage. He tossed it to Gonzalo. "Let's get this girl to Monterey and find a new ship and crew. We must be ready to sail as soon as we have Ventura's gold in hand. If he lives up to his reputation, he may very well pursue us, after the girl is safe."

With a guttural sound of frustration, the mate wrenched my arms behind me and tied my wrists, every movement harsh. I submitted to it, uncomplaining, knowing I could neither outrun them nor fight them both off. No, I had to bide my time. Take them on, one and then the other.

"Go on," Gonzalo said when he was done, his sausage-like fingers caressing my hips, pulling me against him a moment, before shoving me forward so hard I almost stumbled. The captain was already a good distance ahead. I gritted my teeth, gained my footing, and trudged forward.

"You think you're safe, sweetness," Gonzalo said, drawing his sword and pricking me between the shoulders.

I scowled back at him and quickened my steps, trying to stay out of his reach. But he kept pace.

"You think it's over. Well, it's not. We get a bit of water, a bit of food, and the capitán's attention will again wander. There are other forces at work here, you see. Beyond the gold."

Again, with the vague references! "What other forces?"

"Ahh, nothing for you to worry about, sweetness."

I could practically feel his gaze on my hips, my butt, my bare feet as they peeked out from beneath the hem of my gown with each step. I didn't care what it cost me. If he or the captain attacked me, I would die fighting. It made me feel even stronger, thinking that they would lose their last bargaining chip for Javier's gold if I went down fighting. Maybe I'd even take one of them with me.

Their last bargaining chip. The phrase ran through my brain as if on repeat. *Oh, Javier.* He would be devastated. Over Mateo's loss and then mine. Thinking of his potential pain drove my own fear into a corner, and I teared up, thinking of how glad he'd been that I was still in his arms after trying to return to my own time. He'd been exultant, nearly delirious with joy, and it had been so palpable it had spread to me. He'd wanted to tell me he loved me…and I'd asked him to wait. It had been too much in that moment.

I smiled through my tears. I had to get back to him, had to be reunited, even for only a moment. I wanted to hear those words from his lips. Tell him I loved him too.

But that meant I wasn't willing to die. Not really.

I glanced over my shoulder to the steadily climbing sun.

And knew that I already dreaded the coming night.

CHAPTER 15

JAVIER

The road north was deeply rutted from wagon wheels and horse hooves. Most people traveled the length of Alta California by sea, but a fair number still traversed it by land. When I first saw something in the road, several hours into our morning ride, I wondered what it was. A heap of rags? Something that had fallen off the back of a wagon?

Centinela, Zara's odd wolf-dog companion, loped toward it as if she were curious too. She'd joined us—at a distance—from the start, as if she'd sensed our goal—then gradually eased nearer. She reached the lump of rags, sniffed it, skittered left and right, looked at me, then loped off.

No, es imposible, I said to myself, chagrined that I'd even *hope* it was possible. But as we drew nearer, my heart pounded. It was him! Wasn't that his curly hair? His wiry adolescent body, beneath the strips of his battered shirt? But he wasn't moving.... I kicked my mare in the flanks and leaned forward in the saddle, closing the distance between us. I hopped off before she came to a full stop, running the rest of the distance between my brother and me.

"Mateo," I panted as I knelt beside him and tenderly lifted him up, frightened that he was dead. The other men on horses thundered up and around us. *"Mateo!"* I pulled him against me as if my love and hope would send life into his bones.

His dark lashes fluttered and then slowly rose. His eyes were unfocused for a moment, but it mattered not. He was alive!

"Ja-Javier?" he rasped out, squinting as he tried to focus on me.

"Water! Get us water," I said to the nearest man, then looked directly back to him. "Mateo, how did you get away? Where is Zara?"

"I do not…know," he said, closing his eyes and leaning back, wincing in pain.

He was injured badly. I loosened my grip and gently assisted him down again, pulling aside the remains of his shirt to see alarming, sprawling bruises that told me his injuries were deep and serious. "Mateo, Mateo," I whispered, lowering his head to the ground. "What has happened?"

"Shipwreck," he said simply, gasping out the words. "Zara…saved me."

"Saved you? Then she was with you? Might she have survived too?"

"She did," he said, looking to me through hard, narrowed eyes. "But they have her…Javier. The captain and the…mate. They tied her up and are—" He grimaced, as if a wave of pain overtook him. "North," he managed after. "They head…. north."

I lifted my head and stared hard toward the coast, but much of it was hidden behind the intervening hills. *Shipwreck.*

And the only survivors were two of the crew, Mateo, and Zara? I closed my eyes to give brief thanks to God and crossed myself. When I opened my eyes, the men around me were doing the same.

"Four of you will remain with my brother. Build a travois and get him home to my mother. She will see to him or send for a doctor. For the rest of us," I grit out, looking about at each of them, "this day is not over until we see Señorita Ruiz safely away from her captors."

ZARA

We stumbled upon a nearly dry streambed at about noon and hurried up to where we might find a deeper pool. The two men squatted by a foot-wide, shallow pool, ignoring me, sitting there on my knees as they dipped again and again, splashing their faces and drinking until the pool was muddy. Only when their thirst was somewhat sated did Captain Mendoza glance back at me, as if remembering.

"Cut her loose," he said.

"But Capitán—" the mate began.

"Cut her loose. She is weak with hunger and thirst. She will not attack again." He stared hard at me as he said it, as if warning me not to try anything foolish.

Gonzalo went behind me, grunting and huffing as he bent and untied the rope. As soon as I was free, I scrambled forward, cupping my hands and bringing the murky, brackish water to my mouth again and again. I didn't care what parasites or giardia or whatever else I might get. All I cared about was getting a drink, a blessed drink, and then another...

The captain lolled to his side on one arm, staring at me like I was an exotic animal at the zoo. He laughed without mirth and then rose, pulling a bag from his side, opened it, and tossed Gonzalo a piece of dried jerky, now rather mushy after the swim to shore. Still, I stared at it, my stomach rumbling.

Mendoza eyed me. "Forgive me, but there will be none for you, girl. You've had your fill of water; that will keep you alive. But I prefer to keep you in a weakened state until we reach Monterey," he said, subconsciously beginning to lift a hand to his bruised jaw.

I looked away. I would not give him the satisfaction of a reply. It was almost better to know that he feared me than to have a bit of their lunch. In my world, the only men who feared strong women, who needed to make their girlfriends or wives weak in some way, were men who doubted themselves. It was good, *good*, if the captain had this need.

But I glanced up at the sun, high above us, and knew we had only eight or nine hours until nightfall. After a full day's walk, little water, and no food, how would I be able to fight these two off if they decided to follow through on their threats?

I had to find a way to dissuade them. Or preserve enough strength to fight them with all I had remaining in me.

JAVIER

I divided up the men when we found where Mateo had reached the road. Eight were sent ahead and would double-back along the shore, setting a trap and lying in wait. Eight of us would go after the pirates and Zara from the south, driving them into the trap if not capturing them outright on their own. The eight remaining would patrol the road, in case the miscreants evaded our closing trap on the coast.

"If we catch up with them," I said to Rafael, Hector, and the others, "draw your sword and yell with everything in you. I want them frightened; it will be our greatest opportunity for them to give Zara up instead of using her as a shield. And I want them taken alive. I want to savor the moment those fellows are sentenced to death and are forced to climb the gallows, contemplating the price of their transgressions."

Somber faces nodded in agreement all around me, and we set out.

We easily picked up their trail in the sand, but they'd already made it past the point, so they were not in sight. We hung back, allowing the other group time to get ahead, to the north, and find a spot to lay their trap.

Waiting made me mad with worry, knowing that Zara might be suffering even at this very moment. She'd already been through so much. All I wanted to do was whip my horse into a dead run, leaning low in the saddle as we raced along the water's edge, until I could leap upon the captain and the mate and beat them both senseless. But I could almost hear my older brother's counsel in my mind: to tear out headlong would be a young man's indulgence of will, not the way of wisdom.

And the way of wisdom was the only way I might find Zara safe again in my arms by nightfall.

I looked about for Centinela, knowing the wolf-dog would bring Zara comfort, but she had disappeared.

CHAPTER 16

ZARA

We followed ten strides behind the captain. He'd insisted Gonzalo stay behind with me, one hand on my elbow at all times.

The mate smirked at me when my stomach rumbled so loud that he could hear it too. "I have a bit of jerky left in my satchel here," Gonzalo said, patting the pack slung across his shoulder and hanging near his groin. "What would you trade me for a bit of it?" he whispered wickedly, and then glanced ahead to the captain to make sure he hadn't heard.

"Mark my words," I said, not looking his way. "The moment I get the chance, I'll take that wad of wet jerky and stuff it down your throat until you choke on it."

The big man huffed a laugh and yanked me closer. "Fine words from a little bit like you." We were walking by a sea cliff, and the captain edged out of view for moments at a time as he made his way between boulders. He was now a good twenty paces ahead of us. The rocks we crossed were frequently sharp, and all three of us were barefoot, forcing us to pick our way forward. I could feel the mate's wandering eyes on me, the increasing distance between the captain and us. The next time Mendoza disappeared around the bend, Gonzalo grabbed me and pushed me against the cliff, pressing into me. "I'm going to teach you how to respect a man," he said, leaning in to kiss me, his hands moving upward.

I reacted on instinct. I rammed my knee up to his groin. As he bent over in pain, I shifted a pace away, centered myself, then kicked him in the face. I gasped as my bare foot met his nose, knowing I'd hurt myself as much as him, but I didn't care. It felt good to do something to defend myself...even better to show him I wasn't about to ever *respect* him.

I madly sawed the rope at my wrists against an exposed ridge of sharp rock, desperately trying to free myself, when the mate rammed into me, knocking me into the wet sand. My head hit an outcrop of rock, stunning me. I blinked slowly, trying to get my vision of my attacker to focus back into one instead of three. His crooked nose dripped blood into his mustache and beard. With a growl of disgust and menace, he straddled me, driving my still-bound hands beneath me into such a horrible position I feared they'd both break. He swore at me and then lifted a meaty hand to slap me.

But in our fall, my skirts had flung upward, and my legs were free. I lifted both of them, wrapped them around his neck and wrenched him backward, his eyes rounding in surprise.

It was his turn to know the pain of head meeting rock. Even before I was fully upright and seeing clearly, I had no doubt his head was at an unnatural angle.

He was dead. *Dead.*

I stared at him in shock, panting for breath. I'd wished

him gone, even wanted him dead. But now that he was, it made me sick to my stomach. My belly heaved, but there was nothing in it to bring up.

A low chuckle sounded behind me, and I turned to eye the captain. Then I looked back to the sand, still trying to come to grips. *I'd killed a man. It was self-defense, yes, but I'd killed someone!* Again, my stomach turned, but there wasn't even bile coming up.

"Perhaps I won't ransom you back to the ranchero," he said, squatting beside Gonzalo and reaching to check his pulse. The captain's dark eyes ran over me. "I could make a fortune with you in the ring. Such a pretty little thing, but with such *fight* in you." He rose, strode over to me, reached down, and hauled me to my feet. We stood, face to face, a mere two inches between our noses. "It appears that it is only you and I now, Señorita Ruiz," he said silkily.

We paused there for two breaths, then three, before he abruptly let me go, pulling me behind him by the arm. He left my wrists tied behind me.

I glanced back over my shoulder. "Are you not even going to bury him?"

"No. Come high tide, the sea will claim him, as she does every dead sailor," Mendoza said.

As we rounded another point and saw another sprawling curve of beach, I began to tremble violently. *Shock*, I assessed distantly. It was all too much. The attempt to go home to my own time, the attack, the kidnapping, the shipwreck, and now the mate's death. In turns I found satisfaction in it, and then deep regret. I hadn't wanted him to die. I'd only wanted to defend myself. To get Gonzalo off of me. To not let him break my wrists.

I loved Javier. I did.

But I couldn't do this. Couldn't live like this. Where people had to fight for their lives, every single day, in some way. For food. For shelter. For defense.

I thought again about Abuela's apartment. About being home, where I could take a long, hot shower and slip on underwear—real store-bought, mass-produced underwear—a pair of yoga pants and a big ol' sweatshirt. Flop down on the old couch and flip on my cell to watch something mindless on Netflix. I'd have to get my GED now, since I'd probably missed the last couple weeks of school and graduation. The colleges that had accepted me would demand that...

"Watch yourself!" the captain said, yanking me toward him. In my reverie, I'd narrowly missed stepping on a sea urchin, clinging to a water-filled crevice in the rock we were crossing.

He turned me in order to fully face him and peered into my eyes with some concern. He patted my cheeks, pinched my chin, and leaned closer. He swore under his breath. "Come," he said, pulling me to a small sandy spot in the sand. "You're trembling with cold."

I didn't bother to tell him it was shock, not the cold. I didn't care. It would be a blessing of sorts to slip into unconsciousness. I couldn't really feel his hand on my elbow, and I stumbled. Grumbling, he leaned down, swept me into his arms, and carried me ten more strides, then set me down in the sand. He peered behind me, looking at my numb hands, then pulled a dagger from his waist. Sawing at the rope, he cut through it at last, then brought my hands around to my lap, carefully massaging the blood back into them.

He reached into his own small bag and drew out some jerky, stuffing it into my mouth when I didn't grab it. I couldn't seem to focus on it—or him, or the rocks. It was all starting to whirl about me as I told myself to *chew, Zara, chew, and now swallow,* remembering from some far-off place that protein and salt would help me deal, in more ways than one.

But then the idea of needing salt after all the seawater I'd swallowed, clinging to that timber among the incessant waves, made me giggle. The kind of giggle that you get in church, during a quiet moment when you know you shouldn't laugh— absolutely shouldn't. I managed to swallow just before I began laughing so hard that tears ran down my face.

"Perfect," said the captain dryly. "Now I have a hysterical female on my hands." He flopped to a seat beside me, leaning against the rock and lifting his head to the sun, eyes closed.

His comment, of course, made me laugh harder. Hysterical? Well, he didn't know the half of it. But the laughter seemed to clear my head, and gradually my trembling stopped. I could feel my hands on fire as a million blood cells began to prick their way forward through deadened palms, knuckles, and fingertips. I watched as they literally turned from blue to rosy pink.

"He tied your rope too tight," the captain grunted.

"So you will leave me free?"

"That would be rather foolhardy. But I doubt Don Javier would be pleased if I delivered you with two hands in need of amputation. No, I intend to deliver you whole, so I get my full share of the gold promised. But I've experienced enough from you, Señorita, to recognize that it is prudent to take precautions if I wish to deliver you at all."

My trembling had ceased, and my vision was steadying.

His knife was at my throat just as I was contemplating making my move, while I was still free. "Did you truly take me for a fool?" he asked. "I said I wished to deliver you whole, but if you press me, I shall make you regret it in a hundred different ways."

"But then you would get only half the promised gold."

He tipped his head to one side and studied me. "Rest assured, there are other ways I shall capitalize on this arrangement, so I have some leeway."

I frowned. There it was again. A reference to something else going on...some other way this whole deal would benefit him. How was that possible? When he had lost his entire ship and all the stolen goods? One or two chests of gold could not possibly make up for all that. Maybe I was fuzzy-headed now, shock keeping me from adding two and two to make four. "Other ways?" I forced myself to ask. *There's something here, something important.*

"Come now," he said, ignoring my question. He rose, his hand on my elbow. "We must find a place to be out of the wind and rain for the night."

The bit of jerky and rest and the break from my bonds continued to do some good as we walked. My head was clearing, my heart steadying. We had to be getting closer to Monterey. He was nearly as tired as I was; I could see it in his gait. And now my hands were free. Perhaps I could outrun him. Hide somewhere.

"Feeling better, my dear?" He smirked and pulled me roughly along, his grip tight on my wrist, as if he could read my mind. I thought again of twisting, breaking his grasp on me—it'd be easy enough to do—but I was just so tired. Could I really outrun him? Fight him off, when he had a knife? And if he caught me, what would he do to me?

"I think it would be best if I tied you again," he said, pulling me to a stop and studying my face as if he could read my thoughts. "No sense giving you any ideas that you can escape me."

CHAPTER 17

JAVIER

The sun was near to setting when we came across the dead man's body.

The men fanned out around it and then paused, waiting for me to draw near. The incoming tide was pushing us closer to the cliffs. I hoped that around the next point the beach would broaden, or else we'd end up in sodden clothes, even atop our horses.

"So we're down to the captain and Zara," Rafael said, gloved hand tapping his lips in thought. "Think the captain killed him for insubordination?"

I dismounted, crouched down, and studied the victim's broken nose and then the imprints in the sand, traced two sets of footprints over to the rock wall and others that went ahead and then doubled back. "Remember how she handled Lieutenant de la Cruz at the rodeo?" I asked Rafael, rising and walking over to where two people had stopped for a while and sat. Before or after the mate was killed? Footprints were to the side. Zara's smaller feet and a larger man's. In two different places, as if they had scuffled. I clenched my teeth so tightly that they began to hurt.

Rafael's mouth still gaped open when I turned back to him. He was staring down at the dead man. "You think *Zara* did this?"

A couple of the men laughed. But I remained grim. I could see what had happened. I pointed to the imprint of where she'd fallen to the sand. "See how deep that is? The man fell *upon* her. See this?" I gestured toward a deep divot near the center of where her back had been. "Her hands are tied behind her back." Then I waved toward the smooth swashes, indicating where her legs had moved. Heat rose from my neck to my cheeks as I thought about all eight of us considering her bare skin. "She was free of her skirts for a moment," I muttered. "She used her legs to wrap around his neck and thrust him backward, off of her. His head hit the rock, and it was over."

As one, all the men looked from the indentation she'd left to the dead man, then back again. Hector whistled softly. Rafael took off his hat and slowly shook his head in admiration. "That's some woman who's stolen your heart, my friend," he said.

"Indeed. And then I managed to lose her," I ground out, reaching to the smooth area where her back had been, as if I might touch her, encourage her.

"We'll find her again," Rafael said.

"The others must have their trap ready," Hector said. "I say we let that captain know we're behind him and chase him into it. We'll have your woman free by nightfall."

Your woman. His words echoed in my mind as I climbed back into the saddle. Again, I wondered if this was all my fault. That if I had loved her—truly loved her—I would've prayed that God would take her home, to a safer time where she could live and flourish, not suffer as she plainly had here.

Yes, she had defended herself. Managed to kill one of them. But what had brought her to such a point? What had she endured? And what would be the repercussions? I'd killed only three men in my lifetime, and that had all been during the attack at the harbor, when I had no choice. It was one thing for a man to wrestle through the guilt of such a thing. How would a woman tolerate it? She was from another time, which made her stronger in some ways and weaker in others.

My hands clenched into fists.

I knew what was right.

But if I managed to have her safe in my arms again, would I truly have the courage to let her go?

CHAPTER 18

ZARA

The sun was setting in shades of coral and rose, and it was a lovely, tranquil night, with gentle waves—behaving as if last night's hellish storm was simply a distant nightmare. And yet Captain Mendoza's firm grip on my elbow reminded me constantly that this was far too real.

"Do you plan to walk all night? Can't we make camp here?" I hated that my voice trembled on that last word. I didn't want to think about spending the night alone with this man. But I was literally counting down the steps I thought I could take without collapsing, and we were down to about ten.

"Exactly what I was considering myself," he said, looking ahead up the beach and then down an arroyo we were passing. He looked behind us again, as he had been doing all afternoon, checking whether someone was in pursuit. My eyes followed his, hoping. But as always, it seemed like we were the only ones for miles. California in 1840 was like a different planet, I decided. In my time, it was pretty hard to find a space to be alone for an hour, to say nothing of an entire day.

I was just falling back into step with him when he froze, his grip tighter on my elbow. "Ow," I grimaced, "What are you—?"

But he covered my mouth and hauled me into the arroyo. He dragged me up a small stream meandering through this tiny canyon that led from hills to ocean. Around a bend, he abruptly set me before him, swore under his breath and was trying to gag me again before I realized what was happening.

He'd seen someone.

Someone he didn't want to see. Someone who might help me?

I rammed my heel down on the top of his foot and heard his pained *oomph*. He bent over. I spit out the wadded cloth, intent on running, but at my first step, a sharp rock yet again cut my bare foot. I paused just a half-second... which was enough for him to lunge forward and grab a handful of my skirt.

Using the arc of my skirts, he swung me to the side, and as if in slow-mo, I lost my footing, rolling in the finer sand of the ancient riverbed until I came to an abrupt halt against a boulder. I blinked, watching as my vision narrowed, widened, and then narrowed again.

Mendoza fell upon me, panting and growling in frustration as he shoved my wrists back to the dirt with both hands. "Cease your attempts at escape, woman," he demanded in a hiss, but he was looking over his shoulder. Was that fear etching his face?

What was happening? Why could my brain and body not remember all that my instructor had drilled into me? I was not myself. Too weak, too battered...and yet I was not.

Using everything I had left to focus on my inner fury,

I took a breath to scream, but he stuffed his foul handkerchief into my mouth again. I gasped, choked, tried to steady myself, and choked again. In seconds he had me turned over, a knee to my back, the gag tied around my head. It was all I could do to concentrate on breathing through my nose, longing for my balance to return. Again, he tied my wrists.

I felt Captain Mendoza's cruel fingers digging into my arms, lifting me to a standing position. Dazed, I tried to keep my feet, knowing I was about to collapse. With a grimace, he bent over and lifted me over his shoulder, immediately climbing back into the arroyo. I managed to lift my head once, waiting, longing for someone to appear in the gap behind us. For someone to see us and recognize what was happening—for rescue. He'd seen someone, and it had frightened him. But all I saw were the waves, the endless waves, making their way to shore.

And yet...and yet...there were our footprints. Might anyone who was coming our way follow them? Or were they merely travelers who would decide the footprints belonged to local Indians setting off for home after a day of fishing?

When we'd gone some distance, Captain Mendoza dumped me in the sand where the stream had worn a curve into the stone. Then he cautiously edged out to peer toward the ocean. He was panting, clearly struggling to maintain his fast pace and still carry me. And I was fighting to focus, to keep him in my line of vision, as the dark walls closed in.

JAVIER

My heart sank when we saw the point where the other group of men lay in wait for Zara and the captain, but the beach was empty in between us. Two sets of footprints still stretched out before us, until they disappeared where the waves had washed them away. I dug my heels into my mare's flanks and raced ahead, trying to make sense of it. Had the tide come in and covered their trail? Had they been picked up by a boat? Surely we would have seen it.

But then, as the yawning mouth of the arroyo emerged in the cliff-face to my right, I understood what had happened. I reined up, and my mare danced left and right, recognizing my agitation. The other men joined me, and wordlessly I gestured into the canyon. The footprints emerged again out of the meager stream of fresh water running down the ancient riverbed, showing where Mendoza had hauled Zara inward, scuffled with her, then picked her up, his prints becoming deeper. But then I fretted over the reason for that. Was she injured? What had happened?

I seethed with the desire to get my hands around the man's neck.

Turning, I gestured for Hector to come closer and then whispered for him to take a man and go meet the others. For them to divide, leaving two guardians along the beach, but for the others to come around and spread out along the north side of the arroyo. I sent four of my other men to cover the south side. "Keep watch. Wait for them to emerge. I don't want you to frighten him into any rash action."

"Understood, Don Javier," my guard whispered back.

The plan in place, I forced myself to wait. We last four had to move before twilight gave way to stars, while we still could see what—or who—was ahead of us. But saints, it took a strong dose of fortitude not to give chase right now. I counted to a hundred, then two hundred, and finally headed inland. The shadows were deep, but I knew we'd have a good hour of light left. Perhaps they were just heading upstream to camp for the night. With any luck, we'd find them and sneak up on them come nightfall.

That thought forced me to the ground. I handed my mare's reins to Rodrigo and hurried forward, easing around each corner, peering ahead, my eyes straining in the gathering dark. Rafael followed immediately behind me. I winced as I heard the horses' hooves clicking and scraping against rocks, knowing the sound would likely carry along the arroyo. Hurriedly, I motioned for Rodrigo to hold back with the horses and for the two other men to come with Rafael and me.

But we were too late. Around the next bend, I started in surprise and then slowly rose, seeing Captain Mendoza atop the twenty-foot cliff, holding an unconscious Zara in his arms. How had he gotten up there? I wondered madly, glancing about the deep canyon.

Slowly, I clenched my hands. Bested, yet again. I grew weary of how the man seemed able to stay one step ahead of me. But my eyes raked over Zara. She was gagged, her hands tied, and she was clearly injured, but she was whole. *Breathing.*

Which, in turn, allowed me to take a breath too.

Mendoza was looking over his shoulder and then across the arroyo. Obviously, he'd seen my men closing in. He glared down at me. "Come up here, Don Javier. Alone," he barked. "The rest of you stay where you are. Just around this bend, you'll find a way up." He nodded to his right.

I glanced at my men, giving them a silent nod to obey. By the time I reached the top, Mendoza had set Zara's unconscious form at the edge of the cliff, on her side. His foot was perched on her hip, his threat clear.

"Tell your men to dismount," the captain barked.

I did as he asked. The men in the arroyo were already on foot, but on either flank of the arroyo, the guards complied.

"Now send up the mule with my gold, along with that horse," he said, gesturing to my own mount.

I lifted my chin to Rafael, and he went to the mule, untied him from another horse, and then took my mare's reins.

"What have you done to her?"

"Ahh, she's fine. She simply took one too many blows to the head," he said, moving Zara's body a bit with his foot. Part of the dirt beneath her crumbled away and fell. "I understand that I will have to settle for just one chest of gold, according to our agreement. But you'd best hurry—"

I lifted my hand. "Wait. Simply wait, I beg you."

A moment later, Rafael emerged behind him, with the mule braying his complaint and the mare's ears shifting in agitation. She clearly knew something was wrong.

Captain Mendoza's eyes shifted from the mule, loaded with

CHAPTER 19

JAVIER

I forced myself to watch her roll to a stop twenty feet beneath us, her head beneath a limp arm.

"*Javier,*" Rafael said, hoping to stop me.

But I was already over the cliff, sliding, somersaulting toward her lifeless body. There was nothing that could keep me from her.

I spit out dirt and blinked, trying to see as I made my way to her. "Zara? Zara!" I cried, pulling her into my arms. I couldn't see her well enough in the waning light and deep shadows of the arroyo. Did she live? I hauled her into my arms, frantically pulling the gag free and leaning my ear close to her lips, willing my own panicked breathing to cease for a moment so I could hear.

A dim, slow whistle sounded, and I gasped, a lump forming in my throat. "Praise God," I said, pulling her even closer and looking at my friends above me on the rim, and moving toward me along the tiny remains of the river. "She lives. She lives!"

I pulled away, frantically searching her long neck for any sign of a cut, bleeding, but the captain had not hurt her. At least in any obvious way. But she was still unconscious.

"Don Javier," said Hector, placing a gentle hand on my shoulder. "Do you wish for us to fetch our horses? And give chase?"

Slowly, I gathered Zara in my arms. "I wish for you to find your horses and make camp," I ground out. "We shall track down Captain Mendoza in the coming days. Tonight, my only desire is to see to Zara's well-being."

ZARA

I awakened and squinted against the terrible throbbing in my head, trying to see, but recognizing that it was just barely better if I kept my eyes closed. Still, my mind struggled to make sense of what I'd glimpsed. A Madonna and Child? I dared to take a quick peek again.

It was true. A disintegrating fresco on stucco was directly above me, on the inside of a small dome. It appeared that I was in some sort of tiny church.

Slowly, ever so slowly, I turned my aching head to look to the window. Javier stood there, his hand on the sill. A huge monarch butterfly was on one knuckle. He lifted it higher to peer at its magnificent wings, and I could see others fluttering just outside.

I was dreaming. Had to be dreaming. Javier, here, with me? In a church? Where was Captain Mendoza? The thought of him sent my heart pounding, which in turn, made my head ache more. I moaned and shut my eyes.

"Zara? Zara!" Javier said, racing to my side. He took my hand in both of his and brought it to his lips, his cheek. "Are you well, my love?"

"Not quite," I said, feeling a strange urge to pull my hand from his. I did, then, to rub my brow. "My head. It aches terribly."

"Rafael thinks you may be concussed. You were out for some time, and when you came to, you weren't yourself."

Concussed. The 1840 way of saying *concussion*, I guessed. Which explained the headache.

"Hector is brewing you a feverfew tea," Javier said. "The priests left a sizable garden behind. It's overgrown with weeds, but we've found a fair amount of vegetables and medicinals there."

"Priests?" I managed to ask. "Where are we?"

"We're in an abandoned mission. It's suffered from earthquakes and scavengers, except for this chapel and a small kitchen. We will abide here until you are ready to move."

Which in my estimation might be never. I concentrated on taking one breath after another, but even that slight movement seemed to make my head throb more. Still, I had to know. "What of Captain Mendoza? And your gold?"

"He had a good hour on us and was riding my mare, the fastest of our lot. I wager he still heads to Monterey, where he will likely use my gold to slip onto a ship as passenger. I sent Rafael and his men to track him and follow at a distance. Rafael will speak to Patricio and make certain no captain takes him on. When I get there, we will see him to justice."

"When *we* get there," I corrected him gently. *Patricio….*
I fought to place him. I knew his name. Why couldn't I remember
who he was? "Who is Patricio?"

He stilled and stroked my brow and cheek with a knuckle.
"Patricio," he repeated, his brow furrowing in worry. "You
remember Patricio Casales. My friend? The shipping agent
from Monterey? You met him when you met Rafael."

I frowned. "I…I don't." The effort of trying to remember
made my head pound anew.

"Zara, you must rest. Make your full recovery." He lifted
my hand again in his and brought it to his lips, kissing the palm.

Again, I pulled away, his touch grating at me rather than
soothing. I didn't want to be touched, I realized. By anyone.
It reminded me too much of Gonzalo. And Captain Mendoza.
"I must go with you," I mumbled. "I must. I must see him brought
to justice. After what he did…" A lump formed in my throat.
Did Javier know? "It's because of him that Mateo was…that he—
Javier, I tried—"

"Oh, my darling," he said, eyes widening. "You do not
know. Mateo is safe! Whole and hale! Well, he *will* be hale
in time, just as you shall. We found him on the road. It was
because he made it that far that we knew that Mendoza and the
mate had you in hand and were heading north."

"Oh," I breathed in relief, in thanks. "Mendoza said they
searched but could not find him. I'm so glad." Mateo? Safe?
A single tear ran down my cheek and I wiped it away. *Thank you,
Lord. Thank you, thank you.*

"I sent him home to recover," Javier said. "Just as I will
send you. And then I will go after Mendoza. Alta California

has not seen a pirate dare to attack in these waters or along our shore in some time. We cannot let others think that this is new hunting ground. Too much relies on our trade. And I have a personal score to settle with the captain."

His last dark words faded away, and while I could not yet bear to open my eyes again, I could feel the tension in his grip, the rapid pulse. He was likely imagining ten ways to slice and dice Santiago Mendoza.

Javier thought he could send me back to the rancho. But in truth, the rancho wasn't any safer than anywhere else within Alta California. I wasn't safe anywhere…not in this time.

JAVIER

She slept then, and I crossed myself, silently giving thanks that her pain was momentarily abated. Hector came in a bit later, the sharp scent of feverfew rising from the steaming water of a battered pot. Rodrigo was right behind him and left at Zara's feet a wooden basin of warm water and bandages he'd found somewhere. Last night, we were all too exhausted to note the cuts amid the dirt. This morning, I'd seen them. So many miles, Zara had been forced to march barefoot, so many miles. She'd borne kidnapping, shipwreck, threats from the captain and his mate—so much more than any woman should ever have to bear.

Especially my woman.

I'd kill him. So help me, I'd kill Mendoza myself if the magistrate in Monterey refused or failed to string him up on the gallows. I would make certain that the man never hurt another and would rue the day he dared to steal from me and mine. I'd stuff some of my gold coins down his throat…watch as he gagged on them—

"Do you need our assistance, Don Javier?" Hector asked quietly.

I shook my head, returning from my reverie, embarrassed to be so clearly caught musing. "Oh, no. I can see to her."

I turned toward Zara's feet and Rodrigo's steaming basin and bandages. Gently, I lifted one leg, bent her knee, and placed one foot in the basin. She stirred and moaned softly, but then her face slackened again. I let the water work on the dirt for a minute and then another before setting about gently washing it away. Tenderly, I worked at each cut on her foot, glad to see that only one appeared deep, and cleaned away every particle of dirt. It would've been good to put a few stitches in, but none of us carried either sinew or thread, and we were a solid day's ride from Monterey. A thorough bandaging would have to do.

I wrapped her foot, bleeding here and there anew, but all in all looking far better than before. I saw a button on one strip and knew that Rafael had sacrificed his extra shirt for her, leaving it behind with Hector. It made me glad to have such good friends—brothers, really—with us.

I moved to Zara's other foot and tended to it in the same manner. I was almost done when I felt her stir. She was so beautiful, with her dark hair strewn across the pile of blankets behind her. Her cheeks and arms were bruised, her eyes narrowed in pain, but I still believed her to be the loveliest woman I'd ever come across.

She groaned, frowned, and then sat up with a start, her hair in a mass around her shoulders. Her eyes widened, her pupils narrowed, and she screamed, pulling away from me. "No! No!"

She got to her feet and stumbled to the corner of the room, glancing madly back at me as if I were a lion on the hunt rather than a man.

"Zara? Zara!" I said, rising and following. "What is it?"

"Stay away!" she yelled, bending to pick up a bit of fallen stone and throw it at me. "Get away from me!"

I understood then. She was dreaming. I lifted my hands and came no closer. "Zara. It is I. Javier. *Javier. Your* Javier," I said.

My men arrived at the doorway and window, eyes wide in fear. They'd heard her scream. "It is all right," I said, gesturing toward them without dropping my gaze from the terrified girl. "Leave us. She is simply dreaming."

The guards sighed in relief and faded away into the dark to take up their positions again.

Zara seemed to be trying to focus on me, to put meaning to my words. She dropped a second stone and put her long, thin fingers to her face. "No…I…No."

"You are safe, Zara," I said gently, taking a step closer. "Mendoza and his men are far from you. It is only I, Javier. My men surround this place and keep watch. No one else shall harm you."

"Javier," she said with recognition and a hint of hope, brows arcing above her wide eyes. Candlelight danced across her face, leaving some of it in dark shadow. "Javier," she said again, her voice cracking now. Tears ran down her face. She crumpled, but I reached her just in time, gathering her into my arms.

I turned and sank to the floor, the corner of the old church behind my back. "Shh, shhh," I said, stroking her hair and pulling her huddled form tighter against me on my lap, as I might've with one of my little sisters, trying to soothe a hurt.

But the hurt in this one was wide and gaping, the open maw of some dark monster within her.

ZARA

I'd had a choice in that moment. In that split second, I had recognized that my resistance to Javier, my terror, was because I'd felt his masculine hands on my skin and remembered Gonzalo's. Mendoza's. Not his. *Not his.*

Part of me still wanted to resist, to be alone, and not to be touched at all, but a bigger part wanted this. Javier's gentle ministrations, his soothing. I wanted to remember what it was to be held with care by a man, not manhandled. I'd never known my father or grandfather, and Javier's warm, gentle touch felt like something I'd always been missing but had never known. I focused on his careful movement, his breathing, the comforting smell and way of him. He was strong, so strong, and yet he didn't use his strength against me, only *for* me.

This was Javier, *my Javier*, I reminded myself, as I continued to weep, letting out my anguish, my frustration at being powerless to free myself, my anger for the harm that was done to me. On and on I wept—and in the end I was even crying for my abuela…and for never having known my parents…and for how I'd worried I'd never see Javier or the Venturas again.

Through it all, Javier did nothing more than hold me, gently stroking my shoulders, my neck, my hair, while I soaked his shirt with my tears and running nose and probably put his legs to sleep. He simply waited, was there for me. As if he'd never want to be anywhere else.

Finally, my tears spent, I sniffed and snorted and lifted my head to look at him.

Carefully, he lifted a hand to my cheek and pushed back some of my unruly hair to look into my eyes. He did not hold me captive in any way—only gently urged me to meet his gaze. "Zara," he breathed, calm but very intent with his look. "How are you hurt? What did they do to you?"

I sniffed again. "I was not raped," I said. "I was threatened…" My voice cracked. I coughed, sniffed, and forced myself to look into his eyes. "The second mate came close. But…" I shook my head, remembering Gonzalo's awful, still form on the beach, and the rush of relief and regret that surged through my heart.

He eased me back into his arms, and I sank against him, grateful that he demanded no more from me. It was enough for it to come to mind again. And he knew enough, at least for now. He could plainly see the other abuse I'd suffered, at least those visible on the outside. The bruises, the scrapes, the cuts.

"I'm sorry, Zara. So sorry," he said, stroking my hair again.

"For everything you've endured."

I could hear how he felt responsible and wiped away new tears. Somehow his compassion freshened wells of tears I'd thought spent. "If I'd done as you asked and returned to the rancho, perhaps I would not have endured any of it. It isn't your fault, Javier. It is all mine."

JAVIER

I grimaced for two reasons—because she left my lap with those words and because of what she'd said. I wished to argue it, to tell her what was on my mind and heart, but I didn't wish to tax her throbbing head any further at this point. I only wanted to bring her comfort, soothing aid. No more trial or trauma.

"This place is pretty," she said, glancing around the church again before leaning against a crumbling pillar, crossing her arms and then closing her eyes. "Why did they abandon it?"

"The Franciscans pulled out of all the missions at once, about seven years ago. The Church called them to return the lands to the Indians and move on to other tasks."

"To work so hard to build something like this and then simply walk away?" she said, eyes open again. "It seems foolish." The swelling of her left eye had gone down, but the bruise was now a greenish-purple. She'd suffered such abuse because of me. *Me.*

"Sometimes things change," I said, rising to gently lead her back to her pallet of blankets. "We build because we believe it is what we are supposed to do." *Like this, between us.* "And then we learn there might be a better path for us." *Such as letting you go.*

"Javier," she said, her dark eyes now studying me closely. "What is it?"

I feigned confusion. "Of what do you speak?"

"Of what do *you* speak?"

I gave her a false smile and turned to cover her with a blanket again, covering feet that were cut and bruised *because of me.* Legs that had had to swim and walk for miles *because of me.* "I speak of Franciscans and God's winding path, of course," I lied. "Is that injury to your head robbing you of memory?" I winked at her, so she'd know I was teasing. But she looked puzzled and concerned.

Hector arrived then, with another pot of steaming water, a dented tin cup, and a spray of feverfew in hand. "I did find a bit more. It has not the finest flavor, but it should ease your aches."

"Thank you, Hector," Zara said, lifting a hand to her forehead. "I think the first of it did, last night. I had some then, right?"

I answered, "You managed to take a few sips before you were out again." I leaned toward Hector. "Do you mind if I step out for a moment? Can you keep watch on Señorita Zara?"

"Certainly."

I ignored her searching eyes and walked out of the tiny church then, needing to be outside, away from her. When I was close to her, all I wanted to do was sweep her into my arms. To kiss her and know that she would always be at my side.

But if I was to let her go, I had to begin to separate my heart now—niggle free the ends where we were bonded, like Mama tearing out a hem in a dress—so that when the time came, I could set her free, truly free.

CHAPTER 20

ZARA

I took the cup of tea from Hector. "What troubles Javier?" I said.

"Other than that his intended has suffered much at the hands of an evil man?" he asked.

I swallowed the bitter drink and gave him a small smile. "Yes, aside from that."

Hector shrugged and sat back against a brick column, which held up one side of the roof's remaining arch. "There is a great deal on the don's mind. Mostly retribution and revenge, I'd wager. He is very angry that the pirates dared to attack us; he's even angrier that the Mexican garrison did not come to our aid."

"Which draws him closer to thoughts of supporting the Union's claim on California?" I guessed. "And farther away from what his mother most desires, to remain a true, loyal son to Mexico."

Hector nodded slowly. He picked up a stalk of the medicinal flower and idly began peeling more leaves from the stem. "I've had similar thoughts since this attack. If Mexico cannot protect her frontiers, then she is of little use to us here. And if she gives way at her center, how long until we follow?"

I tried to think back to Mexican history from this time. I knew of the Alamo, of Santa Anna, Mexico's ruler, but little else. Was there something in history that might give me a clue as to what truly drove Mendoza?

"Why do you think that Captain Mendoza chose to attack Bonita Harbor and Captain Craig's ship? Craig is a Union supporter. Do you suppose that Mexico hired him to attack those who might oppose them, under the guise of piracy?"

Hector frowned and paused his stalk splitting. His dark eyes shifted left and right. "It's not impossible," he admitted. "What makes you ask?"

"He was so willing to risk his ship and his stolen cargo in the storm," I said, thinking aloud. "And he said some things that made me wonder. I think he expected to gain from the attack in ways outside the cargo's value. Even above the ransom Javier agreed to pay for me and Mateo."

"More than four chests full of gold?" He looked doubtful.

"Honestly, he seemed almost fine with just me as his captive—as if Mateo would've been too much bother. They may not even have searched for him." I swung my head to look back at him but realized my head wasn't doing well enough for me to risk such movements.

"More tea?" Hector asked, seeing me squint in pain.

"Please," I said, holding out my tin cup.

He took it from me, filled it, and handed it back. "Javier has asked me and seven of the men to escort you back to the rancho, when you are up to traveling."

I scowled at him. "So then he will go north without seven of his best men? That makes little sense to me. We could be waylaid on the road. Would it not be best for us all to stay together?"

Hector frowned. "Don Javier only wants to know that you are safe and far from danger."

I sighed. "Danger is everywhere. I might return to the rancho and contract a fever that would kill me."

Hector crossed himself and cast his eyes upward, hands clasped, *"Protégela, bendito Señor, de tal maldición." Guard her, Lord, from such a curse.*

"Am I wrong?" I pressed. "Have you not known people to die in their own homes? Javier's own brother was gored to death in the rodeo. Does not disease run through the Indian villages? The towns? There is danger everywhere. I prefer to face it with those I love."

Hector let out a little huff of a laugh.

"What? What is funny?"

"You," he said. He shook his head, his expression half-dismay, half-delight. "No wonder Don Javier is so captivated. You are unlike any woman we have ever met."

"So I've heard," I said. I grew tired of how women were treated in this era, the weak roles they had to play, the lack of equal rights, opportunity. "So will you aid me in convincing him that we are all better off together?"

He scratched his chin, considering me. "Will you do as we ask of you? Stay where we tell you?"

"Yes, yes, anything. I just do not want to be separated from Javier again. And I want to see that devil myself when he pays for what he did to us," I added fiercely. Again, my head throbbed in complaint, and I rubbed it.

"We must cease this talk and you must rest."

"I'm weary of resting," I said, stretching out an arm and gingerly coming to my feet. "My body aches as much from being in one spot as it does from what I've endured. I need to move. Where did Javier go?"

"I do not know."

"Well, let us go find him."

Hector yanked off his boots. "These are far too big for you. But you must protect your feet if you insist on going about. Don Javier worked too long on them for you to get them filthy on the mission grounds."

I began to protest but knew he was right. Still, I was so antsy that I had to move a little, stretch my muscles, and get the blood flowing. "You truly are a kind man," I said, slipping my foot into one warm boot and smiling as he bent to lace it up for me. "With big feet."

"Big?" he chuckled, as if amused.

Then, in stocking feet, he offered his arm. "Now come, m'lady. Let us find Don Javier. It will do him good to see you a bit more restored."

The thought of it made me a little nervous. I ran a hand through my curls, knowing my hair must be a sight. "Is there any sort of mirror around?" I asked. "Or a brush?"

"The priests did not put a high price on outward beauty," he said, "so we'd be hard pressed to find either. Not that they would likely leave such things behind."

"Right," I said. It was a stupid thought. I straightened my

shoulders and turned toward him. "Then tell me. How bad is my face? My neck?" I knew that a few of the pirates' blows must have left marks. Javier's pulsing neck vein when looking me over had told me it made him furious.

"It's not too bad," he tried.

"Hector," I said. "The truth, please."

Hector hazarded a sidelong glance or two and sighed. "A bruise here," he said, gesturing toward my right cheekbone. "Turning rather green. A scratch here," he said, lightly tracing his left temple to his eye, "with a good scab, but it might leave a faint scar."

A *scar*. I frowned. I hadn't thought of lasting evidence of my scuffles with Mendoza and his men.

"Another bruise here," he said, gesturing toward my lower right cheek. "This one is more brown." He frowned now too, anger gathering in his brow, but there was little more than concern in his dark eyes. "You clearly endured much, Señorita. And for that I am deeply sorry. We tried to get to you in time. You know that, yes? Don Javier did not sleep. From the time he left the *Crescent Moon*, last night was the first he allowed his eyes to close for more than minutes." He stared at me with sorrow, guilt, compassion, as if he wanted to wrap me into a brotherly hug.

I swallowed, refusing to cry again. What was it about compassion in a friend that made me want to sit down and sob? And remembering each blow I'd taken made me angry again too, which would for sure make me cry.

I sniffed and lifted my chin. "Well, I survived, as did Mateo. I think we must concentrate on that gift rather than what was lost, yes? But am I a hideous sight? Is that why Javier had to leave the room? I'm too battered to look upon?"

Hector's face twisted in a look of surprise. "Hideous? Oh, Señorita Zara. Do you not know? You are beautiful, no matter what bruises you bear. In fact, they make you seem more heroic. Fearsome, in a way, even wrapped in your womanly form."

It was my turn to stifle a laugh. "Fearsome?"

"Fearsomely *beautiful*," he returned, lifting a brow. "Like a warrioress, after returning from battle." He tucked my hand through the crook of his arm, and we resumed our slow walk out of the church.

We emerged into a small courtyard, where I saw Javier standing to one side. The courtyard was surrounded by a half-roof, falling down in places. I was certain that it was once a contemplative, prayerful place to walk, protected by the elements. Seeing us, Javier turned and moved toward me, silently taking my arm from Hector. We could all see I was trembling.

"It's fine," I said, waving them both off. "I need to move. Walk."

"I'll fetch more tea," Hector said, eager to have a task.

Javier turned to face me, looking me over. "Do you need to sit?"

I nodded reluctantly. My knees suddenly felt made of jelly, despite my brave words.

He led me to a stone bench, and I half-wished he'd pull me into his lap again, but he sat down at my side instead, one arm around me. Silently he rubbed my arm and hand, as if willing his calm and courage into me. When my trembling finally stopped, he took my hand and gazed at me. "Zara, I doubt anyone will inquire, but in case they do, I must know. Did you kill that pirate on the beach?"

I was silent a moment. "The second mate intended… down on the beach, when I—"

Javier bore my half-sentences, filling in the blanks. "You were defending yourself when he died," he said gently. "There is no culpability in that."

I didn't know what *culpability* meant exactly, but I could guess. He didn't think I was to blame. I thought of the captain striking me, ramming me against the rocks…and again began trembling. "I hate it that I am so weak. That even the thought of it sets me to shaking and—"

"What?" he interrupted. "No. *No*," he said more firmly. He lifted my chin so that I had to look into his eyes. His dark, beautiful eyes were full of sorrow and admiration and fury and hope. "Zara Ruiz, you are the strongest woman I have ever encountered, other than my mother."

I laughed at this. A short bark of a laugh and then giggles that brought tears to my eyes. He smiled with me at last, and it was a relief to finally see him smile again. And it did make my heart and mind feel more steady, the fact that he equated my strength to his mother's. Because I had never met a more formidable woman than Doña Elena.

"Maybe the golden lamp only comes to strong women," he said. "It takes a great deal of fortitude for one to travel to another time, yes?"

"More than you know…"

When he'd handed me a handkerchief to wipe my eyes and nose, he slowly caressed my cheek, tracing my lower lip, clearly thinking about kissing me, but trying to resist. "Is it all right, *mi corazon*? God help me, I shouldn't—"

No, you should, I wanted to whisper back. I could feel my draw to him rise, expand, warming me from within. And yet...

"I'm trying not to press, after all you've been through," he whispered, with a slight rasp to his voice. His lips moved toward mine, whisper-close, but he did not press. "Are you certain?"

I considered him, focused on all that was good in him, driving back the shadows that Mendoza and Gonzalo had cast in my mind. He was light. Light, light...

"You do owe me a kiss," I whispered back, watching as his dark eyes searched every inch of my face as if he could read my deepest need. "You remember? Our wager?"

He didn't laugh, didn't even smile. Just waited for me. Deciding then, I ran my fingers through his dark hair and pulled his lips toward mine. We kissed at first softly, then with deepening intensity. He tasted of salt and sage, of fresh air and leather and sweat—and all of it tasted like comfort to me. Memory. Falling back into the *known*. Blessed, comforting *known* after all the unknown I'd faced. This was the man I loved. This was the man I'd wished for, from twenty-first century California, but could find only in the past....

His kiss quelled my fears and stilled my trembling as passion replaced my hurts.

The sound of applause made him hesitate and brought my head up. Across the courtyard, four of Javier's men were clapping and grinning, like silly college boys full of bravado. I giggled and felt the heat of my blush as Javier's arm tightened around my shoulder, silently encouraging me not to slip away. He lifted one hand and dismissed them with a wave; they dragged themselves away, laughing and chatting as they went.

His gaze returned to me, and humor faded back into intensity. "I am so glad that you survived this ordeal, Zara. To think what might have happened, how you might have suffered…" He ran his fingers through his curls, pushing the mass back from his anguished face.

I took his hand and caressed it. "It was terrible," I whispered. "But you came after me, Javier. Rescued me."

His eyes searched mine, and he opened his mouth to say more but then stayed silent, as if thinking better of it. What was it that he held back? A promise? An apology? Our long-awaited *I love you?*

Whatever it was, in the end, he gave up, sighed, and looked to the sky as if pleading for help.

CHAPTER 24

JAVIER

My mind was screaming at me, even as my heart and body yearned to turn and kiss her again. To tell her I loved her. But I couldn't. Had I not *just* decided that I had to let her go? That it was in her best interest to free her, allow her to return to her own, safer time so that she never had to go through such terror and abuse again? I was a weak fool in her presence, and I had to get her back to Tainter Cove where she could—

I abruptly stood and felt the color drain from my face even as I covered it with my hands. The lamp. The golden lamp that had allowed her to come here, my mother to come here—I hadn't seen it since that day we were attacked.

"Javier? What is it?" she asked, wobbling to her feet. She hurried behind me as I moved toward where the horses were tied up.

"Your golden lamp," I said over my shoulder, just loud enough that she could hear. "I haven't seen it since the day you tried to return to your own time."

She frowned, still keeping pace. "Why are you thinking of that now?" But something in her tone told me that she was now worried about it too. I was right. Clearly right. She still harbored thoughts of returning to her own time. And who could blame her? After all that had transpired?

"Because it belongs to you," I said, making up an excuse. If she didn't want to discuss it plainly, then neither did I. "And you've lost so much—so much has been taken from you—it grates at me to think it's gone as well. I think I slipped it into my saddlebag that day. Do you remember?"

"I don't," she said.

I wished that my mare were here, now, that we could go search her saddlebags this instant. I strode a few paces away, arms crossed, trying to remember. I'd been so relieved that God had left Zara with me, in my time, rather than taking her away....

"You helped me mount your horse, and we rode together," she said, coming to stand beside me.

"So did you have the lamp or did I?"

"I think I handed it to you at some point. Or..." She lifted a hand to her head as if she could force the memory to emerge. "I think you put all my things in the saddlebag. Right as you helped me mount?"

I nodded, dimly remembering something like that. In that moment, all we'd been able to concentrate on was each other. "There's no way I would have left it behind."

"We reached the harbor, you sent me toward the rancho..." she said distantly, lost in memory. "I came across the dead guards, Mateo's horse, and turned back. I hobbled her right across the dunes from the storehouse."

"Where you were captured," I said. "So the pirates might

have searched the bags and stolen it."

She paled. "So it…might have gone down with the *Crescent Moon*. Or it remained in the saddle bag and…and Mendoza has it now. He was carrying a bag with him. I mean, not a saddle bag. But a bag. He had jerky and more in there…But Javier, if he didn't, doesn't have the lamp…"

I turned toward her, my face feeling numb and stiff. "You might be trapped here," I finished for her.

Her eyes searched mine, confused. Fearful. Hopeful. Angry. A myriad of emotions played across her face, one after the other. I believed I recognized each of them because I felt them all as well. I wanted Zara to remain here if she chose to stay, not because she had no choice. Did I not know the chafing nature of such a life firsthand? How I had longed for the sea, the university rather than the sprawling rancho? I'd come to partial peace with my lot as Don Javier de la Ventura, largely due to Zara's influence. But I could not demand the same of her.

"We'll find Mendoza in Monterey and learn whether he has it. Or we'll return to the beach near the wreck. Scour it to see what washes ashore." Even as I said those last words, I know they sounded futile.

"If Mendoza has it, we now have twice the reason to catch him." She gave me a steady gaze—steadier than I'd seen her yet. Determined. "Shall we be off then and make some distance before nightfall?"

"*You* shall be off for the rancho, along with seven of my men. I shall take the rest, track down the scoundrel, and see him to justice, as well as recover your lamp if he has it."

She stiffened. "I will say it again. I prefer to remain with

you. Am I not safer by your side than anywhere else? I might
return to the rancho, but then Lieutenant de la Cruz, Gutierrez,
and their companions might come to call. Am I not as much in
danger with him as I am with the pirate captain?" She stepped
closer to me. "Please, Javier, consider my wishes as well as your
own. Can you not see the value of my opinion, too?"

I sighed. She was headstrong. But also clearly used to having
her way. I reached out and tucked a coil of her hair behind her
ear, unable to resist touching her. "Is it commonplace, in your
time," I whispered, "for women to insist on their own way?"

A devilish smile lifted the corners of her lips. "For certain,"
she said, tapping my chest. "But you cannot tell me that your
mother or sisters ever hold back their opinions or desires.
Not for long anyway."

I covered her hand, capturing it against my chest, and
staring into her eyes. "So it will be, then. Together, *tomorrow*,
we travel north. You need a night's rest, as do I, before we
encounter Mendoza again. And I am certain that Rafael and
Patricio will ensure that he does not escape Monterey before
we arrive."

But, as we walked hand in hand up the hill to watch the sun
set, I couldn't help but wonder what Monterey would bring us.
And while I had the best intentions, with the feel of her hand
in mine—after all we'd been through—I found myself silently
praying, *Lord, let us find the lamp. But please Lord, please, let her choose
to not use it.*

CHAPTER 22

ZARA

After hours in the saddle, my backside hurt. I had not slept well—agitated over all that Javier and I had and had not discussed—and on top of my injuries from the kidnapping and shipwreck, I knew no feverfew tea could soothe every pain. But I forced myself to sit upright and not let my face betray it. It had taken a great deal for Javier to allow me to accompany him; I didn't want to give him any reason to second-guess himself. I knew he was likely doing that already.

We passed ranches more often as we approached town. In my day, I knew Monterey was famous for the aquarium, and a friend's dad had been stationed at the naval base, but I'd never been this far north. Abuela and I had never traveled farther from home than Santa Barbara, because she never wanted to travel faster than fifty miles an hour on the freeway for more than half an hour. I smiled, thinking of her, barely taller than the steering wheel, driving her huge, wide Buick.

The coastline was rugged alongside the road here. Craggy

black-rock cliffs stood sentry against battering waves that crashed against them. One after another roared up and nearly over, sending up a shower of white foam and spray as the cliffs denied them entry and sent them scurrying into retreat. We paused at an inlet, watching as otters played in the wash of surf and turned on their backs to hold mussels in their tiny paws, expertly cracking them open.

I wondered if we paused so long because we couldn't decide how eager we were to reach the town…or encounter Mendoza.

As we entered town, I knew there likely weren't any buildings here that would survive to my own era. Most were one-story wooden buildings, hastily erected. Horses ran wild along the streets, with men capturing and riding any stray they could and then releasing them to graze. *The first sort of public transportation,* I laughed to myself.

There were many men but also a fair number of women, dressed in far more elaborate gowns than anything I'd seen in or near Santa Barbara. Clearly, these women had more access to imports from around the world. Many of them looked me over as if I were so much riffraff, with my matted hair and filthy, torn gown. Maybe they even thought I was a prostitute, riding with all these men—though I hardly acted like some of the girls I'd seen walking by, boldly making eyes at Javier's company.

All the posturing made me want to laugh. It was like girls being in the coolest outfits possible, back home in my own time, but walking along the sidewalks of the poorest neighborhood. Except, you know, these were boardwalks. Honest-to-goodness boardwalks. They were a thing. Not just in Abuela's spaghetti-Westerns.

"We'll find a shop near the hotel," Javier said, watching me and clearly noting my discomfort. "There you can get a dress and boots—whatever you need."

I smiled at him, grateful. *And a brush*, I thought. *I so need a brush and soap. And maybe some lotion of some sort.*

Javier divided the men into two groups. One was to find Patricio Casales, the shipping agent, and the other Rafael Vasquez, to see what each of them had learned. "Keep an eye out for Captain Mendoza," he demanded. "Be certain he doesn't catch sight of *you*. Then return to us here at the hotel and we shall take a meal together."

They agreed and departed, leaving Hector, Rodrigo, and Felipe with Javier and me. We entered the hotel, and Javier booked six rooms. He then told the black-haired hotelier, a short Mexican man in a fine suit, that he was searching for a seaman named Santiago Mendoza. "Have you checked in any male guests that are about my height? He is about thirty or thirty-five, with a mustache and beard. He'd likely be carrying a bag of some sort and a small, heavy chest."

I tensed as we waited. I knew that there were probably more than ten hotels in a town this size bordering the harbor. But what if Mendoza was right here, in this very building? The thought of it made me feel oddly faint with dread—and with hope, too, for the lamp...and kept me on the lookout.

The hotelier frowned, considering, and then shook his head. "None have arrived that fits that description. As you can see from the registry, only an older couple and four young men have checked in over the last two days. It's been a slow week for us, but I hear tell that three sails have been sighted on the horizon, heading our way. That will certainly bring some new guests to our hotel. It is good you secured these rooms before they arrived."

Javier nodded. "Both Señorita Ruiz and I are in sore need of a bath. Might you arrange for a tub in each of our rooms before we take our noon meal?"

"Consider it done," said the hotelier.

Javier passed me a key and then handed the rest to Hector, Felipe, and Rodrigo, quietly telling them to figure out the sleeping arrangement for the rest of the men. I studied the big brass key, thinking about the magnetic key cards of my own time. There was something enormously satisfying about slipping a classic skeleton key into a big lock.

He instructed the men to go together and do as he'd just done with the hotelier, covering the other hotels and boardinghouses in town to see if they might turn up Captain Mendoza. "One of you keep watch as you question each hotelier," he said. "I do not want him to overhear that you're seeking him if he's about. Rafael has likely already done this, but I want to be certain we find the pirate as fast as we can and that no stone has been left unturned."

They set off, and Javier offered his arm. We moved down the wooden boardwalk, and half of me expected the Magnificent Seven to emerge, guns blazing. But I supposed that was more likely to happen in forty or fifty years. In 1840, guns only had one or two bullets in them, and men still favored swords, from what I could see. I'd feel the same. It took far too much time to reload if you missed.

Javier paused at the window of a mercantile and then moved on, obviously thinking we might do better. "I think I recall Mama liking a store around the corner," he said.

"You brought Doña Elena here?"

He smiled. "She and my papa brought me and Dante here a year before I left for university. That trip along the coast, weighing anchor here, was part of what sparked my passion for the sea and sailing. I was just a boy, but it made me wonder what it might be like to travel the world, exploring new harbors and ports, meeting people from far-off lands."

I squeezed his arm. "And you still might get that opportunity. Someday. When Mateo is of age to keep watch over the rancho? Or Francesca or Estrella."

He looked at me as if I were crazy. Or joking. "My sisters? Running the rancho?"

I nodded. "In my day," I whispered, "women run companies with hundreds, even thousands of employees. Do not doubt your siblings, any of them, just because they wear a dress rather than pants."

He didn't disagree, but his expression clearly told me he thought this idea preposterous. It didn't bother me. If I were to remain with him, there would be time enough to change his mind about what women were capable of. And yet I had to admit there was something romantic, reassuring about some of the gender roles of this time. Far too confining for women, absolutely. But it felt good to be looked after. I liked how all of Javier's men automatically protected the women, as if it was part of their genetic code. And it made me feel girly in good ways, while at the same time, agitating me a little. *Yeah*, I thought. *Figuring all that out will be a challenge, if I stay.*

If I stay. Not that I'd have much option if Captain Mendoza had sold my lamp or lost it at sea. Still, the question in my own mind chafed. Had not God made it clear, the night before the attack? I'd tried to leave, hadn't I? Tried every trick and prayer possible? And I'd awakened in Javier's arms on the beach.

"Here we are, just as I remembered it." Javier reached for the handled edge of a carved door at the center of the next shop, with the Spanish *MERCANTIL* hand-painted in ornate golden lettering above the door. I peered in, blinking as I waited for my eyes to get used to the relative dark. There was really no "window shopping" in this town. Perhaps glass was too expensive to import or not yet mass produced. Even the windows at the rancho were empty except for shutters, I recalled.

But inside, an enormous chandelier with nine oil lamps illuminated the center of the store, and four other, smaller lamps lit up the corners. Sighing, I moved immediately to three pre-made dresses, each in multiple sizes. Not the ten or twelve options that my local Target carried, but a few that seemed like they might be possibilities.

The proprietor, a fat Mexican woman in black finery, her hair in an elaborate updo held by an abalone-shell comb, moved toward us. "Buenos días," she said in a fine Castilian accent. "May I be of assistance?"

"Sí," Javier said. "My dear friend here has survived a terrible shipwreck. As you can see, she is in sore need of a dress or two and much to go with it. Boots, too. I need a new shirt and jacket as well. Might you assist us?"

The woman, perhaps fifty years old, sniffed and looked me up and down the way many of the fine ladies on the street had done. Did she suspect I was something *more* than Javier's friend, with me being such a mess? But eying Javier and the thick bag of coins he casually weighed in the palm of his hand, she elected to pretend I was nothing but the finest sort of lady, regardless of her suspicions. In short order, she had me trying on a formal bronzed-brown gown, as well as a more casual one in a sunny yellow.

She crowded into the tiny fitting room each time I changed, uninvited, and swiftly pinned the bodice of each, assuming we would purchase them. And I suppose we had little choice. Judging from Javier's mother's preference, these were likely the best I'd find in town. But she was pinning them like a tailor would. How long would it take to get one or both back?

"You are tailoring the gowns for me?" I dared to ask the formidable woman.

"But of course!" she said, frowning as if I'd somehow offended her.

"I see. But will I then be able to pick them up tomorrow?"

Her frown deepened. "Of course not. I shall have a boy run them to your hotel within an hour or two."

"I see," I repeated as if that should have been obvious to me. I didn't know whether some poor seamstress was chained to a machine in the back of the shop, but apparently this was just part of the deal.

"By the time you finish with your bath," she said with a sniff, not appreciating my B.O. any more than I did, "your gowns will be delivered."

"Wonderful. And I'll need some underthings as well. A new camisole, stays, petticoat."

She waved me off impatiently. "Of course, of course," she said. "All will be in order, señorita."

She left me then to dress again in my tattered gown, after which I padded out to look at fine leather boots. Javier had already placed a crisp white shirt, pants, and jacket on the counter. Together we added a horsehair brush, lilac-scented soap, and a jar of cream.

"The girl needs this," said the merchant, placing a small brown hat with netting on the pile, "to go with her new bronze gown. And this," she said, reaching for a comb with freshwater pearls on it, "to go with the gold."

"Oh, I couldn't," I said hurriedly. It all must be adding up to a lot of money, and I didn't have a dime—or whatever currency they dealt in here.

"We can," Javier said, opening his heavy purse and sliding out five gold coins.

"Javier, it is too much," I said, belatedly thinking it all through. "I can just get the yellow dress and the boots. And the..." I felt the burn on my cheeks as I searched for the right word to describe all the feminine unmentionables.

"We'll take it all," he said firmly, staring straight ahead to the proprietor.

Her fat cheeks spread into a Cheshire-like grin. "Very good, sir," she said. As she slipped the coins into a box behind the counter and fetched his change, she seemed to think of us as people-people for the first time. "May I ask how long you plan on sojourning in Monterey?"

"A few days," he said. "We are to meet with a sea captain here. Captain Mendoza. Have you met him by chance?"

"Captain Mendoza?" she repeated. "I fear not. But the town is not all that big. Ask about him, and you'll likely be sipping port together within the hour."

"I hope so," Javier said innocently, as if instead of slowly strangling Mendoza, he meant to toast his health. He wrote down the name of our hotel and our room numbers, and then we departed.

I breathed a sigh of relief to once again have socks and shoes. You could make it in flip-flops in a beach town. But, with your feet cut up, and stirrups and dirt roads, barefoot-and-bandaged was pretty much the worst idea ever. A huge infection waiting to happen.

But these boots felt tight and confining after those I'd borrowed from Hector. I hoped it was just because they were new. Probably would take a bit to break in. Still I felt less vulnerable, more *me* with them on, and couldn't wait for that bath back at the hotel and the new dress.

Though we kept an eye out for Javier's men, we didn't see any of them on the way back to or in the hotel lobby. "The tubs are in your rooms," said the hotelier, lifting his chin, eyeing the paper-wrapped packages in Javier's arm. "I'll send maids up directly with the water."

"Very good," Javier said. "And the señorita is expecting a delivery within the hour. You will send it up with a maid when it arrives?"

"Of course," he said with a curt nod.

Together, we climbed the narrow stairs and turned down the hall. Javier took the first room, leading me to the next—and I knew then that he'd formed some sort of guard between me and anyone who came up the stairs. Looking at the numbers on the doors, I knew his men would be on the far side of my room, as well as directly across. He'd figured that out as he passed out the keys, and again I felt a rush of warmth over his quiet protection, that reassuring, unspoken care.

I pulled my key from my pocket and bent to slip it into the lock, peering closely to watch it connect, feeling the satisfying turns and hearing the click inside. I felt as if I was entering some sort of secret room in an ancient house.

"It's as if you've never handled a key and lock before," he said with a chuckle.

"Not like this," I said. I turned the porcelain knob. The tall, heavy door swung open on a modest room, with only a single sagging cot, small table, and oil lamp. A deep tin tub took up almost all of the extra space in the room.

"No window, good," Javier sniffed, setting my packages on the foot of my bed.

"Don't want me to escape, eh?" I teased.

"I don't wish for any to gain *entry*," he corrected, pulling me into his arms, "that *you* do not invite in."

I smiled and stretched up on tiptoe to kiss him. We could hear footsteps in the hall, as well as the brush of wood against the walls, and Javier released me and opened my door wider, revealing two waiting maids. He gestured for the first to enter the space he'd vacated. She carried two massive buckets, hooked on what looked like a yoke she carried over her shoulders.

He eyed me over her head. "Lock the door behind her."

"I will. Thank you," I said. "See you soon."

The other maid followed him to his room, while my own set the buckets down beside the tub. "Do you want me to pour them in, señorita?"

"No," I said. "I'll see to it. Thank you." There were maybe six gallons between them. I wanted to meter them out myself.

I locked the door behind her and hurriedly pulled off my gown and underthings, crusty with salt and sweat, and then unwound the dirty bandages around my feet. Naked, I poured three-quarters of the steaming, hot water into the tub, sad to see it was only a few inches deep, and then three-quarters of the cold. It still wouldn't cover me by any means, but it was fresh water, and it would do. I stepped in and immediately rinsed my whole body, reached for the parchment-wrapped soap, lathered up, and rinsed again.

I didn't think I'd ever appreciated a bath as much. There'd been one at the rancho that was close. But to be clean, to feel the water wash over skin that I felt had been defiled in some way after my days with Captain Mendoza and Gonzalo—I only wished I had access to more hot water. But I would take what I had and be thankful for it. I washed my hair and then stood, using the remaining clean water to rinse the tangled brown mess, and the rest of me one last time. Then I reached for the rough, tiny towel the maid had left beside the buckets and quickly dried off.

I unwrapped the pantaloons, which tied at the waist with a drawstring, then slipped on a petticoat that did the same. The silky camisole felt good against my torso; I'd just need help to lace up the stays. I picked up the brush to begin working out the knots in my clean hair.

About the time I finished with that task, I heard a soft knock at my door, removed the key to peek out the hole, and saw a maid's gray skirts. I reinserted the key and opened the door to invite the maid inside, spying the paper-wrapped bundle under her arm. Seeing my conundrum, she gestured for me to turn around and silently laced me up without ever saying a thing. Then she politely bobbed once and left. I locked the door behind her, sank onto the soft cot, and worked free the string from the package. It was the bronze-brown gown on top, and I decided it was most suitable for the rest of the day and into dinner.

It was truly lovely, and I hurriedly slipped it over my shoulders, wishing I had a mirror to make sure but feeling as if the gown suited me well, now that it was properly sized. I could breathe well in it, but it hugged my breasts, waist, and hips before it fell in abundant skirts, as was the fashion. The bodice allowed a bit of cleavage to show but nothing like the scandalous necklines I'd spotted among the prostitutes in town—or even the blue gown that Captain Mendoza had given me.

I bent to slip my new stockings over my battered feet and then the boots again. I wound my hair into a tight, low knot so that I could pin my new hat atop it. A hundred times I wished for a mirror or even a window where I might catch a bit of my reflection, but I just had to go with my best guess and then wait for Javier to confirm I was on track—or gently tell me how I had to fix it.

But when he knocked at the door and said, "Zara, it is Javier," and I opened it, I felt as if I'd been dressed by Cinderella's mice and birds, crafted into some sort of princess by the way he gaped at me. "Heavens, woman," he said, stepping tentatively toward me and taking my hands in his, "Will I never cease being surprised by your beauty?" He spread apart my arms to brazenly look me up and down and then lifted one arm to urge me into a slow spin.

I laughed and felt the heat of a blush rise on my cheeks as I completed my turn. "And you don't look half-bad yourself," I said.

"Half-bad?" he said, pretending to take offense at my modern phrase. "I am head to toe the Don de la Ventura, do you not see?"

He lifted a freshly shaven chin, and I admired his clean hair, neatly washed, oiled, combed, and pulled back into a leather band at the nape of his neck. His new shirt smelled of fresh cotton and the sea, and was crisply tucked into his new breeches. His boots came to his knees, and as I looked back into his melted-chocolate eyes, I noticed that this man—this glorious, handsome, wonderful man—made my own knees weak. Literally weak. I'd always thought it was an odd phrase until now.

"No, Don de la Ventura," I whispered, stepping closer to him. "Not half-bad at all."

CHAPTER 23

JAVIER

It was with pride that I escorted Zara down the stairs, transformed as she was. She was every bit the lady on the outside now, as I'd known she was on the inside. In the foyer, between the small restaurant and the hotelier's desk, the men milled. And as one they turned to watch us, looking as proud of Zara's restored appearance as I was.

But my mind was quickly captured by the look of hesitation in Hector and Rodrigo's eyes. Clearly, they had not found Mendoza.

"What of Rafael and Patricio?" I said to Hector, not bothering to ask about the captain. "They have not learned anything either?"

Patricio himself moved through the group then, clasping me arm to arm in greeting and pulling me closer to thump my back. "My friend, I am relieved to see you and your lady safely arrived." The shorter man turned toward her, took her hand, and bowed smartly over it. "You are most fetching, Señorita Zara. I beg you to attend a party I am hosting this night." His round face dimpled as he grinned at her, as if she might be on his arm rather than mine.

I was relieved to see her eyes widen, and knew she remembered him. Back at the old mission, she'd struggled to place him, but clearly her head was clearing. But a party? I grunted in dismay at the thought of it. I leaned closer to my friend. "Patricio, what of *Mendoza*? What have you and Rafael learned of him? I expected news, man!"

"Peace, peace," Patricio said, waving me down and reluctantly looking from Zara back to me. "The man is about but taking the utmost care to stay out of sight," he said under his breath, his smile finally fading as he noted my fervor. "He booked passage on the *Siren's Quest*, captained by Señor Flores, which is due to embark tomorrow morning. He registered under an assumed name and paid with a pretty gold coin from the Ventura chest."

"Did Rafael not tell you?" I growled. "I wanted you to see that he could not do such a thing!"

Patricio frowned, scoffing at my concern. "Is this not better, my friend? This way, we know *exactly* where he'll be and when. Rafael and I agreed that blocking passage might have simply frightened him away. He'd ride north, for Oregon, I'd wager. Find passage there." His face soon returned to his easy, homely, engaging grin. "*This* way, we can sup together. Enjoy the evening. Attend the party. And capture your enemy come morn."

I wasn't ready to smile with him. "*This* way," I muttered, "my enemy remains free to prowl about all night. Who's to say our presence won't scare him away?"

"He's not here, Javier," Patricio said earnestly. "Not *in* town. He arrived, purchased provisions, and then left to wait for dawn tomorrow to emerge from the shadows. I have checked every manifest and spoken myself to every captain of the ten ships harbored here, every proprietor of every hotel." He reached up to pat me on the shoulder. "Take your ease, friend. Relax for a night. You need the rest, as does your lady. As well as a modicum of distraction?"

Zara turned from chatting with Rafael, who had just arrived and was fawning over her "refreshed countenance," but I slowly shook my head in answer to the silent question in her big, brown eyes. As frustrating as it was to not have Mendoza in immediate custody, I had to admit that my friend's plan was the next best thing. Maybe even his party was fortuitous. For if I was to soon send Zara home to her own time, I wanted every hour with her that I could manage to capture. So I could remember it…forever.

That night, Patricio sent his own carriage to collect Zara, Rafael, and me. Our men all went there on horseback separately, so as not to draw attention. According to Patricio, his mother had been looking forward to the Feast of John the Baptist's nativity for months and had been importing goods for it all along. There was to be a dance and everyone in town of note would be invited. In town, people were already celebrating, but hardly in a Christian fashion. For many, it was nothing more than Summer Solstice, an excuse to drink and carouse. There'd be a fair amount at the Casales estate as well, I was sure, but in a far more genteel fashion.

"You established guard duty among the men?" I asked

Rafael as we bounced along the dirt road out to Hacienda de Casales, one of the finest homes in the region.

"I did," he said with a single nod, "though I don't think it's truly necessary. Would not this party be the one place in town that Mendoza would want to avoid carefully? He got what he was after." He paused to glance at Zara, who stared out the tiny window of the carriage. "Why would he engage any of us further? What would he hope to gain?"

His words mollified me. "You're likely right. I simply want to be overly cautious."

Rafael nodded again and smiled. "Of course. None of us want further harm to come to your lady. But tonight, my friends, you can simply enjoy. Tonight you may revel. Tomorrow you shall see justice done."

"We hope," Zara said.

"We shall, we shall," Rafael insisted. "The rat cannot escape this hole."

"How can you be so certain?" I asked. "What if he's caught wind of our plans?"

"We have a man watching the stables where Mendoza boarded your mare. Two men on every side of the town, keeping watch. He'll likely come to town again tonight, for food and supplies, perhaps for diversion. If he does, he shall not shake those who follow him. Captain Flores of the *Siren's Call* will be in attendance tonight. You may speak to him directly about how you would like to proceed come morn."

I offered my hand to Zara and after a moment, she took it, but she returned to looking out the window. Because she wanted to see this new land? Or because she was thinking of the golden lamp? I'd dispatched two men that afternoon to check every shop in town and on the outskirts—even other traders who might have come across such an item. Hastily, I'd sketched its shape, described its missing spout and the odd lettering barely visible about the circumference. I'd given each man three gold coins—more than enough to purchase it, if they found it.

Patricio's family's estate north of town sprawled across hundreds of acres, from crashing sea to green, rolling hills. The fields were verdant, crops of wheat and corn and grapes all showing the height of summer's pulse. As the only son in his family, he was expected to return to the hacienda and run the estate in time; he and I had both chafed under that expectation, which had drawn us together. For now, while his father lived, Señor Casales allowed his son to explore his business as a shipping broker in town, recognizing that he developed certain relationships that would benefit the estate over time. But I knew that Patricio would end up returning to the hacienda in time. It reminded me of my discussion with Zara—and the idea that I might return to the sea in time, leaving the rancho in Mateo's hands. *En tiempo…* The words rolled through my head and I looked to Zara as the carriage pulled up before the beautiful, pristine hacienda. *In time…*

Where would Zara be if that ever transpired? In my own time? Or hers?

I ground my teeth together and exited first, turning to help Zara descend the tiny stairs in her voluminous skirts.

Señor and Señora Casales stood there, waiting to greet us, with Patricio's little sister, Camila, beside them. Patricio was already mingling among the guests, his loud laugh helping me immediately find him in the crowd. I shook my head. "Everyone loves Patricio," I said to Zara as we strode forward. "He has an uncanny way of becoming everyone's dear friend."

"Including yours," she said.

I introduced her to Señor, Señora, and Señorita Casales. Camila hovered over my hand and turned with me to look for her brother. "He is over there with the Diazes," she said with a small shake of her head, as if half-amused and half-chagrined. "It's impossible to keep Patricio where he is supposed to be."

"Indeed," I said with a laugh and squeezed her hand as we headed in his direction. He now was flirting with three young women, each in impeccable gowns and elaborate hair ornaments. I was glad the proprietor had encouraged us to purchase both comb and hat for Zara. Even in her fine golden-bronze silk and smart little hat, she was outdressed by the majority of these women. But still, none was more beautiful than she, to me. And I knew I wasn't the only one to think so; many men gazed our way, and their eyes were not on me.

Servants moved among the crowd, serving champagne in crystal glasses. Outside of Mexico, I had never seen more than twenty goblets in one room; here there had to be over a hundred. Patricio joined us then, grabbing two glasses and handing one to Zara and one to me. Clearly, he'd already been imbibing; his grin was wider, his gestures more exuberant. He took a third from another passing servant and lifted it high between us. "To your health and restoration, my friends. Cheers."

We clinked our glasses against his, mine sloshing a bit over the edge, and I had no choice but to smile along with him. He was simply so full of life, my friend, intent on squeezing every moment for everything it was worth. Hadn't he been the one who first nudged me to admit that I had more than a passing interest in Zara? Now his small eyes twinkled as he looked from me to her and back again, raising a brow as if our marriage vows were surely about to be said. But there would be no marriage vows, I told myself. I had to set her free, really open my heart to set her free this time.

Quickly, before he mentioned something of our love, I bent toward him. "So tell me, Patricio. Any word of our friend?"

His smile faded a bit, and he looked again to Zara as if he'd much rather tease us, but I put a gloved hand on his forearm. He sighed. "Nothing more," he said under his breath. "But all is in place for tomorrow. You shall have your quarry then. Tonight, we celebrate, no?"

Rafael joined us as the music began, a group of musicians playing tunes from the mother country that made us all smile. Some moved into groups and then divided into lines when the next song was announced. Zara shook her head when I asked if she wanted to dance, whispering that her feet were sore. She demurely declined invitations from others who boldly approached us, several braving my scowl. Perhaps they thought me a cad, not inviting her to dance, and thought they might press their luck. Little did they know that if her feet had permitted it, I would have already had her in my arms.

We picnicked on blankets spread out across the lawn, under the trees, and beside the vineyard. The musicians played statelier music as the sun set in the distance. Captain John Worthington joined us then, along with a number of Anglo sailors, and Zara flew into his arms in the most inappropriate way. He laughed and turned her about, casting me a grin that told me he didn't intend to challenge my suit. Perhaps it was the way of her own time, to be so informal and familiar with others. Perhaps it was the relief of seeing the man who had discovered her after she stole my horse and was desperately trying to find her own way that first day she arrived on the beach….

After I clasped arms with Captain Worthington, he turned back to her. "So I hear tales that you survived both pirate and shipwreck, Señorita Zara," he said, shaking his blond head in wonder. "Do you intend to build an entire life of making tongues wag?"

She smiled and shook her head ruefully. "Trust me, that is not what I intend. And had it not been for Javier and his men…I am uncertain I would have lived another day."

He sobered, seeming to understand that he'd raised a tender memory in a rather cavalier way. "Forgive me, friends. I did not mean to make light of something so terribly serious." His blue eyes softened as he glanced between us. "I am relieved to know you both have survived and fare well enough to engage in a party such as this."

"Not that Patricio would have allowed us to decline the invitation," I said.

"True. He's insisted upon every captain in the harbor attending this ball, along with their officers and any lady of repute they can find."

I laughed under my breath. In a town like Monterey, the men outnumbered the women three to one, if one didn't count the prostitutes. The idea of someone bringing a lady of the night onto Señora Casales's estate… That would not end well. But I also knew that Patricio meant to aid me in finding Mendoza, even if it meant he'd suffer his mother's wrath.

There were whispers of poker being played in Señor Casales's drawing room, and I felt the tug of interest, but I refused to leave Zara's side, even as she spent half an hour hearing of Captain Worthington's trade in the six weeks they'd been apart. "I've been to Seattle," he said, "and am fully loaded with pelts. We'll embark for Panama as soon as I trade pelts for other supplies here. Do you wish to return home by way of sailing with us to Bonita Harbor?" He looked over at me. "Your men could bring their horses—"

But Zara was already slowly shaking her head. "I love the sea, and I would love to sail with you, but…" She cast me a look of apology, knowing accepting John's offer would be the quicker way to get us home.

"Ahh," John said, taking her hand with both of his in brotherly understanding, "'tis too soon. I should have thought of that. Some sailors who survive shipwreck never take to the sea again, once they kiss the beach and draw a blessed free breath of air."

"That won't be my way," she said, squaring her shoulders. "I simply need…a bit more time."

"And when you and Javier are ready, permit me to be your captain. It would be my honor to show you how sailing can be more a joy than a sorrow."

"We'll be certain to do so," I said. Briefly I thought of him taking us south to Mexico, on our honeymoon, where I could introduce her to my extended family.

But there would be no wedding, no honeymoon. She would learn to love sailing in her own time, when ships and sailors were likely far safer.

She leaned toward me as I frowned. "I've saddened you, saying no to John?" she whispered, brows in an arc above her beautiful brown eyes. They always reminded me of the earth, of soil just turned, ready for seed.

"No, no, it isn't that," I said.

"Then you are frustrated that we'll have to ride home."

"No. Woman, permit me to keep my own counsel for once, would you?"

She sighed. "Very well. But I must find the…uh…" She shifted uncomfortably.

"The privy?" I guessed in a whisper, judging her discomfort. After all, I'd grown up with sisters. "This way."

Gratefully, she took my arm, and we went around the house to the back, passing several of my men, who seemed to be relaxing more than keeping watch. Seeing my scowl, more than one straightened and hastened about his task.

"I really can do this by myself. It's not necessary to stay here and wait, Javier. Look at all the people about."

"I will wait," I said calmly. "Right here."

She rolled her eyes and moved away from me, gingerly opening a wooden door into a temporary shack that I knew formed the communal outhouse. In there would be servants to help the women with their skirts, keeping them from getting dirty. The men…well, the men just wandered into the cornfields to relieve themselves. In many ways, it was far simpler to be a man, I thought, feeling sorry for Zara and my sisters as I paced and waited for her to emerge.

But when she did, she appeared shaken.

"Zara, what is it?" I whispered, taking her arm firmly in hand. "Are you unwell? What happened?" I shoved back my frustration of wanting to attend her, even in *there*, knowing there was no way I would've been welcomed. Besides, had there not been twenty women entering and exiting? I had seen them as I milled about outside, with a few other men, waiting.

She did not speak until we gained some distance from the nearest people, under an old oak tree, with a chandelier hanging from its biggest branch. "You must go and play poker with the men inside," she said urgently, putting her fingers on my arm and nodding toward the house. "I heard a woman say that her husband was playing, and there was the strangest golden *lamp* on the table, part of what another man was wagering."

I swallowed hard. The lamp? Here? Did that mean that Mendoza was about too? I pulled her close and looked around, feeling a rush of fierce protection.

John and Rafael both caught my worried eye and hastened our way. Quickly, I told them what had happened. "Zara and I will head inside. I want you, John, to attend Zara as I play. Rafael, alert the others that the pirate may be about and then join us at the tables. If this man didn't bring the lamp to the party, I must find out who did."

Both men agreed, and Zara and John followed me inside. There were a few other women inside the den, standing about, watching as their men played, so it wasn't so extraordinary that Zara was there. Still, John gestured to me as I sat down and then to the man next to him, smoking a cigar. "That's my good friend, Don Javier de la Ventura. Care to make a bet on the outcome of his game? He's the best in all of Alta California."

"Not from what I hear from the men of…" the man said, dropping his tone and turning away so I couldn't hear the rest of their chatter. I strove to ignore it anyway, now that the man to my right, a heavyset, perspiring man named Señor Manuel, was dealing the cards.

ZARA

We stood outside the gaming room, thick with cigar smoke, in a small parlor with windows open wide. Many women milled about, clearly waiting on their dates, but some men too. John and I chatted with one person after another, but he kindly positioned himself so that I could glance over his shoulder and keep an eye on Javier. There had been no room at the table where my lamp sat in the middle, surrounded by coins as prize, so Javier had taken a seat at the table next to it. Clearly, the stakes had risen at the lamp table. And as word spread of the growing bounty, more crowded into the den, intent on watching the game come to its end. I chafed at so many seeing the lamp and wondering over it.

But my attention hovered on the man John was now speaking with, smoking a fat cigar. Focusing in on the conversation, I figured that he spoke of the crew from the *Guadiana*. My mind raced, trying to remember where I'd heard the name of that ship before. It was John's pointed look that helped me remember. It had been the men of the *Guadiana* who had raced after Javier, the day I first arrived on his shore—the day I'd met John, after I'd stolen Javier's horse. The men had been set on killing him, it seemed, and crossed from Vargas land onto Ventura land as if they had every right.

"Have you spoken to the men of the *Guadiana* recently?" I interjected, studying the man in his early forties, puffing on the cigar, next to John.

"As recently as this evening, señorita," he said, sidling me a curious glance after blowing two perfect *O*'s of cigar smoke. "Do you know of her captain?"

My mouth went dry. If the men of the *Guadiana* were here, and they favored gambling, how long would it be before they entered this very room? John's eyes narrowed, as he obviously came to the same conclusion. If they found Javier here, when he'd once escaped them, would they still be seeking to make him pay? I still didn't know what that all had even been about.

I knew I had to warn Javier. I stepped into the room, John right on my heels, and made my way through the crowd.

Cards were laid with some flourish on the lamp table, just as we drew near. There was a grumble from one young man about "uncommon luck," and an older man on the other side of the winner bit out, "That's not luck."

I edged around three men to get a better look at the winner. I had been able to tell from the back that he wasn't Mendoza— his hair was too thin and a lighter brown.

"Gentlemen," the winner said, gathering toward himself

the pile of coins and the lamp and scooping it all into a leather bag, "do you wish to continue bemoaning your own poor luck and make a formal claim about my ethics, or continue playing?"

I gasped, as I registered the lines of the bag. It was the one Mendoza had carried. Somehow, it made the lamp's presence more concrete, more real.

"Wh-where did you get that bag?" I asked, pushing my way through the remaining men to get to the edge of the table.

The young man paused from gathering his winnings and peered up at me. "I purchased it just this afternoon, señorita."

"From whom? Where?" I said, my tone more like a shriek, even to my own ears. I saw Javier rise behind the crowd and push his way in, just as John did so beside me.

"A man, down on his luck, outside of town," said the man, now rising too, eyes shifting warily among us.

"A pirate, you mean," I bit out. "Captain Mendoza. My captor, the one who robbed the *Heron* in Bonita Harbor and stripped everything from Javier de la Ventura's storehouse." My fists were clenched. "The man who kidnapped me and Mateo de la Ventura, holding us for ransom! A killer!"

The young man was lifting his hands in surrender, but I saw that he already had the bag strapped across his chest, preparing to make an exit.

"And I am Javier de la Ventura," Javier said, crossing his arms and giving the man a menacing glance. "I believe we should sit down and hear all you have to tell us. If you are truly innocent, we will know. And if you are not—"

"He is not," cried the man who had lost so badly at the table. "I wager he was cheating throughout our game!" He rose, red-faced, obviously seeing this as an opportunity to regain some of his losses.

"Did someone claim he was Javier de la Ventura?" thundered a man from the doorway of the den.

As one, we all turned to see who had come in, and I instantly recognized the three men who had given Javier chase that fateful first day I arrived in 1840.

It was suddenly hot in the room—dreadfully hot—and far too much champagne and wine had been consumed by those inside. The air was charged, practically sparking.

And then everything exploded at once.

CHAPTER 24

ZARA

John shoved me down to the ground as a chair came swinging through the air.

Women screamed, and men shouted. Others cursed. More chairs flew through the air and a man fell beside me, knocked out cold. Another was pushed across the table and came down four feet away, surrounded by cards and gold coins. But my focus was on the winner—the man with my lamp…and possibly Abuela's shawl and the fossil, too, in the saddlebag. I thought Javier had put them all in the saddlebag, that day when Bonita Harbor was attacked. I didn't care about the gold, but there was no way this evening was coming to an end before I had the lamp—and hopefully the rest of my treasures— in hand. Each was special to me, for different reasons. And I'd lost so much in recent weeks, so much, that there was no way I would lose those three things.

I got to my feet and dodged two men who were both trying to choke each other, careening past. Another man lunged for his adversary, narrowly missing me. I saw that Javier and John were fighting the men of the *Guadiana*, two against three, and others were joining in—some on Javier's side, some not. A young woman was screaming—simply screaming, eyes squeezed shut, fists at her sides, totally still except for her open mouth.

Meanwhile, the young gambler with Mendoza's bag smiled a little to himself, as if this was the perfect exit strategy. He, too, ducked past grappling men, refusing to engage anyone who threatened him, with his hands up as if to say, "Peace, I'm on your side." They let him pass, and he made fast time to the doorway. I dodged to one side behind a column when he glanced backward, obviously to see if anyone was watching his escape.

I bent down and grabbed hold of an unconscious man's sword, sliding it from the scabbard. It was more an ornament than a true battle sword, but at the moment, it was the best I had. I hid it among my skirts as I hurried down the hall, as others moved in—led by the portly Señor Casales—clearly bent on ending the spectacle that was about to totally ruin his wife's John the Baptist feast. The gambler ahead of me again paused at the front door, turning for one more look, but I slid behind an open door and waited, counting to three. After three, I peeked out, and he was gone. In trying to remain unseen, had I given him too much of a head start? I ran forward. If I lost him…if he disappeared into the crowd…

But when I reached the front porch, I saw him entering the stables to my right. More men rushed past me into the house, either excited to enter the fray or eager to assist in stopping it.

I ran to the stables, searching the crowd for Hector, Felipe—any of Javier's men—but seeing none. Javier would kill me if he knew what I was about to do, but I couldn't see any other way. If I gave the gambler even another minute, he might be on his way out at a full gallop. I might already be too late.

I crept down the dimly lit stables, with single-flame lamps hanging three stalls apart. I hated the swish of my skirts across the straw and halted, trying to hold my breath, listening. But there was no movement apart from a few horses dolefully swinging their heads my way as if hoping for a carrot or a handful of hay. "Come out!" I whispered loudly. "I know you're in here! I want only three things from you. Give them to me, and I'll let you go. Refuse, and I'll scream."

"I think you won't do that," he whispered back, lifting a sword to my neck. He'd been in an empty stall almost directly beside me.

I stilled and groaned inwardly. Who did I think I was? Charging in here alone? And what did I plan on doing with the sword hidden among my skirts? The closest experience I had with one was watching *The Three Musketeers*.

"Listen to me," I said. "All I want is the lamp, the fossil, and the shawl. They are mine. Then give me a bit of information, and I will let you slip away."

He paused. "Those things are yours?" he said doubtfully. "I thought you said the bag belonged to Javier de la Ventura."

"I did. But the things within are mine."

I could almost feel him waver.

"Give me those things and I will let you go."

He scoffed a laugh. "I can go now. Even if you scream, none will come in time."

"But some might give chase."

He stepped closer, considering me, forcing my face toward the light with the tip of the sword. "You are the girl that Mendoza kept captive."

So he'd lied. Clearly, he knew the man.

"And you are the man who has my stolen goods. Keep the gold. I only want the lamp, shawl and the fossil. The lamp is worth nothing, broken as it is, but it is a family heirloom."

"And the fossil?"

"Javier gave it to me. It was once his dead brother's. He has one just like it. He wanted me to keep it always, knowing he had the other."

This small intimacy seemed to move him. "You also mentioned a bit of information, señorita. What is it you seek?"

I swallowed hard. "Well, I would like to learn anything you know of Mendoza. Where is he hiding tonight? Why did he risk his ship during a storm? Who is he working for and why?"

He studied me, intently, and came around to face me, his sword still at my neck. "That is more than a bit of information, is it not?"

I hesitated. "Well, yes."

A man shouted outside the stable door, then another. The young gambler's eyes shifted to the door and he held his breath. We both did. When it became apparent the men were not yet coming in, he said, "Are you a gambler, Señorita?" he asked, stepping closer, so he could whisper.

"Me? Uhh, no. I don't play cards."

"Gambling goes beyond cards. We gamblers enjoy a bit of risk in our lives to keep the blood pumping, and testing if we can trust our own intuition, as well as how we read others…"

I considered him. "No. I'm not really a gambler."

He dropped his sword and patted his pursed lips with his gloved finger. "Pity, that," he said. "Because I am about to ask you to gamble in order to retrieve what you seek."

I eyed him warily, waiting.

"I do not have your shawl or fossil here. Allow me to go now," he said, leaning closer to whisper in my ear, "and I will not only get you your lamp, shawl and fossil, I will tell you of Mendoza's greater gain in all this. That will prove far more important to you than his current location in time, no?"

He leaned back to watch my eyes widen, and I knew I'd played into his hands. I hadn't yet managed to hold on to any sort of poker face, and this was a man well-schooled in the art.

"Ahh, yes, I thought that might please you. You already know there is something beyond the Bonita Harbor and the *Heron*'s treasures that greased Mendoza's wheel. You just do not yet know who…or how. I can answer those questions."

"How? When will you tell me?" I said, pulling back angrily, even as my heart pounded with hope.

"That is what you shall have to gamble upon, Señorita," he soothed. "I shall deliver all to you within a fortnight, back at Rancho de la Ventura. Not here. It would be far too dangerous." He moved to the next stall, turning his back to me, and threw a saddlebag across a gelding, stuffed his own bag inside one, and swiftly mounted. "If you betray me now, you will lose not only the hidden shawl and fossil—though it mystifies me why they might be so important to you—but also the lamp. If I am captured, you can rest assured that your lamp will be in the sheriff's custody, not yours."

"For a time."

"For a time. Until someone steals it from him. Trust me. This is your best option."

Trust him? I didn't even know what a fortnight was! I couldn't let him go! I whipped out my sword and aimed it at him as he slipped on a low, black hat, typical among the Spanish here.

He stared down at me as if I were a first-grader trying to take on a sixth-grader. "Do you intend to use that, Señorita? I think *I* shall gamble that you will not. Because you *want* what I have promised. And your only chance at it—your only true chance—is to allow me to go now."

With that, he dug his heels into the gelding's flanks, and I dropped the sword point to keep from stabbing the poor horse. Shouts sounded from the yard as he was spotted, but I heard the clatter of horseshoes on cobblestone for a time until he reached the dirt road.

When I reached the stable door, he'd disappeared into the dark.

CHAPTER 25

JAVIER

I came to and winced, immediately closing my eyes again.

Zara took my hand in hers. "So it's now my turn to play the nurse and you the patient," she said.

"Would that a pretty nurse could make a man's head cease aching," I muttered.

"Exactly what I said yesterday," she teased. I laughed until it sent an arrow through my temple and abruptly stopped.

Her tone gentled. "Truly, are you all right?"

"I will be. The *Guadiana* crew simply paid me what they thought I was long due."

"And more," Rafael said, sitting on a chair beside me, elbows on his knees. "Had your men not arrived, I fear they would have beaten you to death."

"My men and Señora Casales," I muttered, lifting a hand to my throbbing brow.

Rafael looked down at me. "Señor Casales brought aid. Señora Casales restored order. And you can thank Patricio for convincing her not to toss us outside the hacienda gates with the rest of the 'troublemakers.'"

"Ahh, yes," I said, "so I owe the entire Casales family."

"Indeed you do."

I turned to Zara. "And what of you, love? Where were you during the melee?"

"I—I escaped outside," she said.

She was hiding something, not telling me all of it, but I didn't have the fortitude to pursue it. My cursed head was about to explode.

"Hector," she said, "see if you can find some feverfew, will you?"

"Ahh, turnabout is fair play, sí?" I muttered.

"Sí," she said, taking my hand. "What is it about those men from the *Guadiana*? Why did they want to kill you as much today as the day I met you?"

"Well, for one, they are friends of the Vargases."

"Granted. And?"

I paused and chanced a glance, squinting. "Truly, I am not the same man I was the day I met you, Zara."

Her beautiful eyes narrowed at me, waiting.

"The day I won at the *Guadiana* crew's card table in Santa Barbara," I said with a sigh of confession, "I made certain that I also stole a kiss from every one of their women."

Rafael laughed under his breath, shaking his head and putting his long fingers on either side of his mouth, staring in dismay at me. Zara was shaking her head too, but was that a hint of a smile about her lips? I hoped so.

I took her hand in both of mine, pulling it to my chest. "Clearly, that would not have happened since. At that time, I simply wanted escape. A reprieve from the long, straight road that Rancho de la Ventura represented for me. You changed that, Zara."

"I hope I did," she said, squeezing my hands. "If only to keep you *alive*."

"So the young gambler slipped away?" I asked Rafael.

"He did."

"You have men tracking him?"

"Heading north, south, east and west."

"I'm sorry, Zara. We'll do what we can to find him again," I pledged. I refused to think what might happen if the man managed to escape town with the precious lamp still in the bag. But as much as I wanted the lamp for Zara's sake, I wanted Mendoza for all of us. "How many hours until daylight?"

"Three, maybe four," Rafael said tiredly.

"We must rest, then," I mumbled, blissfully glad for the excuse, as my aching, weary body begged for nothing else.

ZARA

Rafael studied me as Javier drifted back to sleep.

"Where were you during the fight?" he whispered, glancing down to make sure his friend did not stir. He took my elbow and ushered me several paces away. "Javier didn't demand an answer, but I would have it now. You're hiding something." There was nothing of his usual playful, genteel manner as he pinned me with his gaze.

"Will he be all right?" I gestured toward Javier, stalling but wanting to know.

"Javier? Certainly. He's taken worse. Now tell me," he growled. "Where were you during the melee?"

"Where was I?" I repeated, buying time, rising and going to fetch a cup of water from a crystal pitcher.

But he followed right behind, clearly glad to get even farther away from Javier. "It is a simple question, señorita, no?"

"What question?" Patricio said, entering the den then, lifting his wide, blunt hands, a wry grin spreading across his reddened face. "Have you now taken to interrogating Javier's intended as he lies there, unconscious?"

I practically melted in relief. I didn't know what had awakened Rafael's suspicion and ire so, but I was glad to have his keen attention now focused on Patricio rather than me... and Patricio practically put himself between us.

"I simply wished to know where she was during the fight," Rafael hissed, hands on his hips. "And why she is not *forthcoming.*"

"Why does it matter, my friend? She is safe. You are safe. Even our friend Javier, though battered, is safe. Now we must rest, for morning is soon upon us, and you know what that means. My men are here," he said, gesturing behind him to servants in the hallway, "to carry Javier to his room." He turned back to me. "Come, Zara. My mother will have my hide if I do not see you to the guest room myself. You must sleep in the bed she has prepared for you, or I will never hear the end of it. And I pray you are ready now, because I myself am asleep on my feet."

"You do not seem sleepy," I said, taking his beefy arm and allowing him to lead me out. I looked over my shoulder as the men entered, gathered around Javier, and carefully lifted him on the blanket beneath him. I knew enough of 1840 culture that Señora Casales would not rest herself until I was in my own room—there would be no nursing Javier through the night, not when we were unmarried and under her roof. And Patricio would not rest either until he could reassure his mama.

"He will be well, Zara," Patricio said, patting my hand as we walked. A maid silently padded behind us. To protect the master's reputation or mine?

"Will he?"

"Oh, he will. Right and true, come morn. It's been a big night, a fine night," he said, pausing outside my door. He turned the glass knob and pushed the tall door inward. "*Buenas noches*," he said, gesturing inward. "The maid will see to anything further you require. See you in but a few hours, no?"

I wished the proper answer was *no*. My body ached from head to toe, and suddenly I could barely keep my feet. "*Buenas noches, mi amigo*," I muttered, even as the maid shut the door.

With one swift look, she took me in from head to toe and then firmly, silently turned me around. She unlaced my gown from the back, then sat me down and swiftly unpinned my tiny hat—I had forgotten I had it on. What an odd custom it was, I thought distantly, to wear a hat when it was for fashion alone, not any measure of practical function. She carefully set it on the table beside me. I wanted to ask her name, make polite conversation, but all I could think was *I am out! Totally done.*

Cooked. Over this. And so I just succumbed to her ministrations, waiting as she loosed my hair from its pins, obeying her gentle command to rise as she lifted the heavy gown from my shoulders—up and over my head—and oh, what a relief it was....

She turned me again, moved to my stays, untied the stiff laces and then laid them across a chair. Then she took my hand and led me to the bed, pulled loose the comforter, and beckoned me silently to slip in, *like an angel to a child,* I thought.

I slipped beneath the covers and watched through half-lidded eyes as she drew them over me. Then she blew out my lamp, and her silhouetted figure silently padded through the door and softly closed it behind her.

In the back of my mind, I thought I should rise and peek in on Javier to make sure he was all right, or at least lock my own door, but it was in the back of my mind. The way, *way* back part of my mind.

CHAPTER 26

ZARA

The knocking at my door was at first a pile driver in my dream, surrounded by orange-vested workers, and then it gradually became the stark, spare knock it truly was. I turned and blinked, trying to focus, trying for a moment to figure out *where* I was, as I stared at the high ceiling lined with crown molding...let alone *when* I was.

And then it all came into focus. I was in Hacienda de Casales. Patricio's family home. It was morning, the potential morning of Captain Mendoza's capture.

I sat up with a start, my heart skipping a beat. I stared at the window and the gauzy curtains stirring in the breeze. I rose and looked to the door. "I hear you," I said at last, as the person outside rapped again. "Who is it?"

"It is Hector, Señorita," he said from beyond the door. "Pardon the intrusion. But we leave in half an hour for the wharf. Do you wish to accompany us or remain behind?"

I thought that over, eying the beckoning bed, still sleep-warm, for only a moment. "I will accompany you," I said. "Come back for me when you are ready to depart." I sank back down to the edge of my bed and brushed the stiff pillow, as if saying good-bye, even as I pondered the fact that I now said things like *I will accompany you* and *depart*. I didn't think I'd ever used the word *depart* in my life, other than driving a friend to an airport, where she left from a *departure* gate.

I've never even flown on an airplane, I thought. But here, now, I'd traveled farther than anyone I'd ever known or read about. *1840. 1840, Alta California. Top that, Buzz Lightyear...*

I looked about the room, idly wondering if somewhere along the way I'd lost it, like Tootles in *Hook*, searching for his "lost marbles." I felt kind of like that old man, scrambling to collect the bits of what he had lost, even as he tried to take in what he had found.

Another knock sounded at the door. It was a maid, the same maid, I figured, who had put me to bed last night. When I opened the door, I was sure of it. Her eyes were purple-rimmed and sleep-deprived, just as I was certain mine were. But she carried a steaming pot of tea and a biscuit on a tray, entering with a bob, and I welcomed her. "Thank you for coming," I said. "I apologize for your short night."

She set down the tray as I closed the door and immediately poured a cup of tea. "No matter, miss," she said, in English. "If it hadn't been you, it'd have been another. Now let's get you set for the day, yes?"

Half an hour later, I emerged in the hall in my golden yellow dress, hair piled high and affixed with pins and the comb that

Javier had purchased for me. He stood there, waiting, and his mouth dropped open for just a sec as he took me in. He tilted his head and then took my hand, lifting it to his lips. "You look… resplendent," he breathed.

Judging from his expression, I guessed that was his equivalent of pretty.

"And you look…battered."

"I gave worse than I received," he said, a bit chagrined.

I laughed under my breath and took his arm. "Shall we go and capture a pirate now?" I asked, casting him a daring look.

"Of course," he said, setting off with me in tow. "What else does one do with a Tuesday morning?"

So it's Tuesday, I thought. Ever since I'd arrived, I had struggled to get hold of the year, let alone the month and day of the week. Something about his mention of it steadied me, centered me. It was a Tuesday. *Tuesday.* "What is the date, exactly, Javier?" I asked.

He paused, either taking in my need for such exacting info or trying to remember himself. "I believe it is Tuesday, the twenty-second of June, the year of our Lord 1840."

"Quite clear about that, are you?" I teased, pulling his arm closer.

"I am, my love, despite last night's exploits." He slowed his pace. "Can you forgive me for that? For giving sway to fight, in the midst of all that was transpiring?"

I looked up at him but continued walking, urging him on. "Of course, of course," I said.

"You are not angry? For the reason the crew of the *Guadiana* was so angry?" Again he slowed, but I urged him on.

"No, no," I said, heaving a sigh. "My only concern is for you, Javier—you. I am not lost in some jealousy about a day I was not even a part of."

He pulled me up short. "But you were a part of that day. The biggest part of that day, in retrospect."

I looked up into his bruised face, his left eye now as puffy as I guessed my own had been a couple days ago. I met his steady, intense gaze and accepted his palm as he caressed my cheek. "Yes, I was a part of that day. The *end* of that day. But you owe me no apologies for the beginning of it."

"You were the end," he whispered, running fingers across my cheek, my temple. His caress sent shivers down my neck, shoulders, back. I turned to face him fully, aware that others were looking our way, but ignoring them. He lifted his other hand and cradled my face between his palms. "You were the end," he repeated, "but also the beginning. Before you, Zara Ruiz, I was racing toward death. When I met you, I began racing toward *life*."

I stared back up into his brown eyes, wondering what tortured him so. Why he pledged such love, as if it pained him to do so. As if he were saying good-bye.

I frowned. "Javier?"

He stilled, took a deep breath, then looked down, letting it out. Taking my hand, he secured it around the crook of his arm. "Come," he said, "let us go and capture your captor. Perhaps he can point us in the direction of that young man who has your golden lamp as well."

"Javier? Is there something else going on?" I tried again, as we walked down the road, straight toward the harbor, skies pink as the clouds caught the rising sun's reflection.

But even though he was distracted by a newcomer's greeting, I had the distinct impression that he welcomed the interruption. My stomach turned into a tighter knot. What could he be keeping from me? And why? I wanted to demand he tell me, right then and there, but he was engaging the other man, shaking hands, exchanging small talk. And by the time they were done, he whisked me into a carriage, while he rode astride his mare, found that morning on the outskirts of Monterey.

Kinda convenient, I thought. Me riding in this vehicle, him outside. I shook my head. It didn't matter. I'd get it out of him eventually. For now, we both had the same goal: Capturing Captain Mendoza.

CHAPTER 27

ZARA

Captain John Worthington welcomed us aboard his ship, the *Emma Jane*. The men carried our few bags and even led a couple of our horses across the gangplank—to make us look like passengers, Javier explained. But it was all a way for us to covertly watch the ship moored just off the pier, the *Siren's Quest*. This was the new ship that Mendoza was to board. Then our men and Worthington's crew would attack, all in an effort to ferret out the pirate and take him to the magistrate in town—in chains.

"They've been taking on provisions and goods all morning," John said to us, his back to the *Siren's Quest*. "My man in the crow's nest has been keeping a keen eye out for our friend, but so far, no passengers have been taken aboard."

"So he has yet to come," Javier said, casually leaning against the rail, as if he hadn't a care about any other ship.

"Or he somehow boarded under cover of darkness. My crew was watching, but we both know a pirate can find ways to accomplish his goals." He turned to eye the neighboring ship a moment and then crossed his arms. "They're taking on stores of water now. It won't be long until they hoist sail and head out. If we're to make our move, it will have to be soon."

Javier offered his arm, and we began to walk the deck. I was on the interior, looking out to sea, Javier on my right. "Tell me what you see," he said.

"Three masts, an American flag. An efficient crew going about their tasks. None of them seem nervous; none are looking about, only tying knots, fixing sails, hoisting cargo from rowboats below and whatnot."

"Hmmm," Javier said, as we reached the stern of the ship and then resumed our walk up the other rail. Now he could look across my shoulder to study the ship himself.

"Do you think Patricio got it wrong?" I asked. "Or that Mendoza booked passage as a ruse?"

"It's possible," he said, his brow furrowing further. "But I hope not. If so, we might have lost both our enemy and your lamp."

I looked to the harbor. "The lamp was never truly mine or your mother's," I muttered. "It comes to those it's supposed to, I believe. If it's supposed to come back to me, it will."

He pulled me to a stop as I turned. "You seem very certain of that."

He didn't know of my deal with the gambler. That I'd let him slip away with only a promise to do what he said he would. Had I been a total fool? Or would it prove to be a wise decision? Regardless, I doubted I would've gotten the lamp back, even if I'd screamed. The man had been easy on the horse, fully in control. And it was as he said…if I screamed, he'd likely have been well away before anyone gave chase. In the *dark*.

"I am certain," I finally said, daring to raise my gaze to his. "There's only so much control we have in this matter, Javier. Any of it." I lifted my hands. "With Mendoza," I said in a whisper. "Or the lamp. Last night…well, let's just say I'm coming to decide that we must make the most of the time we have, with the people in front of us, rather than always wondering about what it might be like elsewhere, with others. An entire life and all kinds of love might be wasted if we're always panting after what we don't have rather than appreciating what we do." I put my hand on his chest and looked up to him. I wished he would kiss me or hug me. I needed him to.

But while he covered my hand briefly with his own gloved hand, he didn't. Because we were in such a public space? Instead, he took my hand and set it on the crook of his arm again. "I hear what you are saying," he said. "But I want you to have a choice, Zara. About the lamp, about your life's path," he said carefully, as two crew members passed us.

"I tried to make that choice," I said quietly. "The night before the attack on the harbor, right? You were with me. We said our good-byes, and I tried to wish my way home. But God clearly denied me that passage."

He pulled me to a stop and turned to face me again. "I believe that is because as fervently as you were praying, wishing your way home, I was as fervently praying that the Lord would leave you right beside me."

My eyes widened, and I stared at him. *Was he saying…?*

He nodded and took both my hands in his. "I do not know if my care for you would have such power to anchor you here, with me, Zara." He lifted one of my hands and kissed the knuckles tenderly, even as his gaze never left mine. "And it is my dearest hope that you will decide to stay. But I shall not press you until I know it is what *you* want, as much as I want it. This life, in this time," he finished in a whisper. "And after all that has transpired—" He broke off then, looking to the sea, then back to me. "I have to believe that your best interest is served in returning to your own home. That you would be safest there. It would tear my heart in two to see you leave me, Zara Ruiz," he said, reaching up to tuck a tendril of my hair behind my ear. "But it would tear my heart in four to see you hurt again and know that I could have been the bridge to your safest harbor, when instead I was your barricade. And it kills me that last night, I was held captive by the sins of my past, as your precious lamp was spirited away."

So there it was. At last. Why he was holding back. Why he'd been holding back since we were reunited, really.

He blamed himself that I was still here.

"Javier, as much as you loved me, as much as you prayed that I would stay, I think if God wanted me to go back, it would've happened. I confess that I've had doubts, since the day we were captured by Mendoza. Serious doubts. I confess that I've longed for home at times, for the familiar. And I confess that I wouldn't mind having the *option* to try to return again, *if* I decided to." I gripped his hand in both of mine, urging him to feel my passion. "But it wouldn't be to 'stay safe,' Javier. Even in that familiar place, my own time, I would face other dangers. Other things that could hurt me, even kill me. Every day, whether I recognized it or not. There is no safe place in the world, Javier." I smiled then. "There may be *safer* places, yes, and *safer* people. But no place can completely eradicate disease, or attack, or death. People making bad decisions, following evil desires, are everywhere, *throughout* time. But *so* are those who are *good*."

My own words surprised me. But as I spoke them, I felt the passion, the resolve behind them as truth. In my effort to comfort and convince him, I'd done the same to myself.

He studied me, and I could see the hope warring with stubborn resolve in his dark chocolate eyes.

"What of the choices in your own home?" he asked, turning me to the rail, so we could not be overheard by people drawing near. We leaned against it, drawing our heads closer together. "You said women have more choices, more opportunities. To lead, to work—"

"To vote," I added.

He stared at me as if I had sprouted horns. "No."

"Yes," I said with a laugh. "Believe it or not, women vote as well as men do."

"That cannot be," Javier muttered, seeming truly perplexed. "Women would be led with their hearts more than their minds."

This debate will have to wait for another time, I decided. "You'd be surprised how well it all balances out. But I understand what you're trying to say. Lack of choice or opportunity would be one of the most challenging aspects of remaining here," I admitted. "But Javier, then I go back to what brought me here in the first place: my three wishes. What I wanted most was family, adventure, and love. I've found each of those in spades. A bit too much adventure of late," I added with a rueful smile. "But I cannot deny that my deepest wishes have come true."

He turned and brushed his curly hair back from his forehead, thinking, then turned back to look at me. After a moment, he said, "It makes my heart sing to know that your deepest wishes have been answered here, with me. But I will see Mendoza in chains and on his knees before you. And I will get that lamp back. I must have it back in order to move forward. And once the villain that has caused us such heartache is punished and we have the lamp in hand, I will leave you in Tainter Cove, by yourself, while I settle to my knees and pray *only* for God's will to be done. I want you to have the choice, Zara, with no possible chains holding you back. Once more. To either return to your home or forever remain in mine."

I swallowed hard. I had to admit that if I had the lamp in hand this instant, if I were back at Tainter Cove, alone, the pull to return to my own time would still be there. But the thought of leaving... I searched his eyes, even as he searched mine. Then he nodded in silent pledge and turned to leave me alone to my thoughts.

CHAPTER 28

JAVIER

My muscles were tense, head to toe, after my conversation with Zara. But the first of my pledges to her was about to be resolved. If Mendoza were aboard the *Siren's Quest*, I'd either capture him or kill him before the morning was through.

"Permission to come aboard, Captain!" John yelled up to the deck from the center of our lead rowboat, taking off his hat and putting it to his chest. Patricio stepped up beside him. The rest of us remained seated.

Most of the crew of the *Siren's Quest* had already gathered on the starboard rail to watch our four boats row up to their side.

"What is this?" the captain blustered. "On what account do you hail us?"

John slid a letter from the harbormaster out from his jacket and held it up, then gestured to Patricio. "Señor Casales has learned that you might have a fugitive aboard, Captain Santiago Mendoza, charged with piracy, robbery, kidnapping, and murder."

"We have no passengers aboard, at present. Only cargo in our hold," the captain said.

John lifted the letter higher in the wind. "This gives us permission to search your ship before you sail. Captain Mendoza booked passage with you, two days past."

"He did, but he has not shown himself. You have my word of it."

"Begging your pardon, Captain," I said, rising. "But I know this man personally. I would recognize him, even if he has taken on a disguise as one of your crew, because it was I he robbed. It was I who was forced to watch as my loved ones were spirited away."

The captain paused, perusing me. "I am very sorry to hear of your losses, sir. But do you think I'd not recognize the fact that one of my crew was new to me? That I wouldn't *demand* an immediate introduction?" His face reddened beneath his gray beard. "What sort of sorry captain do you think I am? I tell you, there is no member of this crew who hasn't sailed with me for a year or more."

"We mean no offense, Captain," I said. "And we're very sorry to intrude upon your morning. But we shall see this through, sir."

"Bah!" said the captain, flinging up his hands. "Permission granted, then. Just try and stay out of my crew's way as you conduct your futile search, and see to it quickly. I mean to make the most of the morning's wind!"

I climbed up the netting, the seas gently rising and falling beneath us, and glanced back to the *Emma Jane*, where I could see Zara hovering at the rail, watching us. My heart skipped a beat, given that this captain was so certain that Mendoza was not aboard, and then I caught sight of a sail moving past the mouth of the bay, heading north. Could it be that Mendoza had tricked us? That all this was meant to distract us as he left Monterey? I'd been so sure that he would book passage and make a hasty escape, but if he'd learned that we'd set a trap for him...

ZARA

We could plainly see that the men had not found Mendoza aboard the *Siren's Quest*. They rowed back to the *Emma Jane* with shoulders either slumped in defeat or stiffened in frustration.

"So much for an easy resolution," Rafael said, from my right. And Hector, who had stayed behind to guard me, grunted at my left.

"What will we do now?"

Rafael shifted. "Head home, I assume. Javier has already dispatched men to other harbors farther north, in case Mendoza decided to put even more distance between us. He'll likely send others by sea."

"He could've gone anywhere. Even East."

Hector let out a sound of dismay. "A pirate heading overland?"

I lifted my eyebrows and tucked my head to one side, thinking it would've been what I'd do if I wanted to escape a noose around my neck. And a pirate caught in the middle of one of the West Coast's busiest harbors? That's exactly what he would've gotten. I chastised myself for having been lulled into thinking this would be easy—capturing Mendoza, seeing him to justice. But at the moment, I had to bolster my frustrated boyfriend, who was climbing back aboard the *Emma Jane*, thunderclouds of fury and dismay boiling just beneath the surface.

He said something to John, before coming over to me. "Forgive me, love. I've failed you." His jaw clamped shut, and he paced back and forth a bit, fists clenching and releasing.

"You did not fail me," I said. "We thought we had him trapped." I shrugged. "We didn't. The fox outfoxed us. At some point, we'll either run across Mendoza again and see him to justice—or face the fact that he's possibly slipped away forever."

Javier shook his head. "It galls me, to think he's escaped us. I cannot imagine that he could take such losses—his ship, Craig's goods—and decide that a chest of gold in exchange for you was enough. That gold will not buy him another ship!" He shook his head and paced back and forth. "I simply do not understand it."

"But it might see him onto a ship and eventually back into the role of captain. And there was his mention of another way he would gain from all of this. Do you have any idea—any idea at all—what that might have been?"

Javier shook his head and continued to pace, chin in hand. "Over and over I've considered that. I cannot think who would've gained from the attack on Bonita Harbor and Craig's ship, or how. Perhaps if they'd made it to harbor with the *Crescent Moon* intact and been able to sell our goods…but to lose it all and still count it good? It makes no sense. I still can't believe he gambled rounding Point Ruina in a storm."

"If he had not tried, that meant giving you the chance to catch up with him in Monterey before he sold the goods, bought provisions, and set sail again. At the very least, you would've been right behind him—probably on this very ship, the *Emma Jane*."

He shook his head, hands on his hips. "And people think of me as a gambler." He looked up at me, and I could plainly see that he was thinking again of that storm, the ship going down, and how close he had come to losing both Mateo and me. I was thinking of it myself, and it made me suddenly anxious to get back to shore. His eyes narrowed. "Trust me, mi Corazon. Some day, I will find that man. And we shall see him to justice."

"I have no doubt of it," I said, stepping closer to him and laying a hand on his chest. I was suddenly so weary over all of this. Eager to get home to the ranch, to his family. Back to love and security among them. "He has no ship now. If he ever returns to Bonita Harbor, I wager you'll be prepared for him, yes?"

He gave me a slow, solemn nod. "He'd come to regret it if he tried. Never again will a pirate take us unaware."

"And if you become a sea captain one day, will you not have one eye out for him, with every ship that passes?"

"Indeed," he pledged.

"Then can we go now, Javier? You've set your men on the trails that Mendoza might have taken, overland. Can we let it rest in God's hands and timing and go home now, to Rancho de la Ventura? Away from here?" *Far away from anywhere Mendoza might be right now?*

He nodded slowly. "Are you certain you don't want to take

up John's offer? We'd be home in almost two days rather than five."

I shook my head. "No. Overland, please. My butt will complain about it in a day or two, but at least it won't awaken my nightmares."

His mouth dropped open a bit, and I realized I shouldn't have said something like the word *butt*. Abuela had never liked it in my own century. Plainly, in this time, a "woman of good breeding" would never say such a thing. But then he laughed, and there was such utter delight in his eyes that it washed away my embarrassment.

"Overland it is, then," he said, offering his arm. "But what of the young gambler? And your lamp?" he said as if just remembering it.

"It will come to me in time."

His brow wrinkled. "What makes you say that?"

Rafael joined us then, obviously seeking to find out what Javier wanted to do next. Javier began to wave him off, wanting to hear my answer, but instead I invited his good friend in. I'd been reluctant to tell him what had happened, but this afternoon…well, now there could be no more secrets. They made me tired. Quickly I told them both how I had followed the young gambler to the stables.

"You went alone?" thundered Javier, drawing the attention of some of the crew members. They stared and then bent heads together to confer, clearly guessing at what was going on.

"Take your ease," I said, waiting patiently while Javier settled down. Both men were tall and created a formidable two sides to our triangle. But I crossed my arms and stared up at them both. "I admit it wasn't my wisest move. But it was the lamp, Javier. He had my lamp. And I knew I couldn't let him just slip away without at least trying to retrieve it. For all I knew, he might've sold it to me!"

"Why is that lamp so dear to you?" Rafael said.

I looked to him. "It was my only possession when I washed up on the shores of Tainter Cove," I said simply. "It's valuable, pure gold, some think, and quite ancient."

He nodded gravely, his brows lowered as he considered my words.

"But the young card sharp would not give it to you?" Javier asked, pinching the bridge of his nose as if a headache was beginning to form.

"No. I threatened him, saying I'd scream, if he didn't give me my things—the lamp, my shawl, and the fossil—as well as Mendoza's location."

Javier's face softened at my mention of the fossil. He paused and turned toward me. "And he said…?"

"That he'd give me those things within a fortnight, if I let him go. He didn't have the shawl and the fossil with him—they were hidden. If I wanted them, I'd have to gamble on trusting him."

Rafael let out a hollow laugh. "And so you elected to trust one of the most untrustworthy people at that party last night?" He lifted his hand toward shore and then ran it through his hair in frustration. "If you had screamed, we might have caught him! Found out where Mendoza was hiding or what road he'd taken!"

"Or I would've screamed, and he would've *still* escaped,

and I would not have gained the promise of my lamp, my shawl and fossil, as well as some explanation for Mendoza's action," I said steadily, keeping my tone calm.

"What could possibly be more important than his location?" Javier asked, his face a mask of confusion.

"The young gambler never promised me he'd tell me where the pirate was. But he did say he would tell me how the pirate stood to gain from the whole venture."

"How will he get that all to you?" asked Rafael.

I shrugged, squirming under their joint, intense gaze. "He said he'd get it to me at Rancho de la Ventura. Not here."

Rafael laughed mirthlessly, obviously thinking I'd been suckered, and Javier scowled at him, protective of me. But down deep, I knew he thought the same.

"I might have lost in that gambit," I rushed on, "but I had little choice! It was either cling to that slim hope or potentially lose everything."

"Well, that's it then," Javier said, taking a deep breath and letting it out slowly. "I guess all that's left to us is to make the journey home. And there we shall wait."

CHAPTER 29

ZARA

As much as I tried to hold a part of my heart in reserve, it seemed that Javier was on a major charm offensive in the days that followed, whether he recognized it or not. It was as if he remained determined that he wanted me to get my lamp back—and have the option to return to my own time—but in the days we had left together, he wanted to make sure I knew exactly what I'd be leaving behind.

He'd purchased a new riding habit for me, which fit like a dream and allowed me to ride sidesaddle without wanting to kill someone within the hour. We spent much of the journey south riding together in companionable silence or talking, while the six men with us kept a respectful distance. Some of the others had been dispatched to see if they could pick up Mendoza's trail; Rafael and his men had sailed south on the *Emma Jane* with John in order to get home to Santa Barbara faster.

We didn't return to the mission where we had spent the night after we were reunited; he seemed aware that it might awaken hard memories for me, just as being aboard a ship had. We rejoined the central road from Monterey to Santa Barbara, hemmed in for miles by hills on either side, but after our fourth day on the road, we again neared the ocean. It spread out before us, a deep, sparkling blue. It became the most beautiful turquoise where it hugged the shoreline, and from above, we could see where rocks stubbornly resisted the waves or where beds of kelp became their dance partner. Javier grinned at me. "A fine place to make camp for the night, no?"

"Can't imagine any prettier," I said, relieved at the thought of dismounting for the day.

He dismounted himself and came over to help me down.

"Remember that first day on the way to the rodeo?" I asked. "When my legs were so numb I collapsed?"

"Indeed," he said, holding me in his arms a moment and looking down at me. "I carried you to that rock."

"Such a hero," I said playfully, putting a hand on his chest.

He waved to his men, making a circular motion with his finger to indicate that we'd make camp here. After hobbling the horses, I walked down the hill, closer to the cove below. It was picturesque, like something that would grace a California calendar centuries from now. The hills were deep green, the summer not yet hot enough to bake the grasses brown, and the horses set to work, as if bent on eating their fair share. Below us, on the far right, a cliff extended out. Beneath it, the waves had hollowed out what looked like a cave.

I glanced back at Javier. "Want to take a dip?" I said.

"Of what do you speak? Swimming?" He frowned in playful suspicion. "Now? But…"

It was all I needed. I moved to my horse and fetched a simple shift that I'd purchased when Javier returned to the mercantile to buy my riding habit, along with new dresses for his sisters and mama. It was hardly a bikini, but trust me, it was the best I could do in 1840. I pulled out a second shift, along with my gold dress, the easiest gown to get into, knowing I'd have to change in private once we were done.

"Zara?" he asked, casting me a look that said, *Are you as crazy as I think you are?*

"Coming?" I asked saucily, passing by him. "Or am I swimming alone?"

He laughed under his breath and went to his own horse, grabbing some clothes. I noticed he didn't bother trying to talk me out of it or point out the impropriety. Perhaps he knew that I was going to swim, whether he approved or not. Which I was. It was so incredibly beautiful and inviting, I couldn't imagine passing up the opportunity. Down below, I moved behind a group of boulders that would keep anyone but sea lions from seeing me change and hurriedly took off my riding habit's split skirt, the long jacket, and then the lace dickey and stays. I elected to leave my pantaloons and camisole on, thinking that once the shift got wet, there'd be little to hide everything beneath if I didn't have a couple of layers on. But at least these layers wouldn't keep me from swimming freely. Even the shift was bound to ride up around my waist, once I was in the water.

Javier was down on the sand, waiting for me, stripped to the waist. I had to admit to myself that the saying was true, not a cliché—he literally took my breath away. As in, I had to remember to take my next breath when I saw the bare expanse of his bronzed shoulders and chest, narrowing to his waist. He still wore his breeches—apparently okay with getting them wet—and he grinned at me. "There you are," he said, coming closer. "My beautiful sea sprite."

He reached to help me down off the rocks, but I shook my head. With a sly smile, I turned and began picking my way along the cliff that hung over the cove.

"Zara," he warned, "now don't be foolish."

"Not foolish!" I corrected. "Fun!" But I hurried on, spurred by the desire to jump in first. If he got there ahead of me, he might decide it wasn't "safe," and I was weary of him worrying about that.

"Wait for me, Zara," he growled, climbing up and closing in behind me. The rocks were wet and slippery, forcing me to slow down, but I pushed on. After all, he had to slow down too. When we got to the end, I let go of my grip on the rocks and carefully inched around to face the sea, my toes hanging over the narrow ledge. It was farther down than I anticipated—a good twelve feet. Which felt like twenty now. Why was that always the way?

"Second thoughts?" he asked, panting as he neared me. He was still facing the cliff. "Shouldn't you be holding on?"

"But then I couldn't do this," I grinned, catching his eye. I leaped outward, bringing my fingers to a perfect point ahead of me, my toes tucked together behind, and sliced into the water.

I went deep, relishing the feel of the cool after a long, sweaty day in the saddle. And then I slowly let myself rise to the surface, emerging in a cloud of bubbles.

He laughed, shaking his head in wonder as I looked up to him, trying to just keep my eyes on his, rather than that amazing expanse of skin. "What was *that*?" he asked.

"That, my friend, was a dive. And where I come from, pretty much a perfect ten," I said, continuing to tread water and looking up at him. "I think even the Chinese judge would have given me that."

He frowned in confusion, and I waved him off with a laugh. "Never mind. Just something from my time. It was good, no?"

"Better than good," he said, eyes alight. "It was glorious."

"Think you can top it?"

"Of course," he said jauntily. Then he leaped, turned a somersault in the air and split the water. But he'd almost overshot it. He bobbed to the surface and flipped his hair to the side. "What say you?"

"An eight, tops," I said with a laugh. "It was almost a back-slapper!"

"When you got a ten?" he asked, catching on.

"Well, of course," I retorted. "You yourself said it was *glorious.*"

He smiled and then looked beyond me. "Come with me," he said, moving toward the cave that we could clearly see beneath the cliff now. Grinning, I followed. With the waves making the opening a mere six inches, I elected to dive deep again, and then popped up in the center, beside him.

"Ohhh," I gaped, staring in wonder and looking around. The light made the water the most transfixing blue, and the cave amplified every sound we made. "This would be a perfect cave to hide pirate treasure in!"

"Indeed," he said with a laugh. "Do you have any of that about?"

"Not at the moment."

"Come," he said again and moved toward a ledge. With some effort, he got out of the water. I could see that he'd cut his shin on the sharp rocks. "Careful," he said, reaching down for my arm. "Let me help you." Then he lifted me with a grunt and deposited me on the ledge beside him. He wrapped his arm around me, tugging me closer, and water from his nose dripped onto mine as we smiled at each other, enjoying our sudden proximity as well as the privacy. We leaned back against the slope of the cave, and I turned toward him, my hand shyly rubbing across his chest. He had a little dark hair, in the center, but the rest was smooth.

He watched my hand, and his breathing grew shallower. His fingers moved to my wet hair, entwining a handful, and he urged my mouth close to his. "You are no sea sprite, Zara," he growled. "You are a full-fledged siren. May I kiss you? Please tell me I can kiss you…"

But then I was kissing him, crushing my lips against his. He pulled me closer, parting my lips, turning me so that he was now leaning over me. We kissed madly, all the days of pent-up desire exploding between us, over us, through us. My hands danced across his shoulders, his neck. His arms wound around me, pulling me closer, even as his lips covered my eyes, my nose, my temples, my chin, my neck…

Abruptly, he pulled away and rose a bit. "Stop," he panted, and pushed me gently back when I reached for him. "We have to stop."

I groaned in frustration. He was right, of course. I wanted him, I admitted to myself. I wanted all of him, just as he plainly wanted me. And well, that was pretty dangerous territory.

We sat there, inches apart, panting, staring, silently acknowledging that we desired each other but chose not to follow through on that desire. And yet what rang through my head was, *not yet. But soon.*

He lifted his hand, fingers spread wide, offering it to me. I set my palm against his, and then interlocked my fingers. He was still staring into my eyes. "I didn't want to say this before you'd decided, about going…*back*, but I believe I must declare myself, Zara. To be certain that you know my intentions."

"All right," I said slowly, half wanting to hear it, half fearful.

He and I both swallowed hard, and continued to gaze at each other. I hated to even blink, feeling like it somehow robbed me of precious seconds.

"I love you, Zara Ruiz," he whispered, his intensity practically electrifying every hair on my body. "You make me a better man. I want you as my bride. I want all of you, forever. If you decide to stay, know that I will be on my knees, asking for the privilege of being your husband. I already have a ring."

I sucked in a breath, gave a half laugh. "A…a ring? Already?"

He smiled, and a bead of water trickled down his forehead, along his nose, along the rounding line of his cheek, then onto his chest. He nodded.

"Can I see it?"

He grinned and shook his head. "Not until I am on a knee at your feet."

I grimaced, but I was inwardly glad. I wanted to see it, because I was curious. But it wouldn't be right, not really, until that day. "So if I decide tomorrow—"

"No," he said, sobering and sitting up. He looked back to me, and I saw a measure of pain in his eyes. "I don't believe you can say you've decided until you have the lamp in hand. You have to be free, completely free to choose—or at least leave it once more to God—before I will allow it."

I sat up too then. He lifted my hand to his face and kissed the palm, gently, sending fireworks down my arm, chest, waist.

"But what if…" I began, wondering if I could really form the words, what they meant. "What if the lamp never is returned to us?"

His dark, wet brows lowered. "I'm gambling it will, just as you did. It *must* be returned to us," he said, as if the lamp contained some force that would magically guide it home. He leaned over and kissed my cheek again once more, slowly, softly. "Let us go. We must return to the men or they'll fear we've drowned." He jumped into the pool below.

I stared at him—the sheer, gorgeous glory of him. His dark hair, slicked back from his face, allowed me to see every beautiful feature. "How long is a fortnight?" I whispered, the acoustics of the cave making it loud.

"Fourteen days," he said.

I counted back. It'd been three since we left Monterey, four since the young gambler had made me his wager.

I jumped in and moved to Javier. Silently, we each took a deep breath and I moved into his arms. Together, we sank below the surface, madly kissing, our lips parting, sealing together to keep the seawater out and the air in…as if we might seal ourselves together in this time, in this place, forever.

CHAPTER 30

JAVIER

My lungs crying out for air, I took Zara's hand, and together we surfaced just outside the cave. The gambler had ten days then—ten days to reach us. Could I survive even one more without this woman as my bride, let alone ten? It seemed like an eternity.

I cursed myself for making the lamp a prerequisite to our matrimony, but I knew there was no choice in the matter. Either the gambler had to bring it to us, or I had to go after it, track it down. I wanted Zara, but I wanted *all* of her, and she would not be able to fully give herself to me until she'd faced the lamp, the choice, one final time. She had to decide, once and for all, that this time and place, a territory on the brink, was what she wanted—and that *I* was what she wanted—even if she had the option to return home. Or she had to leave it to God to choose for her.

Secretly, I hoped she would decide without asking God to decide for her. I didn't want to leave it to Him. He'd brought her here. He could clearly take her back.

But no matter how it was decided, it wasn't my choice.

That was what I knew. Not being able to guide the outcome was the hardest thing I'd ever faced—other than leaving university to return home to the rancho—and yet I was bound and determined to use these days to let Zara know *all* that she'd be leaving behind. I didn't want to ever think that if only I had done this or done that or said something that I felt like holding back—then she might have chosen differently.

I didn't think that was unfair of me. It was merely using every card in my hand to its utmost advantage.

Ten days…

I'd already instructed Patricio to let every captain he met know that I wanted the lamp back, and I was willing to pay three times its value in gold. Patricio seemed confident that such an offer was more than enough to force the ancient treasure to surface. "It will be known from Seattle to Santiago that you seek the odd little lamp, within a few weeks. Rest easy, man; we'll get your girl's lamp back for her."

Weeks, I thought forlornly, as my toes touched sand. What if it was really weeks…or months? I didn't think I could bear to be alone with Zara any longer as it was. The passion we'd just experienced in the cave…well, clearly it was ready to break through any reserve we still held. It was very good that we'd be back at the villa in a few days, I thought, glancing her way as she stood and her shoulders emerged from the water. My men were hardly guardians of virtue. Even now they cast us smirking, knowing glances as they watched us from above.

I lifted a hand and partly grinned, partly scowled at them. *"Un poquito de privacidad para la dama cuando aparezca, por favor!"* I yelled. *A little privacy for the lady as she emerges, please.*

Reluctantly, they all did as I asked and turned. But once they had done so, she waded to me, brazenly pulled me close, and stood on her tiptoes, silently asking for a last kiss! Aghast, entranced, fearful, beguiled…I obliged her briefly, well aware of the men waiting above us all the while.

"Thanks for the *swim*," she whispered and then waded toward the beach. I finally did as I'd asked of my men and turned back to the sea, waiting for the chill of the water to cool the heat coursing through my veins. *Saints*, I prayed, pushing the curls away from my forehead, *give me strength. Help me honor Zara in every way. Help me honor you.*

And then I waded to shore, hoping with every step that I could be the one man that Zara could not turn from. I smiled at her as she tossed me a grin over her shoulder and disappeared behind a boulder.

Because, God help me, I couldn't imagine never seeing that beautiful smile again.

ZARA

Sadly, there were no further make-out sessions to rival what we'd experienced in the water, and Javier seemed determined to make sure we always had a chaperone around, even if it were one of his caballeros. I was partly honored by such chivalry and partly an anxious mess. But the night before we reached the rancho, Javier shook me awake. We all had laid our bedrolls out around the campfire, as we had each night, and the embers were burning low. One man stayed up for two hours at a time, keeping watch, until he woke another. Apparently, it was Javier's turn, because no one else was awake.

He lifted a finger to his lips, urging me to stay quiet, and I slipped on my boots. When he helped me to my feet, I stretched, feeling every ache and pain of five days on the road, as well as every rock beneath my bedroll. Two of the men were snoring loudly, and I thought it said how tired I was that I could have slept through *that*. Two others were breathing steadily, low and deep. The last two tossed and turned. We waited until they settled before we tiptoed away from the campfire, my hand in his.

I chastised myself for being ridiculous—yes, his hand felt so good, wrapped around mine, as if it were sending sparks up my arm, shoulder, neck, and back—but really, how was that possible? *Get a grip, Zara,* I told myself. But then I was thinking, *No, absorb every second we have together!*

He led me up the hill. As soon as we were away from the fire, I knew what he wanted to show me. The entire sky was bright with stars—more than I'd ever seen in my life—and the higher we climbed, surmounting the hills, the more I could see the depths, the expanse.

At the top, he turned me around, and I looked out across the calm sea and gasped. The stars appeared to dissolve into the sea, and the sea reflected the stars, making it all seem one. "I've never seen the ocean this calm," he said, wrapping his arms around me from behind when I shivered.

I sank back against his chest and stared, not even wanting

to blink it was so beautiful. "Neither have I. Back home," I said, "it's hard to see the stars this way. There are so many people, so many lights, that it interferes."

He took that in but said nothing, even though I thought it would be a perfect opportunity for him to lobby for staying in 1840. But maybe he knew I'd do that myself. "A shooting star!" I cried, covering my mouth as together, we watched the meteor streak across the sky, leaving a trail of flame behind it. And then it was out, but another was shooting in the same direction, and another in the opposite, and another, until it seemed like a hundred were flying over our heads, bent on reaching some far-off realms. "It's a meteor shower!" I said, squeezing his arm in glee. "A meteor shower!"

"A what?" he asked, puzzled. But I could hear the smile in his voice.

"Meteors," I said excitedly. "Bits that come off of comets, passing by in space, and when they hit the earth's atmosphere, they light up like that as they disintegrate."

He was silent a moment. "And here I only thought they were an opportunity for us to make a wish." He laughed under his breath. "Were you at university, then, when you came here? A scholar?"

"No. I was in my last year of school. Thinking about college—*university*, as you call it—this fall."

He was silent again, taking that in. "So then…females attend university," he muttered, sounding partially mystified.

I laughed under my breath. "I think there are actually more women than men in university in my time."

Again he was silent. Then, "You enjoy learning?"

"I do." I turned in his arms. "It's part of what I love about being here, Javier. It's like watching history come alive."

He bent his head down so that our foreheads touched. "But it is one thing to learn like this, learn what life and a ranch and others around you have to teach you"—he sighed heavily—"and another to learn at university. Would you not miss that opportunity to attend and learn there?" He pulled back and traced the line of my hair around my face. "You have a fine mind, Zara."

"I do," I said, pulling him closer. "I can admit that," I said with a smile and squeeze. "But you left university yourself, right? To see to your family, your land. Sometimes life takes us on tracks we don't expect. My abuela always said that the best people she knew were always open to learning, whether they found themselves in a restaurant kitchen or a university classroom."

"A wise woman, she was," he said. "Did she attend university?"

"No," I said. "She left school when she was about twelve. But she was a hard worker and smart in many different ways. Wise, as you say. And she was always open to learning. She would sit down with a lawyer in our restaurant and talk about a case that was going on in our city, wanting to understand both sides. She would watch the construction workers who came to make repairs, and insist they let her swing a hammer or use a saw. She wanted to know what it felt like to do it herself. She read everything she could find, when she was not knitting or running the restaurant."

"You loved her very much," he said.

"I did. And she loved me. The day she died was terrible," I said, resting my head against his chest. He reached up and stroked my back with one hand, my neck with his other. Listening, just listening. "But it was she who first asked me what I most wished for. And it was her death that made me think about our conversation, about what I most wanted in life. And it was being alone in our apartment after her funeral that sent me to the beach that night, when the fisherman pointed me to the tide pool…and I found the lamp among the starfish."

"Hmm," he said. He lifted his chin, again staring at the sky and sea. "Starfish, you say?"

"Yes. So many starfish! More than I'd ever seen in my life in one place. Orange and purple, mostly. And when a wave passed over, they shifted, and I spotted the lamp in the bottom."

"My mother's bait for a bride," he muttered.

"Your mother's *invitation* toward family, adventure, and love," I said, after a moment. "That's how I've decided to think about it."

He paused and seemed to be stuck on my mention of *love*. I hadn't told him I loved him, when he told me. I was holding back on that for some reason.

"Even if she didn't think of it that way?" he finally said.

"Your mother meant well, Javier. To find someone for you."

"And to have a reason to stay."

"Well yes, that too."

He took a deep, long breath and slowly let it out. "I suppose it is the way of peace, to think of it that way. Your wise abuela raised a wise young woman," he said, pulling me tight against him.

I smiled. But then I heard the scattering of rocks, just above

Javier. He was on the move in seconds, pushing me behind him, turning to face whatever approached.

The thing was rushing us.

Javier drew his knife, and at the last second I cried out, recognizing the smell of wet dog and sage and wildness that could only be…"Centinela!"

The wolf-dog raced past us, loping around in a broad circle, then grazed us again, clearly delighted to find us. "Centinela, Centinela," I crooned, going to my knees and waiting for her to calm down enough to approach me. Slowly, warily, she did, until I was finally able to rub her neck, her back. She was too skittish for me to hold her face in mine, to try and see the stars reflect in her round eyes, but it was almost as if I could anyway.

Javier laughed and shouted to the men down at the campfire, who had roused, hearing us cry out. "It's all right! It's only the wolf-dog!"

Two men were already heading our way, and their heads lifted, as if relieved, their silhouette visible against the fire, which another had banked. It rose to life again, sending a shower of sparks skyward.

"I think she was just waiting for us to get close to home," Javier said. "I haven't seen her since we found Mateo on the road, while we searched for you. I don't know where she was while we were in Monterey."

"She was probably keeping watch from afar, or else she returned to the rancho to wait for us. I was worried about her," I said, taking his hand again as we headed back toward camp. It felt like a relief, to know she was close by again.

"With all that's transpired, you were thinking about a

wolf-dog?"

"Yes, at least a little," I said. "I worry about everyone. Not just the dog, but your mama, the girls, Mateo, Jacinto—they'll be so relieved to have you back."

"And doubly relieved to see that you are with me," he returned.

The next morning, his words still warmed me. Thinking of his family—Mateo and the adorable little Jacinto with his gap-toothed grin, sensible Francesca, trying to be an adult, and Estie with her round cheeks and dimples—I couldn't wait to be surrounded by them again. Almost from the start, they'd welcomed me as their own.

Their mother, Doña Elena, was a little more confusing. Eighty percent of her wanted me there...she'd basically thrown the lamp in the water, hoping someone like me would pick it up; twenty percent was held in reserve. It was as if she protected her heart...and Javier's, in case I left them. But as I stared at his back, his beautiful profile as he said something under his breath that made Hector laugh, I couldn't imagine leaving his side. But deep down, I acknowledged to myself that I wanted the lamp back. God had refused to send me back to my own time once, but if I wanted to go back—if I ever really and truly wanted it—and tried again...and God granted me that wish, wouldn't I be glad for it?

Javier glanced over his shoulder, smiling at me, eyes all crinkly at the corners, and joy was what I felt from him most.

As he turned back around, riding on, I wondered if I'd ever find someone like him in my own time—and then felt guilty for even wondering. As if I were connecting with someone else online, while I dated him. Only that, you know, that was impossible. There was no "online" here. No "dating" here—only this headlong dive into forever-1840.

I mused over that, as the sun beat down upon my shoulders, making sweat run down my back and gather beneath my breasts. Making me pit-out in my pretty new riding habit jacket… because razors and deodorant weren't a thing. There was no pretending, no posturing, no protecting yourself in this era. You were who you were, sweaty and stinky, just like the rest. And men and women seemed to approach one another more on the basis of "You like me? I like you. Let's just go for it."

It was a little overwhelming. But mostly it was just a relief. There weren't as many games here. It was as if people knew that life was precious, and they wanted to make the most of it. It was as if they never forgot that a flu bug could take them out tomorrow. So today? They did whatever they were led to do.

I glanced out to the wide, sprawling valley to our left and the sea to our right. Felt the cadence of my horse, the restful rocking in the saddle. And I wondered if we, in our own time, had too much time. To consider. To question.

When God spoke, moved…weren't we simply supposed to respond?

CHAPTER 34

ZARA

The closer we got to home, the less Javier looked over his shoulder, as if his concerns that Mendoza or other bad guys were going to try and capture us again faded. I wanted to tell him to relax, that it would be okay—not because I thought he was overly cautious but because it set off my own PTSD alarms. So the less that went on, the more we could laugh and smile together. He'd been riding ahead with the two guys in front for a while, when one took off at a gallop down the road.

Javier pulled up and waited for me to come alongside him.

"Where is he going?" I asked, looking ahead to the man growing smaller in the distance.

"I sent him ahead to tell the family that we are on our way. Mama would want to know. They'll be glad to have us home." He smiled and reached out for my hand, and for a moment, all I could take in was his big, warm hand holding mine. It felt ridiculously good to be touched by him. I wished there was a reason for him to hold my hand all day long.

We had to ride east for a bit to cross a river, where it widened and grew shallow. The road wound through a small canyon then, where the swallows were building their mud nests among the nooks and overhangs. They swept past us, hunting for bugs, and chirped their high-pitched greetings. "I've always loved swallows," I said. "I think it's amazing that those little wings can carry them all the way to South America for the winter and back again come spring."

He stared at me as if he'd never thought about it before, and smiled.

"What is your favorite kind of bird?" I asked.

He thought about that a moment, one of his brows lowering in the most charming manner as he contemplated. "The pelican," he said at last.

I felt my own brows lift in surprise, since I'd expected him to choose a falcon or eagle. Basically something more…manly. "Why pelicans?"

"On the water, they look rather slow and ungainly, don't you think? All lumpy flesh and bulbous beak. But when they fly— especially when a group of them are together—they're rather elegant."

"It's true," I said, thinking on it. "And they have such an amazing wingspan." I considered him, covertly, as we rode on. I'd never really figured I'd be a pelican girl. But this guy had me rethinking everything.

We continued along our trek, hour after hour, and by early afternoon we were again on Rancho de la Ventura land. Soon we could see two ships anchored in the harbor, but as expected, Craig's *Heron* was gone, apparently seaworthy once more.

I heard the music before we reached the top of the hills

closest to the house, and when we emerged on top, a cheer went up from all those outside the villa. We could smell roasting meat, and it looked like every one of the Indian workers, every guard, every family member, and about ten visiting sailors were outside, waving at us. When we got closer, they cheered and threw flower petals over us, and I saw they'd plucked every purple bougainvillea blossom from the thick vines that lined the front entrance in order to do so.

It was a trio of sailors playing on fiddles and a guitar that we heard, a jaunty tune that was clearly more old-time country than the Spanish-influenced songs I'd mostly heard since I arrived. Crewmen from one of the ships, I guessed.

It was Mateo—*Mateo!*—who helped me dismount, and impulsively I hugged him. He hesitated and drew back, but then he relaxed, kissed either side of my face, and took my hand. "It is good to have you home, Zara," he said quietly.

"I am so very glad to see you, Mateo. I was so worried." He was still a bit pale, maybe even a little unsteady on his feet. Then I wondered if my hug had hurt him. If he'd had internal injuries, broken ribs…

But then my attention was taken by Javier's sisters, Francesca and Estrella, hugging me, all while his little brother, Jacinto, stared at me, smiling shyly while he nibbled on a lip. Their mother, Doña Elena, bustled through the throngs, gently patted Jacinto's cheek, and then took my hands in hers and looked me up and down. "So here you are, my dear, back again." Then she tentatively pulled me into her arms for a hug. "I am so relieved, dear Zara. So relieved."

"Me too," I said, deciding that it felt good to be hugged

by the matronly woman. We'd had our differences, and she'd made me angrier than I'd ever been in my life, but in that hug, I felt the promise of peace on the horizon. Hope. If I chose to stay...

The girls each took one of my hands and led me inside the villa. I looked over my shoulder, wondering where Javier was, and found him shaking hands and hugging everyone he could. I thought about how different he was now, about how it felt to be here on the ranch, compared to when I first arrived. When I'd first come, it was as if he were trying to find the fastest escape route he could; now he looked like there was no place he'd rather be. Could that be? Could I really be seeing that difference in just a few weeks?

Inside, the cook and maids were depositing dish after dish of food on the long table, and after washing our hands in a basin, Javier and I were pushed to the front of the line. But there he paused and raised his arms to quiet everyone. "Friends and family," he said, loud enough that even those in the throngs outside could hear, "I want to pause and give God thanks for bringing us back together—and to remember those we lost."

Together, we bowed our heads. I put my hand through the crook of his elbow, feeling a surge of pride. In response he shifted, widened his stance, straightened his shoulders.

"Father, we pause to remember our friends who gave their lives to protect us at the harbor and ask you to comfort those who lost their husbands or brothers or sons. Thank you that you have made all of us family, so that we might help bear one another's burdens. Thank you also for the safe return of Mateo and for my Zara. Protect and keep us from this day forward. Amen."

"Amen," echoed everyone in the room. But of course, all I could hear were the echoes of "my Zara" in my head. *My Zara.* It had sounded like a claim. A source of pride. Of hope and glory…and above all, love.

I was picking up my plate when I happened to see the Indian workers streaming around the side of the house, back toward the kitchen, where I knew they would be fed. I knew that a couple of the guards who had died at the harbor were not Mexican but Native American. And they had died to try and protect us, and Javier's storehouse. *We can't treat them as second-class citizens. Not today.*

I put a hand on Javier's arm and nodded toward the window, where a couple young men cast furtive glances inside. "Do they not belong with us as much as all these others?" I dared. I knew it wasn't the way of his people or the times— after all, we hadn't even hit the Civil War yet—but Javier had *just* prayed for all of us…*all* of us…as family. "Many of them lost people they loved."

He paused and frowned, with a hesitant glance at his mother, but I stood where I was, still waiting on him. I knew there was no way he could invite a hundred workers into the villa. It just wouldn't fly. His dark eyes moved to me, but it seemed as if the Indian cook bringing in another steaming pot solidified his decision.

"Wait, Jalama," he said. "It's such a beautiful evening, I think we need to take this feast outside, where *all* can join us. Hector, Mateo, Rodrigo, help me with this table. We'll move it to the front.

Jalama, tell the people to come and join us there."

Doña Elena gaped at him, so surprised that she couldn't seem to think of a word to say. Jacinto hopped around, clapping excitedly and exclaiming over the chance to eat outside, and the girls turned those in the villa around, spreading the news that we were all going to head outdoors. Blankets emerged and were spread around the clumpy soil. The workers held back, let everyone else be served first, and definitely kept to their own threadbare blankets, but I decided it was at least a step in the right direction. It seemed like a teeny step to me, but watching Doña Elena, who was clearly out of sorts with how things had evolved, I knew it was a big step for all of them. And their willingness to see it through opened a hug of welcome to me, whether they knew it or not.

My ideas were way different. But they were willing to go with the flow with me…try it out. See how it might fit. And so far, I thought, as I looked around with a grin, it was fitting fine.

We had traditional Mexican dishes like tamales and *menudo*. But there were also ribs and roast. When the piles of meat came out, after we'd already eaten so much, I thought no one would agree to take some. But when I looked fifteen minutes later, the platters were empty, except all that remained of the roast was the bone.

A bit overwhelmed by all the people and activity, with my belly so full that I was feeling pretty miserable, I rose, went to retrieve the massive bone, and then walked around the house and to the top of a hill, where I'd seen Centinela sitting, watching.

"*Everybody* is a part of this feast," I said and tossed the bone to her. She shied away, as if she thought I was throwing a mud-ball at her, but then she returned to it, head low, nose twitching. Then she gently mouthed it, bit down, and loped away, as if afraid someone might steal it from her. I lost sight of her in the longer shadows of twilight and turned to see that Javier was leaning against the back of the villa, arms crossed, smiling, watching me. I paused there, looking back. He had one boot perched behind him, against the adobe, and looked like a still in some fantastic, epic movie scene.

And yet it wasn't a movie scene; it was real life.

I walked down the hill and he stayed where he was, waiting. He opened his arms to me and I gladly leaned against him. He hugged me tightly, smelling of leather and smoke, and kissed the top of my hair. He said nothing for a long while, just rubbed my back and seemed to appreciate holding me close. Then, "You have given me many gifts, Zara, but the greatest gift is contentment," he said, lifting my chin so I would look into his eyes. He stared into mine, intensely, as if he willed me to feel what he was saying. "You have taught me how to appreciate everything in my life— even a wolf-dog—while I have it."

I knew what he was getting at. He didn't yet know if I'd always be a part of his life. I dropped my chin and hugged him again, listening to the warm, steady beat of his heart and thinking I couldn't quite imagine myself anywhere else. But then I heard my name, and Javier abruptly encouraged me to stand beside him—rather than firmly in his embrace—as many of his family members found us.

Mateo had a guitar in his hands, and he offered it to me. "Come, Zara. Gift us with a song. Then we will know that you are truly home."

Others clapped in agreement and anticipation, and I laughed and moved forward to accept the instrument. They moved around me, and Mateo gestured to a stump of a log, where I took a seat. Looking to the skies, the first stars just peeking out—and remembering my starlit night with Javier—I said to him, "This is in memory of our road home. It is called 'Una Noche Estrellada.'" *One Starlit Night.*

The song began slowly, with syncopated breaks, reminding me of when you first see stars emerging in the sky. But then it built, moving faster and faster, until my fingers were flying across the strings, the notes first high and light—like stars distant—then to low and heavier, denser chords. It was the perfect song to remember that beautiful night with Javier, and as I finished and everyone applauded, crying, "Brava! Brava!" I found I was wistfully wishing for another such night with him, and another, and another.

They begged for a second song, but it hit me then—if I didn't get to bed as soon as possible, I was liable to pass out right then and there. Javier saw it too and whispered in Francesca's ear, and she and Estie each took one of my arms and led me away from the sweet crowd, all murmuring "Buenas noches," and up to my room. Estie fetched a pail of steaming hot water, and Maria brought me a cup of tea, while Francesca slipped my riding jacket from my shoulders and hung it on a peg. There were new things in my room, as if they had been preparing for, even hoping for my return—a dressing screen, a night shift, new underthings.

I took a quick sponge bath and slipped into bed, where Estie covered me, tucking me in like she was fifty-two, not twelve, and kissed me on the cheek. Francesca smiled at me and turned out my lamp, then left the room, quietly shutting the door behind her.

And as I stared out my window, I realized what it meant when people talked about how good it felt to be home. Stars began to sparkle in a cobalt sky, but I couldn't watch them for long. I closed my eyes and in one breath, maybe two, gave in to sleep.

CHAPTER 32

JAVIER

As I tried to work on some accounting, Zara paced around the den. She'd go to the bookshelves, pull out a volume, page through it as if not able to make out the words, then slap it closed and put it back on the shelf. Then she would walk to the window, gaze outside a moment, and pace back to the shelf.

I knew what was bothering her. It was the young gambler's last day to deliver what he'd promised, and she kept hoping he'd ride down our road or send a messenger.

I set down my quill. "Zara." I rose and went to her, taking her hand in mine and leaning against the desk. "I cannot replace the lamp or your dear Abuela's shawl, and we might never find out what drove Mendoza to such a despicable act, but we can do something about the third thing."

Her pretty eyes searched mine, then narrowed. "The fossil?"

"Yes. My brother and I didn't find the only fossils up there. You remember. There are tons. Let's go find a new pair— a pair just for us. We can take my sisters and brothers. They're bickering anyway, driving my mother mad. Getting them out would lift the whole household's spirits."

She hesitated. Wrung her hands. "What if…"

"What if he comes while we're gone?" I guessed.

She nodded.

"There is nowhere else for miles for him to rest and water his horse, take a meal himself. And if he came all this way, all the way from Monterey, would he simply leave if he found out we wouldn't return for a few hours?"

She frowned and then shook her head. "I suppose not."

I took her hands in mine and said gently, "And if he doesn't come and you spend all day pacing, won't you be all the more frustrated that we didn't take a little ride to find our own new set of fossils?" Behind her, I could hear Estie and Francesca bickering now, and lifted my brows.

Her face settled into a smile, and she nodded as she squeezed my hands. "It's a grand idea, Javier."

"Good. Go and get ready. I'll fetch my siblings."

ZARA

We rode out an hour later, the youngest children—Jacinto and Estie—back to bickering, this time about who got to ride in front of the other until Javier told them to take turns riding in front of him. Maybe they'd all picked up my tension in the last few days of the gambler's countdown. I think Doña Elena partly wanted to come with us and partly was happy to see us all go and leave her to enjoy a few hours in a quiet house.

I thought about inviting her, but then I thought this was a perfect opportunity for the Ventura "kids" and me to be alone.

We cantered for a while through the hills, then slowed to a walk when Estie started whining that her legs were getting tired. And within the hour, we entered the small canyon that opened up to the sandy, pink-colored remains that had been so clearly underwater thousands of years before.

I remembered how it was here that Javier had almost kissed me the first time. It was Adalia and little Alvaro's departure that had interrupted that fine moment. I knew the Venturas still missed Dante's wife and her son, and they hoped that someday she'd come back for a visit. Just remembering little Alvaro's single-toothed, drooling grin made me smile.

But nearly being kissed right up here? How close we'd come when his little brother and sister burst on the scene, breaking us apart? That made me grin.

"What are you thinking about?" Javier asked, nudging closer to me as the canyon way narrowed.

By the look on his face, I could guess what he was thinking about—our almost-kiss—and it made me blush to be caught with that intimate memory. "Well, *fossils*, of course," I tossed out with a grin.

"Oh yes," he said, with a wink. "Just as I was."

We pulled up near where Javier and I had last time, and each dismounted. Then the kids scattered among the rocks, each crying out every time they saw something. Mateo found wormlike remains, and Frani found a creepy armored-tank sort of creature. She pointed it out as I came closer to get a better look, and I said, "Oooh, I think that's called a trilobite."

She and Javier looked at me in surprise and I shrugged. "Something I read," I said, giving her the truth. But I couldn't add *in my biology textbook*. Science had always been my favorite subject.

Over the next hour, Mateo found a seriously freaky sea spider, and Jacinto discovered clamshells, much like what Dante and Javier had brought home all those years ago. Everyone knew that Javier had promised to help find a pair of new fossils to replace the originals, so every time one of the kids found a pair of anything, they shouted out and made us come and look. But I didn't think I wanted another clamshell. Since we were up here, I wanted something new—something that would help me remember this day forever. We found fish skeletons and what might have been an eel. More worms and clamshells.

But then little Jacinto came and shyly took my hand. I squeezed through a narrow opening in the rocks behind him, but Javier had to take a longer way around. There, behind the first wall of rocks, I knelt to duck under a shelf and see what he had found.

"Oh, Jacinto," I breathed. "They're perfect."

"And we can each have one!" he said, his small hands drawing together in glee.

I considered him, smiling but thinking at first, *No, this is something special, just for us. Me and Javier.* Then, staring into his brown eyes, I thought, *No, that's part of what makes it perfect.* Because as much as I wanted to remember Javier, if I decided to go back to my own time—and could—I wanted to remember this, too. This sense of being a part of a family. Of mattering to them, just as much as they mattered to me. I turned back to the wall, just as

Javier caught up with us and bent to take a look.

"I think we found them," I said, with a tender smile over my shoulder. "Six of them—one for each of us."

"Six!" he said with surprise, eyes widening as he looked at the group.

And as I ducked again to look at the beautiful, detailed, spiraling "lamp shells," thinking how perfect they were— an appropriate symbol for time travel—Javier took a deep breath. "Do we truly each need one?" he asked, with a whining tone and a twinkling eye.

The kids all fell upon him, insisting that they did, that they were beautiful, and it wasn't fair that he and Dante had always had a matched set and yet they did not.

Javier grinned and lifted his hands, looking around at his siblings with pleasure and acquiescence in his eyes. "All right, all right! Mateo, fetch the chisels. Let's see what we can do."

He moved under the ledge, squatting beside me, and then leaned over and stole a brief kiss. And smiling into his eyes, I decided in that moment, I'd fallen just a little more in love with him.

JAVIER

We rode back down to the villa in high spirits, our mission complete.

It had taken a good hour to safely chisel out all six of the fossils—as well as a seventh that Francesca insisted we take to send to Adalia for Christmas—and then a couple of different fossils for Jacinto and Estie, for their new "fossil collections." But the littlest of our group were chattering happily on the way back, rather than bickering, and I knew Mama would be grateful as she looked over our ancient treasures that night.

Coming home the back way, we brought our horses into the corral beside the stables, but Hector greeted me with a worried look, rather than his customary grin. "Doña Elena has need of you, Don Javier," he said with deference. "She has been to the stables three times, inquiring about your return."

"Did someone come? Earlier?" I asked, handing him my reins.

"A messenger," he said, "with a package." He didn't know what it meant to us, this package, but obviously he'd picked up on the tension.

"A messenger?" Zara asked, her eyes meeting mine.

"Let's go find out," I said, taking her hand.

Together, we moved toward the house, Mateo right behind us. My stomach had been rumbling on the way home, though supper was a good hour away, but now I didn't feel hungry at all. I could guess why Mama was upset and anxious for our return. Francesca hadn't heard Hector, because she was back with Estie and Jacinto, helping them rewrap their fossils in cloths because they insisted they wanted to carry them separately.

I strode forward, biting the inside of my cheek. Maybe it was something else. Maybe the gambler had dropped off Zara's things and information but not the lamp. I cursed myself for the hope that rose within me at that thought. I wanted the lamp back, didn't I? So Zara would have her choice? Maybe even return to her own time, where she would be far safer?

Mama met us outside. "A messenger came," she said, staring right at me. "Come to the library. Alone, with Zara."

Mateo departed with a brief bow, realizing he had been dismissed. I knew well how it chafed, being the next-oldest, but not considered in times such as these…not in on everything. Beyond the closed doors, I heard Francesca and Mateo leading our younger siblings up the stairs to wash up and change for supper.

Zara took my outstretched hand, and we followed Mama into the library. She closed the doors behind us and then went over to my desk, gesturing toward it. "A package arrived for Zara," she said.

Zara stepped up beside me and together we stared at it as if it was a living, breathing thing. "A package," she breathed. "And here I thought he would come himself."

I'd never thought he'd come or send anything at all, but I could tell it grated at her, that she wouldn't have the chance to question him. I, too, would've liked the chance…

On my desk was a small wooden box. Tentatively, Zara moved toward it, rested her hand atop it a moment, then unlatched it and opened the lid. She methodically placed the contents on the desk. A letter in an envelope. The fossil, wrapped in a silk cloth that she unwound and laid beside the box. I forced myself to step up beside her. The lamp was nestled in the bottom, atop her grandmother's neatly folded shawl.

Her eyes met mine, briefly, and she picked up the envelope and tore through the wax seal. Swallowing hard, she moved toward the window, ostensibly to get more light, but I could feel her need for a bit of privacy.

"My dear Señorita Ruiz," she read, half to herself, half to us. "I cannot begin to thank you for the favor you bestowed on me in Monterey. As promised, I include the objects you required as payment—the shawl, fossil and the odd little lamp. In addition, I also promised to tell you more of who was behind the attack in Bonita Harbor." Her voice trailed away as her eyes quickly scanned what was next. Did I imagine it, or had she paled, her breath quickened? Her hand went to her slender throat.

"Zara?" I asked. She started, as if she'd forgotten that we were there. She blushed furiously, looking from me to Mama and back again. "Zara," I repeated, this time more softly, more encouraging than questioning. I stepped toward her, as did Mama.

She bit her lip, then straightened her shoulders and lifted the letter. "He says that Captain Mendoza was paid handsomely by agents of the Union to attack Captain Craig and your storehouse."

I frowned. "That makes no logical sense. Captain Craig is a Unionist!"

Her eyes were steady on mine. "This man claims that Craig was in on it. The goal was to sway you to their cause at any cost, knowing that your family is very influential in the region."

"I knew it," Mama said, half furious, half triumphant. "I never trusted that man! It was all part of a tremendous deception! Well, now we know the lengths to which those Unionists will go. They cannot try to win our support in an honorable way! No, they go about it in the most underhanded manner…"

While Mama seemed to immediately believe it, my mind struggled to make sense of it. Would they really go to such extremes to win my support of their goals? Perhaps the young gambler lied. Perhaps it was all a ruse to turn us against the Unionists!

Mama went on, chastising Captain Craig and his companions, but my mind was on all we had lost that day. The men. Four of the rancho's men, all fighting to save us and what had been in the storehouse. I ran a hand down my mouth, keeping it there as I remembered two of Craig's own men, floating facedown in the surf as I swam toward the men who'd captured Mateo. His own men? Had he been paid enough to lose good men, loyal to him and the *Heron*? To see them die? It wasn't possible for a captain. Was it?

I looked to Zara, and she stepped forward and took my hand.

Mama was still pacing back and forth, ranting about the dirty games of the Americans and how glad she was that she was a proud citizen of Mexico. "I will never stoop to joining them!" she said. "I will die before—"

"Doña Elena," Zara said, sharply interrupting her.

Mama was close, and Zara let the letter fall to the floor to take her hand, too. Holding both of us, she looked from me to Mama and back again. "I have to tell you something," she whispered. "Something very important."

My stomach sank. Because I could guess a few things she might say, and none of them were things I wanted to hear. Not now.

"You have every right to be furious about this," she said. "You've suffered terribly because of their efforts to convince you that Mexico would not ride to your aid. But that is what happened, did it not? The soldiers of the garrison never came to your aid, never assisted Javier in coming after me and Mateo, or the pirates. Right?"

Neither Mama nor I, it seemed, could respond.

"Remember that as you consider what I am about to say." She took a long, deep breath. "It's 1840. In a few years, the first gold will be discovered in the north. In 1849, a great deal more will be discovered. But even before that, the Union will have requested that Alta California be the newest U.S. Territory."

Mama let out a sound of disgust. "Let them request it. Mexico will deny their claim and defend us!"

Zara's eyes shifted to her. "No. They will not," she said quietly and assuredly. "Because in the meantime, Mexico will go to war with the States over Texas—and lose."

CHAPTER 33

ZARA

As much as Javier had been considering joining the Unionist cause, as much as he hated the usury of the Mexican soldiers and the government they represented, I knew my words were like knives to his heart, after learning of Craig's treachery. But still, I knew I needed to push on. I'd gone this far, hadn't I? If I was going to change a little history, I wanted to make sure these people I loved came out on top because of it.

"It will be some time before they come this far, but mark my words. They are coming. And these massive ranchos will be divided, and divided again. You must get a surveyor here—a proper surveyor—to map your property." I'd remembered that much from my California state history class. Streambeds and trees marked the borders of early ranches. The only Mexican settlers who succeeded in holding on to most of their land were those who had properly filed surveys and maps with the state. "You must befriend those who will rise to power, both Anglo and Mexican. You must do all you can to show them that you are on their side."

"But we are not on their side," Doña Elena said faintly,

fingers hovering over her eyebrows, as if she were trying to get a grip. She knew I told the truth. She just didn't want to believe it.

"You must be willing to go to their side," I said. "Or your rancho will be lost. You and your husband, your children, you've all worked too hard for this place to lose it. You'll likely have to give up portions of it, but I think if you play this right, you could hold on to a great deal."

Now Javier was rubbing his forehead, as if trying to soothe away an ache. "Mama," he warned, lifting a hand as she began to bluster at me again.

"Remember, Javier, I have seen it," I said. "I have *seen* it. And now that you know what is to come, you have the power to make the most of it. What will you do with that power? Will you lead your friends? Will you not be able to watch with some satisfaction as the garrison is drained of its power and driven from what will become the newest state in America?"

He just stared at me blankly, as if trying to catch up with all I'd said. Maybe I'd said too much. "I'll give you two some time to consider all I've shared." I turned to Doña Elena. "I'm sorry that it isn't the future you envision. But trust me, it will be good for California in time. And especially good for the people here who are anticipating what is to come."

"What if we can use this knowledge to change history in Mexico's favor?" Doña Elena said. "Warn them that they will lose this territory, if they are not careful."

"How, Mama?" Javier asked. "By telling them that a girl from the future landed on our shore and told us?" He shook his head.

Doña Elena stared hard at me, arms crossed. "What if… what if Zara is misleading us?"

Javier gave her a sharp look. "*Mama.* What would she have to gain from doing so? You know I've had Unionist leanings, especially in this last year. We've discussed it. And this revelation about Mendoza's attack—if it's true, well, it hardly ingratiates me to the Americans, does it? It actually makes me wish I could stand against them! I cannot abide by such manipulation. And yet, if what Zara says is true, how can we do anything but move in their direction?"

She shook her head. "I don't know. I don't know." Her mournful tone and the obvious wrenching of her heart made me forgive her even before she stepped toward me, brushing my shoulder with her hand. "I am sorry, Zara. This is all so much—"

"It-it's all right," I said.

I hated this. Hated that I was in the middle of so much trauma, frustration, fear. Hated that Doña Elena could doubt me and my intentions…even for a second. I felt like their whole world was crumbling and I was the cause.

Javier was picking up the letter from the floor and scanning it. Doña Elena dropped her gaze from me and moved to the window, to stare outside. I put my shawl, fossil and lamp into the box, closed the lid, and then quietly left the room. I just needed…out. And Javier and Doña Elena needed time to sort out their thoughts together.

I stood there a moment, my back against the library door. This tearing, this fear, this doubt—they weren't the feelings I should be having when I was with family, were they?

No, I should be only feeling love, joy, acceptance. Trust. Right?

Suddenly, I felt the urge to escape, fast. And yet also a deep calling to stay. I bit my lip, trying to figure out what I should do.

Run! Run, my mind said. *Get out. Leave this place, this stress, this uncertainty.*

The kids were still upstairs—I could hear Jacinto and Estie, once again alternating between laughing and bickering. But I didn't want to see them or talk to them. I could hear Jalama humming in the kitchen and the back door slamming shut as people went in and out. I caught the scent of melting lard and smoke.

Run.

Heart pounding, wondering if I really had the gumption to think about leaving, I ran upstairs, grabbed my new spiral fossil, carefully set it into the box, wrapped my shawl around my shoulders, and hurried back downstairs. I hovered in the foyer.

Stay.

The word rang through my heart like a gong, reverberating for several seconds. I stood there, wondering what I should do. Run…or stay? In some recess of my mind, I knew that this was it. That there was some opportunity, some window opening, through which I could really leave this time. That I'd discovered what I needed to, in full, and now it was up to me.

But did I want to go back, regardless of how uncomfortable it was right now? Did I really, really want to leave Javier?

Again, I heard the sounds of the kitchen—the chatter, the chopping, the clanging of pots. As if in a trance, I walked down the hall to the kitchen, wondering over the separate calls…

to go and to stay. But for the next few minutes, I knew where I wanted to be—the kitchen.

I waited until Jalama saw me in the doorway. The round-faced, small-eyed cook grinned and clapped her hands, then lifted them outward. "Señorita!" she greeted me. "What may I do for you?" She shifted forward to grab a handful of oregano leaves, and began tearing them into a pile before her.

"I...I'd like to help. I need to think, and cooking... would help."

"Ahh, yes," she said, giving me a curt nod. "A good task is what you need." After last time, when I'd just jumped in to help make dinner, the kitchen crew seemed to accept me, after they got over their astonishment at a lady wanting to do such a thing. But after years of helping my abuela in her tiny Mexican restaurant back home, it brought me comfort, and the routine of cutting, mashing, stirring, kneading... I honestly did think it would help me figure it out.

Whether to go. Or stay.

I set my box in the corner, folded my shawl atop it and then settled on a stool at the end of the huge wooden countertop. Jalama set five onions and a big knife before me, and wordlessly I set to chopping. I don't know what it was, but the onions they grew on the rancho were mild, not setting my nose to running or eyes tearing. I popped a bit in my mouth, considered the smooth, slightly sweet flavor, and thought about how my abuela would have loved them, finding just the right dish for the aromatic veggie.

This kitchen crew put onions in everything, it seemed. Jalama scooped them into a big pot and began sautéing them, filling the kitchen with a heavenly smell as I turned to knead tortilla dough beside another Indian maid. She smiled at me shyly but didn't seem apt to chatter, which was fine by me.

After that was done, I settled into the rhythm of kneading bread, working the dough over and over again, losing myself in the task. I thought about the hundreds of times I'd done just this in Abuela's kitchen, how she pinched my cheek or swatted my butt as she walked by, yelling at the dishwashing boy who was always falling behind, while putting up four platters for a server and ringing a bell. I kept kneading as I thought about following her up the stairs each night, her gait a little slower at the end, her exhaustion increasing. And yet she always had the energy for a kind word, an encouraging word.

I missed her, oh, how I missed her. But I had to remind myself that going back—if I could go back—would not bring her back to me. I'd be returning to sell her restaurant and apartment, to go to school and start a new life.

And if I was going to start a new life anyway, why would I leave this? This kitchen, this house, this family, these people? Yes, it'd been a rough time lately, and I wasn't ready to meet a pirate ever again. But thinking back to the mission, the city of Monterey and the party, the road home—the butterflies at the mission, more stars than I'd ever glimpsed, the unspoiled beaches and turquoise-green sea, the swooping swallows— and Javier, with his preference for pelicans, but looking at me with pure adoration. *Oh, Javier.* How could I ever, ever leave him behind?

Jalama came over and gently laid a hand on mine, stilling me. "I think this dough was done some time ago," she said quietly.

"Perhaps you can think now, Señorita, *outside* as you walk? Or you might ruin all my bread." Her words were chiding, but her eyes shone with understanding. She lifted a hand to the back door. "Go. It is a pretty afternoon."

Casting her a rueful look and mumbling an apology, I did what she asked, pulling my abuela's shawl tight around me, and picking up my other things. It was true. I needed to think, and it was easy to be so distracted that I couldn't really do anything right. I'd walk, maybe go down to the stables.

The stables. Where there were horses that could help me obey this ringing in my mind to go, while my heart told me to stay. I'd pray, pray with everything in me, that God would direct my next steps.

But as I walked down the hill to the stables, I saw a carriage pull through the front gate in the distance, and all thoughts about prayer left my mind. I felt the sense of urgency, the potential for intrusion that might block what was right. I walked quickly to the stables, even as I watched the carriage come down our road, the dust rising in a plume behind it. It was a beautifully crafted thing—as fine as some I'd seen in Monterey—and pulled by a matched set of black horses.

I paused at the stable doors, and a servant, spying the visitors too now, met me there, opening them wide. The kid was maybe fourteen, dressed in a breechcloth and a jacket that was too big for him. He wore nothing underneath, as did so many servants who weren't in the house. But all he seemed to care about was the visiting coach. He practically thrummed with excitement.

It was only as the driver pulled up that I saw little Alvaro

peek his head out, waving to me and the stable boy. Then I saw
Adalia, Javier's sister-in-law, with her lovely almond-shaped
eyes. The driver climbed down, brushed the road dust from
his sleeves, and then opened the small door, offering his hand
to Adalia. She climbed out, Alvaro over her shoulder.

"Adalia!" I said, hugging her. "What are you doing here?"

"Well, you know how wily Doña Elena can be. She ordered
something special for you, and suggested I bring it and stay
for a little visit. How could I resist?" She looked around, her
round face sweeping left and right, a bit wistful. "I've missed
this place. And all of you," she added, leaning forward a little.
"And Alvaro will delight in seeing his cousins!"

She turned to watch the driver unfasten a trunk from the
back and lower it to the ground. Two servants appeared and
wordlessly carried it toward the house. But when a second
trunk was placed beside us, she urged the remaining servants
to wait.

"This one is for Señorita Zara," she said, black eyes
twinkling, staring up at me.

I frowned in confusion, wondering what Doña Elena could
have possibly ordered for me that would require an entire
trunk. More clothes?

"Go on with you," Adalia said. "Open it. I can hardly wait
to see what you think!"

I set my box to the left of the trunk and leaned down to
unlatch it. In the distance, I could hear Francesca and Estrella
shrieking, so excited were they by the news that their sister-in-
law and nephew had arrived, and now clearly heading our way.
I lifted the heavy lid as the driver pulled the carriage through

into the stables, leaving us alone.

Adalia turned and set Alvaro down, and the little boy began toddling toward his cousins, giggling as they raced toward him. In my peripheral vision, I knew they were picking him up, swinging him around, laughing, but my eyes were on the gown inside the trunk.

Swallowing hard, I brushed off what I could of the dust that always seemed to follow me here and fingered the fine damask. The abundant fabric was thick and a gorgeous ivory. I only had to lift it a little to know that the skirts were wide. The bodice was tight, the sleeves full up top and then tapering. I glanced up at Adalia. "But this…this is a—"

"A wedding dress," she said, her cheeks dimpling with glee.

She turned to welcome her sisters-in-law, hugging each of them, and now the boys, and Javier and Doña Elena were coming down the hill, faces all alight. I closed the trunk and backed away.

Adalia grimaced, bending toward Alvaro in Francesca's arms to smell his diaper. "Would you…?" she asked the girls, and immediately, they were off to do as she asked. She turned back to me. "Doña Elena sent orders for it to be made in Santa Barbara," she said under her breath as the others approached, "just as soon as you returned with Javier from Monterey. I know you haven't yet set the date, but Zara," she said, reaching for my hand, "why wait? Life is so fleeting, at times. And love? Love is rare. You love Javier and he loves you, no?"

"Well, yes," I said. *Stay*, clanged my heart.

"Then?" Her almond-shaped eyes held mine, wondering over my hesitation.

I glanced at the rest of the family, just fifteen steps away. "Go to them, now. I'll consider your words."

She grinned and squeezed my hands, looking up into my eyes. In that moment, I felt another deep *clang* of connection, despite our differences. It was like a bell within, tolling constantly. "Hurry to the house, will you?" she said. "We have so much to discuss!"

I watched her go, feeling confusion strangle me for the thousandth time. I wanted to trail after her. To hold sweet little Alvaro—once he was changed—and watch as his aunties and uncles greeted him. To hear about their last month in town, with her family. Oh, how they'd been missed in ours! *Ours....*

But she'd brought me a wedding dress. A beautiful, tastefully made gown.

Part of me chafed at the idea—didn't every girl want to "say yes to their own dress"? Most girls I knew, back home, had had a Pinterest wedding board since they were fourteen years old. But what did I know of wedding fashion in 1840? And how hard was it to get one? By the time Javier and I got around to it—if we ever got to that point—it would likely have been too late to do anything but slip on my gold gown and call it good enough.

Go. Run, said my mind. *You'll never have choices here.*

No, Doña Elena had ordered the gown as an act of love and generosity and forethought, I fought back. *Not* domination or meddling. *Okay, a little meddling.*

My eyes returned to the trunk.

I couldn't help myself. Fairly alone for a moment, I squatted beside the trunk and opened it, peeking at the luscious fabric between the layers of parchment paper. It was a doll's dress. A *princess* dress.

But then I felt the hair on the back of my neck rise. I suddenly knew that not all of the Venturas has gone back to the house—that I wasn't alone.

Javier hovered in the shadows at the edge of the stables, leaning against the wall, watching me. "You found it," he said simply. "Is it to your liking?"

I hurriedly dropped it and slammed the lid down. "It is… it is beautiful. But your mother was ahead of herself in ordering it. We're…well, we're not really in the right spot to even be thinking about such things as wedding gowns, right?" I grabbed my box, turned, and walked toward the stalls, aiming for the one that held my gelding. I cradled the box with the three things it held—the lamp and my two fossils—and tucked my shawl tighter around my shoulders.

Javier followed right behind. "Zara, you are right. I have been a fool. I hesitated over your news of what is to come, when I should have fully come your way. I should not have let my mother speak to you that way."

"It's a lot," I said, even though my rage and hurt were building now. "A lot for you to consider." But in my heart, I was wondering why he hadn't immediately accepted my predictions, understood, thrown everything he was behind what I'd said would happen—*trusted* me completely.

Doubt and fear and frustration stung my eyes. I moved to the saddle, barely managed to lift it off the post, and ambled down to the gelding's stall. Javier made no move to help me but only followed behind.

"What are you doing, Zara?" The first note of fear entered his tone with my name.

"I need to go to Tainter Cove."

"Not like this. Not now. Let us talk about it."

I ignored him, just kept moving.

"*Zara.*"

"So you wish to talk. About what, specifically?" I dropped the saddle to the ground, suddenly more than weary of holding it. Saddling my own horse, when I was this tired, was a tall order, especially for a short girl. Either I'd have to fetch a stable hand to help me, or I'd have to ride bareback.

B*areback*, I thought. The way I'd arrived at Rancho de la Ventura. It seemed right to leave that way too. I reached for a saddlebag, though, tossed it over the gelding's neck, and shoved my treasured things inside—the fossils, the shawl, the lamp—leaving the small box behind.

He stood there, face taut, a vein pulsing at his neck, watching one item after another slide into the bag. My cheeks burned, knowing he'd recognize the fossils and understand that, in taking them, I proved they were important to me. That *he* was important. That they all were important. And yet it was obvious that I was preparing to leave.

G*o*, my mind screamed. *Run.*

S*tay,* my heart tolled.

I straightened, facing him, thinking, *Dear God, this is it. I'm getting ready to go. I don't want to go. But I don't want to stay. I think…I'm scared.* But pride made me square my shoulders, lift my chin, and look him in the eye. The shadows were long, casting half his face in eerie darkness.

I wanted him to say something, to stop me, to convince me.

But he wouldn't. And if he wouldn't, well then, I wouldn't. Anger surged through me. Wasn't I the one that was giving up so much? Okay, I'd clearly found love here. But what was I giving up? A chance for a career. Equal opportunity. Maybe I'd even find love, there, *then*.

I paused. *Like this?*

It struck me, then, what he was doing, standing there, saying *nothing*, as he swallowed so hard that I saw his Adam's apple bob. He was doing as he'd promised he would: letting me choose, once and for all.

I paused, staring up at him, now in the corner of my gelding's stable, arms crossed, chin down, big, dark eyes upon me. I hadn't seen it going like this. Not *at odds*. Not *silent*. I'd wanted us to at least kiss, hug. I'd expected tears of anguish, not tears of rage and hurt and frustration, like those running down my face now.

He took a deep breath and came over to me. He lifted a finger to slowly raise my chin, forcing me to meet his eyes. "This is not how I wished us to part," he said softly.

"Me either," I whispered, sniffling.

He swallowed hard, as if fighting tears himself. "Looking back, if I were in charge of time, I'd never allow a minute to be spent in anger, frustration, or fear. But that is a part of life, no?" he said with a slight shrug. "I love you, Zara Ruiz. I will forever love you. Would you, could you…possibly…forever love me?"

He dared to wrap a hand around my waist and pull me closer then. I gazed up into his handsome face. Forever?

That was *so* long. My rational mind kicked in, thinking about weather patterns. How one seemed solid for a time and then….

I didn't know. *Didn't know.*

He let out a gasp and cough that made me pause, hard—those sounds told me he wept, even as he bent, grabbed hold of my waist, and gently lifted me to the gelding's back, even as my mind thought, *Wait! I don't know! I don't know!*

My hesitation had evidently been answer enough for him. He put a hand on my thigh, staring up at me, tears running down his cheeks, waiting for a long moment for me to say something.

But my mouth was full of cotton. I might as well have been gagged again. I could only cry. How many tears would I spend on this man and our love? And yet, how could I possibly choose between this crazy past and all that might await me in my true future? But where was my true future? Here, now? Or my own time?

Moving slowly, shoulders slightly slumped in defeat, he slipped a bit into the gelding's mouth—the unnamed gelding—that was what dominated my scattered thoughts at that moment—then lifted the reins to me.

I paused. Took one breath, then two.

Then I grabbed them, and as if on autopilot, urged my gelding to walk out of the stables and down the road. When I passed the gates, I moved to sit astride and kicked him into a full gallop, headed toward Tainter Cove. It felt like an act of defiance, sitting on a horse like a modern woman. And with each stride, I felt stronger, but also…emptier.

Still, it was the wind that dried the tears on my cheeks as

I rode. I wasn't going to bend beneath the pressures of my heart's call. I'd been subjected to abuse, crisis, like I'd never seen before. And I might have a way out…and no matter what I left behind, wasn't that safe place—a safe place that even Javier silently urged me toward—the one I should go to?

CHAPTER 34

JAVIER

What had I done? What had I done? I couldn't believe that I'd *lifted* her to the gelding's back, that I'd *handed* her the reins. Almost encouraged it. Let her go, without another word. And yet I knew I couldn't have done anything else. I'd ruined it, ruined everything. She'd finally told me what was to come, and it was exactly what I wanted, in a way. But then it had unfolded in the worst possible manner.

And somehow she'd been caught in the middle, making her feel like an outsider. Other. Reminding her that she might better fit in a different time. She'd come to the stables and discovered my mother had presumed to buy a wedding gown for her, even before I'd proposed. I'd been such a fool to tell Mama that it was a good idea. I'd simply been so sure, after our ride home, after the fossils, after everything, that she would decide to stay. But I knew that for all I wanted her to feel free, she had to have felt trapped. Her future decided for her. Frantically, I paced back and forth in the stables, rubbing my face, wiping away furious tears. Again and again I caught myself praying, praying exactly what I had once promised her

I wouldn't…for the Lord to keep her here, with me, until we could work it out.

I had to stay at the rancho.

Not interfere. Not again.

All I could do was wait.

"Javier?" Mateo said, from the front of the stables, reaching out to grasp the top of the doorframe. He had the guitar strapped to his back. He'd been strumming at it, trying to learn some of the chords, ever since I'd returned and she'd played. "Mama sent me to come and get you and Zara for supper."

"Tell Mama that we cannot come," I said, still pacing, fists clenching and unclenching.

"What?" He came farther into the relatively dark stable and looked around. "Where…? Was that *her* I saw riding down the road?" he asked in confusion.

"Sí, sí," I muttered.

"Did you two have an argument?"

"Something like that," I said, laughing but feeling nothing but bitterness.

"But she will return…" he said, glancing to the open doorway.

"I am not certain of that."

He gaped at me. "Then go after her!" he said, coming closer to me, and for the first time, I recognized he'd grown a couple of inches since I last took stock. "You two love each other! You can't just let her go! Not after all we went through."

I shook my head and looked up to the stable rafters, willing confidence and patience into my bones. "Sometimes, Mateo, it isn't that clear."

"Isn't it?" he said, reaching out to grab my arm, drawing

me to a standstill.

I turned toward him, surprised by his intensity, his daring to touch me like that.

"Isn't it?" he demanded again, clenching down harder, shaking my arm.

I searched his eyes, and all it once, it *was* clear. Like that beautiful, star-filled night, with meteors cascading above us.

I'd promised that I'd let her go, if that's what she chose. That I wouldn't pray against God taking her home to her own time. And I wouldn't. But I wanted her to *see* me, waiting for her, up on the dunes. For her to *know* I still wanted her and would fight for her, as much as I could, until the bitter end. That was all I could do. The least I could do, really.

I turned at once and saddled my mare. I'd be faster with a saddle. And with luck, I'd reach Tainter Cove in time.

Mateo set the guitar in the corner, helped me finish buckling the saddle, and handed the reins up to me after I mounted. "Wait," he said, moving toward the guitar. He picked it up and handed it to me. "Take her this. Tell her that I either want her to take it with her, so she can remember us, or bring it back with her, so we can hear her play again tonight."

I stared at my little brother a moment—seeing for the first time a friend, not just a follower—then took it. My eyes ran over the strings, remembering Zara's small fingers flying over them, her eyes closed, feeling the music, the sheer joy that practically cried out from her when she played, as if she *herself* were the instrument more than the guitar. That was the magic of my beloved, I decided. She was an instrument, ready to sing with everything her Maker had crafted her to be.

"You, little brother, are becoming a man," I said, slipping the strap on and positioning the guitar on my back. "*Gracias.*"

"Bring her home," Mateo returned simply.

"I will do my best," I said. And then I exited the stables and whipped my mare into a full gallop.

CHAPTER 35

ZARA

When I reached Tainter Cove, I slid from the back of my horse and went to his head, petting his nose and cheeks and neck. "You've been good to me, boy. Thank you," I said, pulling his big face close and kissing him. "I wish I were staying long enough to name you. Make Javier name both you and his sweet mare, okay?" My voice cracked on the last word.

He snorted and pulled his head away and I smiled wistfully. Even he didn't want to say a proper *adios*, it seemed.

I pulled off the saddlebag and then patted the horse's rump. "Head on home if I disappear, boy," I said. He ran off a bit, but as I moved down the dune to the center of Tainter Cove, I noticed he hovered in the distance—as if waiting for me to entice him back, and yet ready to go running off if he chose. Perhaps he echoed what I was feeling...not certain I wanted to go, but not at all certain I wanted to stay either.

I plopped down on the sand, just a few feet from where the waves ended their claim to soil and receded back to the sea, again and again. I wrapped my fossils in Abuela's shawl and tucked them into one arm while holding the lamp with

both hands. The sun was setting behind a marine layer, making
the sky a super-pale pink and purple display, something out of
a winter's eve rather than the heat of summer with its usual
vibrant oranges and corals.

Honestly, I'd hoped for a bigger, better send-off, in my
romantic heart-of-hearts. "Ehh, it figures," I said, deciding the
unsatisfying sunset was just like all the rest of this big exit,
never destined to satisfy—only wrapping tendrils around my
wrists and ankles to hold me back. I lifted the lamp in my
hands and turned it over, wondering over all I'd experienced
since the moment I first fished it from the pool. My fingers
traced the odd, ancient script, and I wished I could Google it,
find out more about it. In 1840, my only chance would be to
travel east and hunt down some archeology scholar to see if he
could tell me more.

And not hope for a whole lot. Because back then—back *here*—
resources were limited.

Some mysteries will forever be mysteries, Grillita, Abuela used to
say, with a shrug of her round shoulders. I'd always wanted
to know the next thing—like if God was the Creator, how
did *he* begin? Or why love didn't find everyone, even *good*
people. Or why good people had to suffer. Now I wanted
to know why he'd sent me back to 1840 to fulfill all three
of my wishes, but then made me realize all the reasons to
go *home*.

Oh, how I missed Abuela. I wished, so wished, she was
here with me now to tell me what to do…or that I could go
home to her. It would make my parting so much easier.

If I could even go at all. I still didn't know. I glanced

over my shoulder to the empty dune behind me, feeling both relieved and hurt at once. There was nothing but clumps of beach grass, waving in the breeze, as if saying good-bye.

Javier hadn't followed me. He wasn't here. He was doing it. Letting me choose. Not interfering.

And while I'd wanted that, recognized that it might open the hidden passageway that was closed to me before, it left me feeling more hollow and sad than ever before. I wished he were here—that we could have a real farewell—but he wasn't.

He wasn't.

I wanted to cry, but it seemed all my tears were spent.

I turned the lamp in my hands again. God had sent me here for a purpose. To grow me, to show me how much more there was to life—even more than what I'd wished for. And while so many bad things had happened, there had been far more good. I'd forever treasure those memories.

Or would I forever be trying to match or better them?

Was it even possible in my own time to capture what I'd found here?

Well, I won't know if I don't try. God wouldn't let me return if it wasn't for my best, right?

Or would he again let me choose for myself, as Javier had? For good or bad?

I let out a guttural cry of frustration. I was making myself crazy, arguing both sides.

With a sigh, I stood up, brushed the sand from my skirts, and moved to the edge of the water, feeling the cool wave wash around my bare toes, the arches of my feet, my ankles. My heels began to sink as the water receded, the water seeping up on the hem of my skirts.

The pale tangerine sun was just meeting the sea with its bottom edge, sinking now, as I might sink into my own time again. I put my hand on the lamp and closed my eyes.

A whine behind me made me pause, and then turn my head.

"Centinela," I said wistfully, stepping toward her and shifting the things in my hands to pet her. She wouldn't understand my disappearing.

Or had she always understood best of all?

I knelt in the damp, cool sand, and for the first time she allowed me to pull her face close to mine. "Thank you, girl. Thank you for being my sentinel, my guardian. You've given me comfort."

Movement at the top of the dune drew my eye next.

Javier.

I glanced over my right shoulder at the sun, a third of the way down now. Something inside me, deep inside, told me that if I was going to go, I had to go now. Before the sun was gone. *Hurry.*

But I could not look away as Javier dismounted and strode down the sand with long, powerful, decisive steps.

He walked all the way to me, wordlessly wrapped one hand around my lower back, the other behind my neck and pulled me to him for a long, tender, thorough kiss. Then he stepped back, leaving me somewhat dazed.

"Ja-Javier," I said. "I-I thought you were going to leave this to me." I looked up into his dark eyes, as he shoved aside his curly dark hair.

"I am," he said, with a firm nod, everything about him that

I loved *back* in that instant. It was as if he'd been shaken out of his reverie, his fear, his frustration, and he had returned to himself. "You will decide this on your own. Or leave it to God. But I could not let you leave without giving you *all* of me, Zara. Reminding you of all the love I have for you."

He fingered the strap on his shoulder, and for the first time, I saw that he carried the guitar. "Mateo sent you this. He wanted you to have it."

After a second's hesitation, I took the guitar from him, and as it passed from his hands to mine, memories of every time I'd played it flooded through me, like flashbacks in a movie, one after the other. It reminded me of all I was, all I had here, in 1840, every time I played it. It made me remember my potential, my breadth and height and width and length in ways that only Javier's love—and God's—had made me remember, like a long-distant promise, awakened and realized.

Then Javier stepped back, palms cupped, head bowed. "Do what you must, beloved," he whispered. *Stay,* my heart clanged, now more like an alarm. *Stay, stay, stay…*

I tore my eyes from him to the setting sun, now just the top third of the oddly pale orb visible. *Run.* My head throbbed, like a drum. *Run.*

I felt the pressure in my chest, my mind. It was now or never.

Now…and forever.

Slowly, I took the lamp, turned…paused…breathed… and stared at the setting sun, wondered one last time if I was supposed to stay or supposed to try and return home. One last try? To see if I was meant to be there, even if my heart sent ribbons around everything it could touch, making me want to *stay here?*

Stay, Zara. Stay.

Run! You idiot! Run!

I weighed the lamp in my hands. Turned it over, tracing the odd lettering, the ancient, burnished gold reflection, the missing spout.

I remembered the magical moment I'd pulled it from the waves, back home.

Thought of when I'd remembered what I'd told Abuela I wished for most. Remembered awakening to this, this time, this place, this reality.

Then I turned as the sun trembled, ready to sink beneath the waves, casting a serpentine golden path in my direction as if it beckoned me one last time. I set the guitar down, along with my things and allowed the shawl to drop with them to the sand.

And then I threw the lamp as far and as deep into the sea as I could.

CHAPTER 36

JAVIER

I was confused, at first, as she set down her things. She was little more than a blurry, dark form against the giant, pale-pink setting sun. Staring in her direction made my eyes water. Distantly, I thought of her as a kind of fairy, blowing into my life like magic, and about to blow out of it again, when my eyes focused on the object she'd hurled, in an arc, toward the sea.

My vision narrowed, and I watched the golden lamp, gleaming in an odd pink and purple reflection as it turned, over and over, sailing past the first two waves and slicing toward the third, farthest out.

She threw it, I told myself, as if trying to convince myself it was true. *The lamp is gone.*

Relief and triumph flooded through me at first. *She's staying!* But then immediately after, angst and horror. *She's trapped here! God, what does this mean? Could it mean...?*

After a brief splash, the ancient lamp disappeared, no sign of it visible when the next wave rose. No rings of impact, no trace of it on the water. Even though it felt like a hundred-foot wave crashing over me.

I blinked, trying to make sense of it, but then she was moving toward me, striding across the sand as intently as I'd moved toward her, jumping up into my arms. I turned her around and around, crying and laughing and kissing her. Was it real? Was it true?

"Zara," I said, setting her down and clutching her cheeks in both my hands, holding her away from me so that I could look into her eyes, "are you certain? Are you *certain*?"

"Never more certain of anything in all my life," she said in a growl, fresh tears running down her face again too, tipping up her chin for more kisses.

I think I laughed more than I kissed her in those moments after the lamp left us forever.

Finally, I released her. Then I bent down on one knee, fishing for the ring in my inside pocket. Ever since Monterey, I'd carried it there. There were moments in the past days when I'd believed *this* moment was destined never to come.

But here it was.

Holding the ring with two fingers, I took her hand with the other and looked up into her sweet face. "Zara Ruiz, you have turned my life upside down and inside out, and it's all been for good. I will spend the rest of my life, in this undetermined land, determined—always and forever—to do right by you and the love we share, so help me God. If you love me as I do you, might you agree to be my bride?"

"*If* I love you?" she whispered, tears streaming down her cheeks. She reached down and cradled my face with both of her small hands. "I think I've always loved you, Javier." She smiled. "Perhaps not on that *first* day we met…but it was not long after." I grinned with her, but waited for her to answer. Slowly, she nodded her head. "And, *sí*, Javier. I will marry you."

I leaped up and held her again in my arms, this time not swinging her around, just standing there, trying to fully comprehend that she was *staying*, that she *loved* me, and that she was going to be my *bride*.

"I think," I began, "that I just got *my* three wishes."

Grinning, I slipped the ring on her finger. It was an old band of gold set with a new sapphire gem that had reminded me of the lamp and Tainter Cove's peculiar green-blue color the moment I saw it.

"I love it," she said. "It's beautiful, Javier," she breathed. "So when shall we marry?"

I bent down to kiss her tenderly. "We have the gown, right? Why not tonight?"

She laughed under her breath. "Tomorrow," she said decisively. "Tomorrow I shall become Zara Ruiz de la Ventura. Here, I think, at Tainter Cove."

"Hmm, Mama will probably argue against that."

"But I shall win that argument," she said with a wink.

And I knew she would.

Then, as if in a dream, we gathered her things, I strapped the guitar over my shoulder, and we walked hand in hand to the horses, who had wandered away to graze along the dunes.

Centinela loped about in a wide circle, again and again, as if sensing the celebration in each of our hearts. And the horses waited, noses together, as if conferring themselves.

"Do you think they know?" Zara asked in a whisper, reaching up to nuzzle her gelding.

"Know what?" I scoffed, feeling no rancor.

"Do you think they recognize pure love, sure love?" she asked, stroking her gelding's nose. "Love that was destined, beyond time?"

And as she turned to look at me, I was already removing the distance between us, taking her fiercely, madly into my arms. "Do they know? Mark my words, *mi corazon*. The very stars will cry out tonight, singing of what *we* know here, now, in *this* time, between us. No?"

She stared up into my eyes, trembling but in an odd way, more sure than I'd ever seen her. "Yes. *Yes*."

And in the midst of her last *yes*, I claimed her lips with mine, thinking with her, *Yes. Yes, yes.*

CHAPTER 37

ZARA

The girls awakened me, pouncing on my bed when they could not wait any longer. Judging from the sun, when I sat up and stretched, peeking out of one eye, it was after eight. After *ten!* I couldn't remember the last time I'd slept past sunrise. *Probably back in my own time…but no longer my time…*

"My goodness, you all must have been so quiet! I didn't hear a thing!"

"Mama gave the whole household very strict orders," Estie said earnestly, "to be ever so quiet. She didn't want the *bride* to be awakened." Her eyes lit up with the word *bride*, as if she'd said something magical.

"She said every bride needs a good night's sleep so she looks her best," Francesca added, sitting down on the edge of my bed after opening up the shutters on both of my windows. It was going to be a beautiful day.

"The maids are bringing up hot water," Francesca said. "For a bath," she added, as if I might not figure that out. "Mama said it should be extra deep. And to bring you her special soap."

"An extra deep bath? Special soap? Sleeping in? I must be a princess," I said. *My little sisters,* I thought. I reached out and took Francesca's hand, and then Estie's too. "Today, we become sisters!" I said with a grin. "I've never had sisters! Or brothers..."

They smiled back at me, looking as happy as I felt. How lucky was I to land with a family who would so easily take me in as their own? "It feels so right," I said, "to be your sister. There's something about your family that makes me feel as if you were waiting for me."

"We were, in a way," Francesca said shyly.

"It's like you were the missing puzzle piece!" Estie added.

I thought about that. They thought of me as the missing piece, while to me, they were the entire other part of the puzzle. *Thank you, Lord,* I prayed. *Thank you for this blessing.* I was overwhelmed to the point of tears.

"No, no, no!" Francesca said firmly, rising in alarm. "Mama also said we must not make you cry! It will make your eyes swell!"

I giggled. "That's true." I'd never been one of those pretty sort of criers. Which made me all the angrier, when I started crying *because* I was angry. Which then made me angrier... The thought of all of that made me laugh. "No more tears," I said, wiping my eyes. "At least until sunset, when I marry your brother."

Their faces lit up, and they squeezed my hands as the maids arrived, four of them, each carrying two buckets of steaming water. A man came with the copper tub, depositing it in the center of my bedroom floor, as if embarrassed. The maids, however, each looked at me with shy smiles. I met their grins with my own, thanking each of them by name as they exited. I knew I was a girl from the future, but I could do my best to bring a bit of the future back to the past.

"Take your bath," Francesca said, unwrapping a treasured, half-worn bar of lavender soap. "And we'll be back to attend you."

They wanted me to keep to my room all day. I felt a little like trapped Rapunzel in her tower, without as much hair. I was in turns, spun up—pacing in agitation—frustrated, and calm, lost in my dreams of what was to come. But as the hours crawled by, even as Maria wound my hair in rags—positioning them high on my head, so they might dry faster—and Consuela helped me dress only as far as stockings, stays and shift. I looked longingly at the beautiful gown, strewn across my bed, and just wanted to get down to that beach. See Javier. Be his, at last.

The girls peeked in every so often, and then Adalia and Alvaro arrived. We sat down on either edge of the bed, letting Alvaro crawl and roll between us. "I cannot tell you how happy this day makes me," Adalia said, smiling so broadly that her almond-shaped eyes became mere slits. "If Dante were here, he'd be with Javier right now, teasing him mercilessly about your wedding night."

I grinned and ducked my head, feeling the heat of a blush rise, and fingered the edge of the blanket. "I suppose he's missing his dad, and his brother, today especially."

Adalia covered my hand with his. "Most likely. But it can only be brief pangs of regret that they are not here to experience the best day of his life alongside him. You should have seen him this morning, Zara. He couldn't stop smiling! He danced around the library with Alvaro in his arms!"

"Danced? *My* Javier?" I knew he was a good dancer, but he usually was pretty formal around the house.

"Danced," she confirmed with delight. "I've never seen him so happy. You have brought him, and this family, much joy in agreeing to be his bride."

"No more than they have brought me." I reached over and grabbed Alvaro as he stood up and toddled recklessly toward the edge. "Now if only you two returned to the rancho, all would be perfect." I kissed Alvaro in the soft folds of fat at his neck and he laughed—and we laughed with him. Was there any better sound than a little one giggling like crazy? It was pure delight to my ears.

"It has been good for me to be at home, with my own family," Adalia said carefully. "But it is grand to be with you here too. It is difficult, being pulled in two different directions, is it not?"

I glanced at her, wondering for a moment if she knew. Knew exactly what this decision meant for me. But she only peered back at me, all innocence. "More than you know," I said. "It took me a long while to decide if I could promise Javier—and this family—my forever."

"I'm glad you took that time. It was wise. And I'm very glad that we are to be sisters."

I kissed Alvaro's neck one more time, eliciting one last giggle, and then handed him to his mother as she rose to go.

"Time to get your nephew in his finest for the ceremony,"

Adalia said with a wink.

Your nephew, echoed in my mind, as she quietly shut the door behind her. Not only had I gained sisters and brothers, but there would be children too. It hadn't struck me before, but my wish for a family—with lots of aunts and uncles and cousins and nieces and nephews—was about to finally come true. Forever.

The stately Doña Elena arrived at the end of the day, as Francesca unwound my curls from the rags, still a bit damp. Elena was dressed in her finest green gown, her own hair in curls and pinned high on her head, with a tiny green hat atop. She carried a comb covered in fresh flowers—roses and more from the garden—that she'd attached to it. It looked a little wilted, but it was beautiful. A gift.

I lifted it to my face and inhaled the sweet scent. "Doña Elena, it is so pretty," I said. "Gracias."

"Not Doña Elena any longer," she returned, laying a hand on my shoulder. "Only Elena. Or…" she paused, as if wondering if she could really dare, "*Mama* Elena, if it pleases you."

I swallowed hard. I knew that Adalia called her Mama Elena. All my life, I'd never had a mother. An abuela—a dear, wonderful woman, for sure. But never a mama.

"I think I shall call you Mama Elena, if that is well with you," I said.

She smiled, and I counted all the wrinkles as joy. She was

glad I was here, truly glad, no matter what troublesome reality I'd brought with me.

"It is time, my dear," she said, nodding past the table full of uneaten food the maids had brought to me throughout the day by the window, to the sinking sun, then back to me. "Today you become a Ventura, and forever will be a part of us."

I laid my hand on hers—still on my shoulder—and looked up at her. "I think…I think there's a part of me that thinks I've always been a part of your family."

Her brown eyes settled on mine, and she gave me a single, firm nod, understanding as only a fellow time-traveler could. "I know this feeling. To be so out of place, and yet home at the same time." She squeezed my shoulder. "It eases, in time. I promise."

I gave her hand a final squeeze, and then she left me to finish dressing.

I arrived in Adalia's rented carriage, and I really did feel like a Disney princess at times—when, you know, I wasn't getting choked by dust or bounced out of my seat by road bumps. By the time we reached Tainter Cove, Centinela making wide, loping loops about us, my head buzzed with excitement.

This is happening, I thought. *It's real. Not a dream. I'm getting married. Married!* I pictured the word in my mind. Eighteen years old and married? Yeah, that wasn't what I'd imagined. Ever. I was supposed to be off to college, chasing down the study of clouds and rain.

But as I lifted my skirts and climbed down the two steps of the carriage, staring into the sun, low above the water, I knew that I was exactly where I was supposed to be. Rafael, also dressed in his finest, bowed and offered me his hand, as well as a grin of appraising approval, looking me over from head to foot. "You, my dear," he said, "look ravishing."

"As do you," I murmured, grinning as I moved past him, knowing I'd shocked him.

He hurried forward to catch up to me, blocking my view of the rest of the beach—and anyone from seeing me. "My friend thought you might like to begin your approach here, where he first found you?"

I dropped my hand from his arm when we reached firm, damp sand and made a slow circle on the far side of the big boulders. The rocks blocked me from the rest of the beach, where I knew the others—and Javier—awaited me. "Yes, yes, this is perfect." I could feel the prick of tears behind my eyes. It was almost like standing in the back of a church, waiting for that moment when you saw your groom at last…and he saw you.

"Now," he said, voice low in soft, comforting, mock-chastisement. "None of that." He straightened. "All is well?"

"Yes," I mumbled, wiping my nose as I did another slow turn among the rocks, thinking about how far I'd come, what I'd experienced, what I'd learned.

And how much there was to come.

He left me, and then there was Mateo, looking like a fine young man in his starched shirt, long, dark coat, and breeches tucked into polished boots. His hands were behind him.

"Javier thought…" he began uncertainly. "In light of the fact that your own father is not here to attend you…" He turned his head away and stroked the nape of his neck, before straightening, settling his mouth in determination. "That is…Zara, may I have the honor of escorting you to your groom?"

His mouth quirked in a grin as he glanced over his shoulder to the corner of the boulder. "Are you ready?"

I nodded, my heart pounding, suddenly not feeling ready at all. But then we rounded the rocks and I looked across the expanse of sand…to the center where Javier, his friends and family, and a small, homely priest stood waiting. I knew the guy had to be thinking of the church in Santa Barbara, or the Ventura villa and grounds, but me? To me, this was perfection.

I focused on Javier, looking like something out of a magazine, with his shoulders back, chin up, dark curls waving in the wind. He was in a crisp white shirt, cropped black jacket, new breeches that disappeared into polished black boots.

"Yes, Mateo," I breathed. "I think I'm ready to get married." To be with Javier.

Ready to get married, was what echoed through my brain, as I wrapped my hand around his arm.

We began the walk along the sand, skirting the incoming waves by a few feet. At one point, I paused, bent, unlaced and pulled off my boots, ignoring Doña Elena's chagrined face, concentrating only on Javier's. But I could tell he knew how much I wanted to feel the cold, wet grains between my toes, to remind myself of the first day I'd met him, but also that this, today, right now, was real too.

I reached him at last and he offered his wide, warm palms

to me. I settled my own in his, and looked into his eyes, and beyond to his family and friends, and then over my shoulder to the setting sun…knowing that I promised him not only my heart, but also my present, my future, my forever.

And for the first time, that thought didn't make my heart beat twice as fast.

Instead, all I felt was peace.

EPILOGUE

MODERN DAY

Dante passed the public-access parking lot and then got down to unlock the chain while Gramps silently waited on his horse, wrists crossed on the saddle horn. When it was open, Gramps urged his mare through the gap, pulling Dante's horse along too by the reins, then waited for the boy to chain up the passage again. It was after visiting hours to the site, but Gramps was strict about such things.

Dante used a big rock to climb back atop his horse and followed Gramps farther into the narrow canyon, entering the area of the fossil-covered cliffs that were usually out-of-bounds to the general public. It was their favorite place to ride.

Gramps took a big breath as they moved into the cool shadows of the canyon, the nearby freeway noise fading away, the deeper they got. Dante looked up, watching swallows dart back and forth above. It was nice and cool in here too, a break from the intense California heat that seemed to hold even after sunset.

Dante expected to take their usual path that wound up and up, until you came out on top, where you could see all of Rancho de la Ventura, the nearby cities, all the way to the beach. But instead, Gramps pulled up and wearily dismounted.

"Gramps?"

The old man just gave him a small smile and motioned for him to dismount with his paw-like hands, weathered and thick with arthritis. Obediently, Dante followed after him. Gramps was already ducking under another chain, climbing up and among the rocks, then squeezing through such a narrow passage that his grandson worried he'd get stuck. But he didn't.

There were more fossils. Everywhere. Curlicues and clams and fish skeletons and crabs…

Dante's hands grazed past both flat rock—blasted smooth by wave and wind, he supposed—and rough, newly exposed rock. Gramps paused across from a small cave, and placing a hand on the edge, bent down and gestured to it to his grandson.

The boy squatted and looked, checking out a section where fossils had obviously been removed, the lines square. He hunched there, in the shade, looking at the expanse, wondering what had been there, and who had taken them. Then, in the top right, he saw something.

He edged closer, trying to make out the letters scratched into the rock.

Zara was here, he thought it said. *6-12-1840*

He shook his head and looked to his grandfather. "Whoa," he said. "1840?"

Gramps smiled. "1840, yes. And Zara de la Ventura was your great-great-great-great…" He straightened and rubbed his forehead. "Well, just say she was your great-grandmother, times six or seven."

Dante looked back to the ancient graffiti. "My great-great-grandmother?"

"Yes. And mine," Gramps said, hooking a thumb to his chest. "She was quite a woman. Some said she was born ahead of her time. She was even kidnapped by pirates and survived a shipwreck."

"Pirates!" Dante exclaimed, having a hard time believing he'd never heard this story before. "What happened?"

"Well, the ship went down around Point Ruina, and Mateo—Zara's brother-in-law—and she survived. Two of only four to do so."

"Whoosh," Dante said, "that was lucky."

"Real lucky," he said, taking a seat on a nearby rock. "Some said that God seemed to smile on her, all her life through. It was because of her that her husband, Javier de la Ventura, was able to preserve as much of the ranch as he could. A lot has been sold over the years, through the generations. But for us to have what we have now today?" He took off his hat and wiped his brow, then shook his head. "That's a definite miracle."

Dante nodded. This was a part of the story he'd heard a hundred times. "What about the pirates? Two survived? What happened to them?"

Gramps squinted, as if trying to squeeze out the memory. "Well, I'm not quite sure about the one, but the other was the captain. And he was caught and hanged a few years later in Monterey."

"Huh," Dante said, turning back to look at Zara's inscription. 1840. *More than 175 years ago.* "Was it her that took these fossils?"

"Best as I can tell," Gramps said. He fished in his old vest pocket and brought out a beautiful spiral-shell fossil and handed it to the boy. Dante had never seen one that was so crisply perfect. "These have come down through the family over the generations. They say they came from right here, 'Zara's Rock.' Some have gone missing over the years, and there are just two left, that I know of. I want you to have mine, Dante. If you remember a few things."

"Wow, thanks, Gramps," Dante said, running a finger over each dip of the shell. His little sister was going to be so jealous. Mining for fossils here was off-limits anymore. The canyon was special, and preserving it without further harm was always the rule. So to get one from here...

"Will you remember, Dante? Me and those who came before me? It's special what we have here, boy. So much family, within reach. Acres of land to farm and run cattle. Someday, you'll find a girl to love, and introduce her to it. Discover a little *adventure* together," he added with a wink.

"*Gramps*," Dante winced. A girl? Maybe someday. But now? *Ewww...*

Gramps laughed under his breath, rose and patted him on the shoulder. "Trust me. Someday you'll want a girl to love you as much as you love her. And a *ranching* kind of girl because you like it, right, boy?"

"Like it? I love it. I never want to be anywhere else."

"That's my boy," Gramps said, standing straight and tall again. "That's my boy. Now let's head home, Dante. I think I can smell dinner on the stove from here."

AUTHOR NOTES

Historically speaking, there really has not been any piracy of note in California waters, other than the mission-raiders mentioned in the text; Mendoza and his crew were entirely a figment of my imagination. I took a little fictional license in getting our characters back and forth between the Central Coast and Monterey—using my best guess in terms of time it would take to travel, but knowing I was stretching here and there for the sake of the story. Ranchos in the time really did sprawl across hundreds of thousands of acres, and many of the original settlers failed to hold on to their property when California entered the Union.

ACKNOWLEDGMENTS

Many thanks to Paul Hawley, Rachelle Cobb, and Hannah Donor for their editing skills. Also big thanks to my committed-reader/proofers: Staci Murden, Andrew and Debbie Spadzinski, Julie Schmidt, Tawny Moore and Sharon Miles. Enid Ruiz helped me with Spanish translations. The flowers were donated by Ponderosa & Thyme (Salem, OR) and the cover model was the beautiful Graziella LiVolsi (who happens to be a River reader). Her dress came from Western Costume in Hollywood! My husband, Tim, helped me typeset the book and design the cover, and Kerry Nietz helped me get it into e. I wouldn't have started this duology (*Three Wishes* and *Four Winds*) were it not for my rabid River Tribe readers—I'll love each of you forever, as well as your passion for time-slip stories! Thank you, thank you to each of you.

ABOUT THE AUTHOR

Lisa T. Bergren is the best-selling, award-winning author of over forty books in all sorts of genres, with more than three million copies sold. Her most recent fiction works include the historical Grand Tour Series (*Glamorous Illusions, Grave Consequences, Glittering Promises*), the dystopian-fantasy Remnants (*Season of Wonder, Season of Fire, Season of Glory*), and the time-slip romance series, River of Time (*Waterfall* et al). She lives in Colorado with her husband, three children, and a little white dog.

WHAT'S NEXT?

Beginning to release April 2018 with Bethany House…

The Sugar Baron's Daughters, a trilogy set in 1770s West Indies (Caribbean). Revolution, pirates, vast sugar plantations, untold riches, unspeakable hardship and tragedy…it's what I'm writing now! In the meantime, I hope you'll look up one of my older books and follow me on Facebook, Instagram, Twitter, or the web!

You can find my web site here: LisaTBergren.com

Find out about upcoming releases, events and sign up to receive my quarterly e-newsletter. Or join me on:
- Facebook.com/RiverofTimeSeries
- Facebook.com/LisaTawnBergren
- Twitter @LisaTBergren

CHECK OUT THE ORIGINAL SERIES!

Loved this time-slip romance? Want to see where it all began?

The original River of Time Series, set in fourteenth-century Italy, is available in paperback, ebook, and audio from your favorite retailers!

Manufactured by Amazon.ca
Bolton, ON